Flood Tide

By Alexander Geiger

Prime Directive (2013)
Flood Tide (2019)
Conquest of Persia (2019)
Immortal Alexandros (2020)
Funeral Games (2021)

Book Two of the Ptolemaios Saga

Flood Tide

*An Epic Novel of the Greek
Invasion of Persia*

Alexander Geiger

Requests for permission to make copies of any part of the work may be sent to:

Permissions Department
Ptolemaios Publishing & Entertainment, LLC
668 Stony Hill Road, Suite 150
Yardley, PA 19067

www.PtolemaiosPublishing.com

ISBN-13: 978-0-9892584-4-9 (pbk)
ISBN-13: 978-0-9892584-5-6 (ebook)

Library of Congress Control Number: 2019937857

Cover Design: Scott Schmeer, Prometheus Training, LLC

The author of this work is available to speak at live events. For further information, please contact the author at Alex@AlexanderGeiger.com

First Edition

Manufactured in the United States of America

To the memory of Emil Geiger,
the smartest man I ever knew.

Table of Contents

"There is a tide in the affairs of men.
Which, taken at the flood, leads on to fortune." [1]

---

[1] William Shakespeare, *Julius Caesar*, Act 4, Scene 3.

Maps and Animated Battle Depictions[2]

Map 1 – Ancient Macedonia and its Environs

Map 2 – Mainland Greece in 336 B.C.E.

Map 3 – Lands Traversed by Alexandros in 335 and early 334 B.C.E.

Map 4 – Lands Traversed by Alexandros between May 334 and November 333 B.C.E.

Map 5 – Miletos and its Environs, c. 334 B.C.E.

Map 6 – Halikarnassos, c. 334 B.C.E.

Map 7 – Movements of the Persian and Pan-Hellenic Armies Prior to the Battle of Issos

Battle 1 – Chaironeia – August 338 B.C.E.

Battle 2 – Granikos – May 334 B.C.E.

Battle 3 – Issos – November 333 B.C.E.

---

[2] In lieu of black-and-white maps and static battle depictions in this book, color maps and animated depictions of battles are available at AlexanderGeiger.com.

List of Principal Characters

Alexandros Aniketos (356-323)[3] – King of Macedonia (336-323)[4]

Antigone (unk-unk) – Philotas's mistress

Antigonos Monophthalmos (c. 382-301) – Military commander under both Philippos and Alexandros; appointed satrap of Phrygia by Alexandros

Antipatros (397-319) – Macedonian nobleman; served as regent under both Philippos and Alexandros

Aristandros of Telmessos (c. 380-331) – Alexandros's soothsayer

Aristoteles (384-322) – Alexandros's teacher in Mieza

Arrhidaios (358-317) – Alexandros's half-wit half-brother

Artabazos (c.387-c.328) – Persian nobleman; father of Barsine and Artakama, among others

Artakama (347-unk) – Artabazos's daughter; Barsine's sister

---

[3] Numbers refer to year of birth and year of death, respectively. All years are B.C.E. In some cases, the actual dates are either uncertain or in dispute. In those cases, the year in question is preceded by a c.

[4] Numbers refer to years of reign.

Barsine (355-309) – Artabazos's daughter; Artakama's sister; Memnon's wife; Alexandros's mistress

Dareios (c.380-330) – Persian Emperor (336-330)

Hephaistion (356-324) – Alexandros's closest friend

Kallisthenes (c.368-327) – Aristoteles's great nephew; accompanied Alexandros as campaign historian

Kassandros (358-297) – Antipatros's son

Kleitos Melas (c.357-327)[5] – A commander in Alexandros's army

Kleopatra (354-308) – Daughter of Philippos and Olympias; Alexandros's sister

Krateros (365-320) – A commander in Alexandros's army

Lysimachos (360-282) – A commander in Alexandros's army

Mazaios (380-328) – Persian nobleman

Memnon of Rhodos (380-333) – Mercenary commander in Dareios's service; Barsine's husband

Nearchos (c.360-c.312) – A commander in Alexandros's army

Nikanoros (358-331) – A commander in Alexandros's

---

[5] The date of Kleitos's birth is uncertain, but he was probably several years older than depicted in this book.

army; Parmenion's son

Olympias (a/k/a Myrtale) (377-314) – Philippos's 4th wife; mother of Alexandros Aniketos

Parmenion (400-330) – Leading Macedonian general; served both Philippos and Alexandros

Perdikkas (359-321) – A commander in Alexandros's army

Philippos Amyntou Makedonios (382-336) – King of Macedonia (359-336); father of Alexandros

Philippos of Akarnia (unk-unk) – Alexandros's physician

Philotas (360-330) – A commander in Alexandros's army; Parmenion's son

Ptolemaios Metoikos (c.364-282) – A commander in Alexandros's army; one of Alexandros's bodyguards

Seleukos (358-281) – A commander in Alexandros's army

Sisygambis (unk-323) – Dareios's mother

Stateira (c.365-331) – Dareios's 1st wife

Chapter 1 – Euphoria

He sat, swathed in a nimbus of golden hair, and laughed. "Never had a doubt," he exclaimed, shaking his head in wonder. Although his physician implored him to keep still, Alexandros was in an irrepressible mood.

"No kidding," he asked giddily. "Sliced the bastard's arm right off, huh?"

His informant nodded with a grin, causing Alexandros to burst into peals of laughter once again. "I don't remember that at all." He fought to regain his composure. "I guess I was pretty much out of it by then."

He was holding court, sitting on a low stool in the middle of a makeshift tent, wearing the remnants of his armor. His helmet was gone but his cuirass still hung by a strap off one shoulder, its shine dulled by shallow dents, patches of mud, a generous coating of blood, and a streak of whitish gore, splayed like a lightning bolt across the simulacrum of washboard abs. His mismatched eyes sparkled in the torchlight, moist with merriment or exhaustion or perhaps pain. He was leaning slightly forward, hands on knees, fingers tapping the upper edges of his greaves.

His best friend Hephaistion was helping him relive the battle, especially the parts Alexandros had missed while lying unconscious on the ground, surrounded by bodyguards waging a desperate fight to prevent Persian cavalrymen from cutting off his head and hands. Of course, Hephaistion had missed those parts of the battle as well, having stayed far out of harm's way, but that didn't inhibit his vivid recounting of second-hand information gathered after the Persians had been routed.

"You're lucky, sire." Philippos of Akarnia was peering into his young patient's darkening mane. "It's a clean cut, though the wound's beginning to spread."

Alexandros shrugged. "It's a scratch."

To me, it looked like a chasm. The scalp was severed all the way to the bone, from just above Alexandros's hairline to beyond the crown of his head, the cleavage wide as a finger and growing wider.

I was standing behind the king, holding a torch, trying to keep the operating field illuminated without setting the patient's hair on fire. My task became more complicated when the surgeon also asked me to use my other hand to hold a rag against the king's forehead in order to keep the wine out of his eyes. *When exactly had I become a surgeon's assistant?* I wondered.

Marooned out of time, I was still trying to adjust to the paradigm shift I had experienced during the battle. Like a gyroscope wrenched from its mounting, I had lost my bearings. Admittedly, disorientation was my customary mental state but this evening I was more discombobulated than usual. *What the hell am I doing here,* I kept asking myself, *and will I make it to the escape hatch in time?*

"This may sting a little, sire," Philippos warned.

Alexandros appeared not to have heard. "Somebody, go get that guy. I want to thank him in person." The scrum of aides milling about in the tent appeared oblivious to his request.

"It was Kleitos Melas, sire," I said under my breath but my whisper was drowned out by the torrent of uncut wine Philippos had started to pour into the wound.

Alexandros winced but did not utter a sound. Wine flowed everywhere: down his back, around his ears and onto his shoulders, and into the rag I was pressing against his forehead. With the wine flowed clots of blood, clumps of hair, clods of dirt, bits of skin, and shards of metal.

After the wound had been adequately irrigated, Philippos used a sharp knife to cut off the hair near the flapping edges of skin.

"Sssmp." Alexandros sucked air through clenched teeth but, embarrassed by his show of vincibility, quickly turned back to Hephaistion. "Do we have a count of our casualties yet?"

"I've prepared a special potion, sire, to dull the pain," Philippos interrupted. "Here, sip a little at a time."

Hephaistion snatched the proffered cup out of the physician's hand. "What in Haides is it?"

"Just wine, with some essence of poppies mixed in."

Hephaistion took a swig and we all stared at him expectantly, waiting for the effects of the poison to manifest themselves.

He was a tall, slender, elegant young man, with a clean-shaven face, penetrating eyes, straight nose, full lips, a sculpted chin. Had he been a woman, he would have been beautiful. As a warrior, he struck some people as soft but that appraisal missed Hephaistion's greatest talents. In addition to his good looks, he was also intelligent, cunning, and a virtuoso sycophant. He and Alexandros, both twenty-two, had grown up together and were inseparable, except possibly on the battlefield.

Flood Tide

As we watched, Hephaistion grabbed his neck and collapsed to the ground. Incomprehensible sounds escaped from his throat; his limbs convulsed spasmodically. His right hand reached out beseechingly to Alexandros while his left hand clutched the tainted cup against his chest. Remarkably, not a drop of the suspect potion had spilled during the entire performance. Philippos the Physician continued calmly to clean the wound.

There was a momentary, stunned silence in the tent, until Alexandros burst out laughing. Tears were rolling down his cheeks. "Alright, let me have some!" he yelled. "This hurts, you know."

Hephaistion sprang to his feet and proffered the chalice to Alexandros with a theatrical flourish. The assembled men broke into boisterous laughter and loud applause in an attempt to cover up their moment of uncertainty. Hephaistion acknowledged their acclaim with a smile and a brief bow.

Alexandros, with Hephaistion's help, drained the chalice in no time. Hephaistion nodded toward the empty cup. "Do you have any more?"

Philippos raised his crimson-stained hands in apology. "Just wine, with nothing in it."

"That'll do." Alexandros winked.

Both Alexandros and Hephaistion were roaring drunk by the time Philippos finished cleaning his hands. He produced a large bronze needle from his bag, dipped it in wine, threaded it with catgut, and stitched the wound together. After inspecting his handiwork to make sure the suture was tight but sufficiently porous to permit pus to ooze out, he covered the wound with a mixture of lint, animal grease, copper oxide, and honey, creating a pleasant smelling but gross looking poultice. A thick, wine-soaked linen cover, secured by leather strips looped repeatedly over the pad and under the king's chin, completed the ensemble.

The effect of the finished job was rather comical and we all started to laugh. Alexandros grabbed a breastplate from the floor, rubbed it furiously with spit and wine, and tried to see himself in the resultant smudge of polished grime. I doubted he could make out anything, what with the limited reflectivity of the smeared bronze surface and the unreliability of the flickering torchlight, but after squinting dubiously at his distorted image for a moment, he broke into loud guffaws. "Now that's a crown fit for a king!"

Parmenion, with his usual impeccable timing, chose that moment to enter the conversation. "You're never going to need to part your hair again, sire." Naturally, his observation brought all levity to an abrupt halt.

Flood Tide

It was as if he had spoken in a foreign tongue. At sixty-six, Parmenion was the oldest man in the tent. Only hours after the battle had ended, his hands and face had been scrubbed clean, his armor immaculate, his beard neatly-trimmed, his eyes tired but hard as ever, his back bent only slightly under the pressures of responsibility, exhaustion, and age. He had been placed in overall command of infantry and allied cavalry at the start of the battle that morning. The troops under his control had performed superbly during the entire day, rolling up the enemy line rendered vulnerable by Alexandros's reckless, albeit ultimately successful, attack against the Persian cavalry.

Every man in that tent, including Alexandros, recognized Parmenion's political acumen and military accomplishments. He'd had a long and distinguished career as one of the leading generals under Alexandros's father, King Philippos Deuteros. When Philippos was assassinated and the twenty-year-old Alexandros acceded to the throne, one of his first acts as the new king was to confirm Parmenion as the commander of the Macedonian expeditionary corps in Asia. After that, Parmenion had maneuvered adroitly to become Alexandros's second-in-command when the long-awaited main-force invasion of Persia finally arrived. Several members of Parmenion's clan, including two of his sons, held important command posts in the army. His third and youngest son, only twelve at the time, was the cavalry's favorite mascot. Parmenion should have been the most important man in that tent, next to Alexandros himself, but he wasn't.

In the two short years since Alexandros had donned the diadem, Parmenion had become the voice of experience, wisdom, and caution. Somehow, he'd acquired the thankless job of trying to contain Alexandros's reckless élan, boundless enthusiasm, and preternatural self-confidence. They were both men of action but Alexandros was also a young man chasing his destiny while Parmenion was an old man trying to preserve his legacy.

"Will it leave a scar?" Alexandros asked Philippos, while glaring at Parmenion.

"No, sire, the scar will be invisible," Philippos reassured him smoothly. "No one will know it's there, beneath all that glorious hair."

"It's a shame you have to wear a helmet, Aniketos,[6]" Hephaistion joked.

Alexandros winked. "Next time we go into battle, I'll let my hair announce me."

"A helmet would do a better job of protecting that stubborn skull of yours," Parmenion observed drily. The man just couldn't help himself.

---

[6] "Aniketos" was Alexandros's nickname. It meant "invincible."

Flood Tide

Alexandros, his effervescence unquenchable, looked over his shoulder toward me. "Hey, Ptolemaios, you're always so damned rational. What do you think? Am I better off wearing my hair or my helmet into battle?"

"Both, I think – with the hair tucked into the helmet."

Everybody in the tent roared with laughter. In the aftermath of victory, every joke was a riot. Most of us – unlike Alexandros and Hephaistion – had not even drunk much wine yet but we were all excited, happy, elated. "We're still here, alive, and the Persians are dead," was the prevailing sentiment. "Can you believe it?"

"There he is!" Alexandros called out when Kleitos Melas walked into the tent. I guess he'd heard my whisper after all. "The butcher of Granikos."

Kleitos broke into a wide grin. "Hardly that, your majesty," he said modestly, giving me a friendly nod when he noticed me standing behind the king.

"Come have a drink with me, man." Alexandros waved his arms for two cups of wine, which promptly materialized in his hands. "Tell me what happened."

"It was nothing, sire. We all fought to keep up with you, which is not always an easy thing to do. You made a hell of a charge, sire. I was sure my horse was gonna drop dead trying to keep up with yours."

"Yeah, Boukephalas was raring to go, wasn't he?"

"Not as raring as you, Aniketos," Hephaistion put in.

"By the time we caught up," Kleitos continued, ignoring Hephaistion, "you were engulfed by the enemy. Mithridates's unit, the best squadron in the Persian cavalry ..."

"Used to be," Hephaistion interjected, to much hilarity, "they're all dead now."

Kleitos attempted to continue. "Mithridates's unit was directly in front of you."

"And I was thrilled to see them." Alexandros's comment provoked fresh gales of laughter.

"I'm sure you were," Kleitos agreed with a broad smile, "but the rest of us were still trying to catch our breaths. Besides, other satraps, with their units, were closing in on us from all sides. I'd never seen anything like it."

"It was the perfect trap," Parmenion observed, genuine admiration in his voice. "They isolated you, sire, with but a small unit around you; cut you off; surrounded you with their best heavy cavalry, led by their top commanders; and prepared to destroy you and your squadron in detail."

"It was great, Parmenion – fantastic!" Alexandros was buoyant. "The perfect trap, as you say. I had them exactly where I wanted them. The cream of Persian nobility, outfitted in their heavy Persian armor, sitting on their weighted-down horses, just waiting for us to mow them down."

"Tell him, Aniketos!" somebody yelled out.

"Hand-to-hand combat against the enemy commanders," Alexandros continued. "For a minute, I thought I saw the walls of Troy looming above us."

"Champion against champion!" someone else interjected.

"Achilleus against Hektor!" This, predictably, from Hephaistion.

"Man on man!"

"Horse on horse!"

"Bullshit on clover!" Kleitos concluded, after which the entire group dissolved into helpless laughter.

"Actually, sire, it was pretty tense for a moment," Kleitos resumed after the merriment had subsided a bit. "I don't know if you remember but when Mithridates threw his javelin at you, from close quarters, and you tried to parry it with your shield, it was like waving an animal pelt to repel a lightning bolt. The spear tip punched right through your shield, through your cuirass, through your tunic, and probably through your skin."

"It hardly left a mark."

"We thought you were dead right then and there."

"I guess I came back from the dead then." Alexandros was reveling in the narrative. "Go on!"

"It was amazing, sire. You jerked the javelin out and threw it at Mithridates, after which you smashed your own spear into his breastplate. Unfortunately, it shattered against his armor."

"Must've hit him too hard."

"He just kept coming. He drew his sword and tried to slash you. You rammed the stub of your spear into his face, dumping him from his horse."

"Wow!" Hephaistion called out.

"You were about to finish him off when another one of their noblemen, Rhosakes, rode up on you from behind and hit you over the head with his sword, slicing your helmet in two and leaving that scratch on your skull."

Flood Tide

"That's the point where my recollection gets a little hazy," Alexandros admitted.

"Well, sire, anybody else would surely have been out cold but you still managed to keep your seat on Boukephalas, to spin, and to slash your sword across Rhosakes's face, killing him instantly."

"It wasn't me anymore, Kleitos. Some supernatural force had taken hold of my body."

"No, Aniketos, it was all you, doing what you do best." Hephaistion was getting to be pretty annoying.

"Just then," Kleitos continued, ignoring Hephaistion, "another satrap, Spithridates, came charging at you from behind."

"Rhosakes's brother," Parmenion observed, drawing an irritated look from Alexandros.

Kleitos forged ahead undaunted. "You were a mess by then, sire, just sitting there, slumped forward, holding on to Boukephalas's mane, helmet smashed, your face covered in blood. I couldn't tell whether you were conscious or not. But I could see Spithridates sneaking up on you from behind, raising his sword, ready to finish you off."

The tent was silent. Those of us who had witnessed the scene relived our own emotions during that infinitely long instant when we had all thought we were watching Alexandros's last moments on Earth.

"And that's when I cut his arm off," Kleitos concluded cheerfully.

It was uncanny. We all let out a collective sigh of relief, as if we had not known, simply from seeing Alexandros sitting there, laughing and drinking, that Spithridates's sword had not completed its predestined arc and Alexandros's head had not gotten sliced in two like a ripe pomegranate.

In my case, I was also sighing for the certainty I'd lost during that brief quantum of time. Up to that instant, I'd known, to an epistemological certainty, that Alexandros would die during the battle. When he didn't, my entire world view wobbled on its axis. Now, hours after I'd witnessed his survival, I was still nauseous, suffering from a form of kinetosis that might more accurately be called chronotosis.

Of course, the story didn't end there. Despite Kleitos's timely intervention, Alexandros was nevertheless rendered unconscious, was dislodged from his horse, and was almost killed by the Persian cavalry that engulfed us. But nobody was interested in that part of the story.

Alexandros grew serious for an instant. "Thank you, Kleitos, for saving my life."

Flood Tide

The king's seer – Aristandros was his name – couldn't stand the moment of genuine gratitude. "It was foreordained, your majesty," he hurried to declare. "This man was but the instrument chosen by the Fates to advance your destiny, great king. Your survival was never in doubt. I had read it in the auguries before the battle, remember?"

"It's true, Aristandros. You did tell me, before the battle, that the signs were propitious and we would emerge victorious. Though you neglected to mention that I would emerge with a new part in my hair."

"Sorry, sire. The entrails can be a little messy."

A tiny, barely audible snort escaped me. No one, except Aristandros, noticed it.

"Well, try to be a little more accurate next time," Alexandros said in mock rebuke. "And you, Kleitos, don't bother waiting until somebody bops me on the head before intervening, got that?"

"Yes, sire."

"And make sure you're close at hand at the banquet the day after tomorrow. I might be surrounded by a bunch of drunkards and in need of your protection once again," Alexandros joked.

"You need no protection from us," Hephaistion assured him.

Alexandros ignored the interruption. "Besides, Kleitos, there is a chance you might be singled out during the distribution of honors and rewards. What do you think, Aristandros? Will I survive the banquet the day after tomorrow?"

"I have to slaughter a sheep before I can tell you for sure, sire. For now, I'd just keep an eye on Ptolemaios here," Aristandros said, pointing at me. "He looks pretty menacing with that torch and that bloody rag in his hand."

"It's not blood; it's only wine." My defensive response was drowned out by everybody's laugher. It was an easily amused crowd but Aristandros's poisoned barb was no accident. He'd maintained an unfailing antipathy toward me since the day I met him.

Surprisingly, Alexandros came to my defense. "Leave Metoikos alone. From what I could see, he fought pretty well today."

I forced a smile. "Thank you, sire."

Ptolemaios Metoikos is what they called me. It was meant to be an affectionate nickname. The word Metoikos meant traveler, alien, stranger, outsider. Having a nickname showed I'd arrived, which was true, both literally and figuratively. I'd arrived in this young, vital, exuberant era as an enthusiastic and naive twenty-one-year-old explorer, intending to observe an initiation ceremony, unobtrusively and tracelessly, and then return home after a few days. Now, nine years later, I was still here but, in the interim, I'd managed to earn a place in Alexandros's elite Companion Cavalry and become one of his personal bodyguards.

Alexandros switched directions abruptly. "Well, don't just stand there. Let's start drinking! And bring something to eat! I'm famished. And where are my reports?"

Parmenion spoke up. "The men are here, sire. Have a bite to eat and when you're done, they'll make their reports."

Several orderlies materialized in the tent, bearing large bronze chargers, heaping with bread – dark, stale, and hard, but tantalizing for all that. They also carried in several small tables to hold the platters, along with a few terracotta kylikes filled with turbid olive oil, barely suitable for dipping. Finally, and to much applause, they dragged in an enormous silver krater and proceeded to fill it with pitcher after pitcher of red wine and local water. We stopped them before they could ruin the wine with too much water and used the water to wash our hands instead. Then, after a perfunctory libation, we all fell to it, acting as if we had not eaten since before the battle, which in fact we hadn't.

"Stop!" Alexandros roared. "Let's thank the gods first, sing a paean, make a proper libation, and then we can eat and drink."

"Easy for you to say. You've been drinking all this time," somebody objected, to catcalls and laughter, but we all stopped eating and did as we were told. Then we devoured the bread and drowned it with diluted wine.

We all did, that is, except for Alexandros, who didn't start eating immediately. "I can eat and listen at the same time," he told Parmenion. "Let's have those reports."

For someone who hadn't slept in two days, who'd suffered a severe blow to the head only hours earlier, who'd just undergone surgery without the benefit of anesthesia, who'd drunk enough fortified wine to render a mere mortal unconscious, Alexandros had a surprisingly healthy appetite and a remarkably clear mind.

While we all ate, and mostly while we all drank, Alexandros listened to a detailed listing of Macedonian casualties. He'd already spoken, in the immediate aftermath of the battle, to as many of his wounded soldiers as he could find, before retiring to his tent and submitting to the ministrations of his physician. Still, he wanted updated reports and repeatedly asked for assurances that the injured men were receiving the best possible care. He teared up at the mention of each comrade lost in combat but in fact our casualties were minimal given the scale of the battle. Only a few dozen of our men were dead, and perhaps as many as two hundred lay wounded. (The twenty-five members of the Companion Cavalry who'd died during the initial, unsuccessful – some might say foolish – assault across the Granikos River weighed especially heavily on Alexandros. In due course, he had statues erected to each one of them at Dion, a city located at the foot of Mount Olympos.)

Our casualties would escalate, and Alexandros's sentimentality would diminish, as our campaigns unfolded, but I didn't know any of that as we boisterously celebrated our unexpected victory over the Persians. Well, at least it was unexpected to me; I had fully anticipated – no, I had known – that the Macedonians would lose. It struck me, for the second time that day, that I was utterly lost. *I've got no idea what comes next.*

Watching my fellow soldiers, whooping and hollering, teasing and laughing, eating and drinking, pissing, retching, and then drinking some more, I stood there, alone, sipping my wine and trying to cope with the deepening realization that I had no better grasp on what fate had in store for us than they did. It was a little disconcerting suddenly to lose my road map to the future but, in a perverse way, my abrupt loss of prescience left me with an odd sense of liberation. *No more Prime Directive[7] to worry about*, I told myself. Of course, I knew better, even as the thought flashed through my mind, but I couldn't bring myself to analyze my situation clearly. It was just too early.

Alexandros's insistent voice cut through my jumbled ruminations. "I need exact figures! How many men did the enemy lose?"

"Sire, it's dark outside," Parmenion protested. "We'll count the bodies tomorrow."

"If we can count that high," someone chuckled.

Alexandros was especially curious to know the fate of the Greek mercenaries who had fought on the Persian side. "I don't want a single traitor to escape the battlefield," he said more than once.

"Most of them are dead, sire, and the few that survived are prisoners," Parmenion assured him.

"I didn't want any Greek prisoners," Alexandros muttered, but he let the subject pass, at least for the moment. "What about the plans for the victory games and the big feast?"

---

[7] The Prime Directive was the paramount commandment, drummed into the heads of all time travelers, to do nothing that might influence, interfere with, or change the future course of events.

Flood Tide

"Tomorrow, sire, tomorrow," Parmenion told him.

"It's always tomorrow with you, Parmenion. I think we'll change your name to Not-Today Parmenion."

The wittiness of that last remark required another round of drinks for everybody in the tent. We had all started out high in the wake of the battle but now, slowly but surely, we were all also getting drunk. Plus, the elation of victory started to give way to bone-weariness and the gradual recognition of niggling cuts and bruises and, in some cases, more serious injuries.

Men started to drift away. Parmenion brought in sentries to stand guard outside the tent overnight while those of us left inside, including Alexandros, collapsed into dreamless sleep, on packed dirt or, if we were lucky, on trampled patches of sod.

******

I was awakened by a sharp poke in the ribs. "Get up, smart ass!" somebody whispered in my ear. In the near total darkness of the tent, all I could see was a man with a long beard leaning over me, holding a knife to my throat.

My training kicked in before I was fully awake. Using my left palm to parry the arm holding the knife, I used my other hand to grab my assailant by the neck, unbalance him, rotate him to his back, and pin him on the ground, all in one nice, smooth movement.

"Help, help! He's trying to kill me!" My attacker unleashed an anguished outcry.

I recognized his voice. "Aristandros? What the hell are you doing?"

"Let go of me, you lunatic!" he yelled. The commotion roused my sleeping companions and brought the sentries running.

Aristandros continued to scream. "He tried to kill me!"

I stood up, releasing my would-be assassin. "He's the one holding the knife," I pointed out to the small circle of people that had formed around us. But when we looked, there was no knife to be found.

"He had a nightmare," Aristandros sneered, brushing himself off. Nobody else was amused. Grumbling, they all went back to sleep or back to their posts.

I lay down as well but couldn't fall asleep. *This guy is a problem.*

At that time, Aristandros of Telmessos was probably in his fifties but looked older. He was bald, with a fringe of long, thin, flowing white hair. His beard was much more robust than his hair but also completely white. His face had the expected furrows, folds, wrinkles, moles and skin tags of a veritable sage and prophet but his small, furtive eyes exuded all the warmth of a venomous snake.

He was a seer, which meant he read entrails, deciphered auguries, interpreted dreams, delivered oracular pronouncements, explained the inexplicable, communicated with the gods, and generally predicted the future. In other words, he was a charlatan.

I couldn't remember the first time I had become aware of his existence. It must have been shortly after my arrival at the Macedonian court in Pella because Aristandros was already well-established in King Philippos's retinue by that time. He had first made his fame, a dozen or more years earlier, by interpreting a vivid dream that had jolted the king out of his postcoital sleep, one night shortly after his marriage to his fourth wife, Olympias.

Philippos had watched himself, in this dream, sealing Olympias's vagina with wax and stamping the plug with his royal device, which featured a rampant lion. Needless to say, the dream occasioned a certain amount of consternation. Philippos's first impulse was to question his new wife's chastity but his advisors, when he recounted the dream to them, gave widely disparate explanations, ranging from incipient frigidity to latent bestiality. One well-established soothsayer even permitted himself an allusion to impotence, which resulted in his instantaneous and permanent banishment from court. None of the explanations sounded the expected peal of revelation in Philippos's mind.

Aristandros, recently arrived at the court, heard about the dream and managed to secure an audience with the king. He told Philippos there was a simple explanation for the dream: Olympias was pregnant. After all, he reasoned, people did not seal empty amphorae. Philippos was overjoyed but Aristandros was only getting started. He also predicted, based on the design of the king's seal, that the child would be boisterous, leonine, and male. When it turned out that Olympias was in fact pregnant and did deliver in due course a healthy, energetic, and evidently bright baby boy, whom his parents named Alexandros, Aristandros became a permanent fixture at court, presumably taking over the job vacated by the unfortunate impotency alluder.

When the prophesied son assumed the throne upon the death of his father, Aristandros's influence at court increased immeasurably. Before Alexandros undertook any new venture, appointed a commander, entered into a treaty, wrote a letter, changed his tunic, went to the latrine, made any important decision at all, he would consult with, and rely upon the prognostications of, his number one soothsayer, Aristandros the Seer.

Flood Tide

And I had to admit, Aristandros was uncanny in the accuracy of his predictions. Until that moment, it had not struck me how remarkable his foresight had been. I'd never thought about it, I suppose, because I'd always been able to foresee the same events with equal accuracy. Of course, in my case, I'd read about all those events in the history books in preparation for what was meant to be my quick expedition into the past. Somehow, I'd never stopped to wonder how Aristandros could see the future so clearly in the entrails of slaughtered animals, in the patterns of cast lots, in the rustling of leaves of sacred trees, in the flights of eagles, or in any number of other, essentially random events. But he was never wrong.

On the other hand, he was an old, scrawny noncombatant. It seemed incredible, even to me, that he would attempt to attack me physically. Admittedly, he'd been unremitting in his efforts to derail any advancement coming my way at the court but his efforts had always been cerebral, not physical. *Perhaps I'd dreamt it after all.* I rejected the thought before I'd finished thinking it. I didn't confuse dreams with reality. On the contrary, I prided myself on my ability to recognize, even amidst a nightmare, that what I was seeing in my mind was simply a dream. And, perhaps more importantly, while awake, I never suffered from hallucinations. *No, it had really happened, but why? Why is this guy so much on my case?*

Despite the nine years I'd spent serving the king, not all my fellow soldiers necessarily accepted me as one of their own. There was a reason why they called me Metoikos. My Macedonian dialect had improved over the years, as had my horsemanship. I'd proven myself on the field of battle and at the drinking parties. I'd become one of Alexandros's leading commanders but I couldn't become a Macedonian. Some of my fellow commanders resented not only my rapid advancement but also my very existence in their midst. Perhaps Aristandros had acted at the behest, and with the connivance, of my enemies in the ranks. *That smacks of paranoia*, I thought. *Besides, Aristandros always struck me as someone actuated by an animosity all his own.* Of course, that didn't exclude the possibility that the insidious fortune-teller and the conspiratorial commanders were proceeding on parallel tracks.

I have to get to the bottom of this, I thought. *This guy's been rubbing me the wrong way for a long time.* I got up and set off in search of the elusive seer. I found him sitting at the edge of the tent, gazing at the stars. I sat next to him.

"I knew you were going to come," he whispered, without turning his head. "I read it in the stars."

The ridicule in his voice set my blood aboil. "Don't bother pulling your pranks with me. I'm not Alexandros. I can see right through you. And the next time you pull a knife on me, I'll bury it in your gullet. It'll be sticking out of your craw, I promise you."

Flood Tide

"I don't think so," he said airily, rising to his feet. "I don't think you can see through anything at all. You're just a blind bastard who's lost his way."

For some reason, his comment chilled me to the core. Until a mere few hours earlier, I'd known exactly where I was going. I'd arrived in ancient Macedonia, nine years before, for what was basically a training mission, intended to last a little less than three days. Although I was a third-year cadet at the Academy, this was my first actual time trip, after having gone through many, many live-fire exercises in the VCS.[8] All had gone as planned (or so I'd thought). After completing my assignment, I'd arrived at the rendezvous point in good time and waited patiently for the appearance of the artificial portal that would get me back to my own time. At the appointed hour, the portal had failed to materialize. I then waited, with rising anxiety and foreboding, for the extraction team that never came. After a while, I was forced to admit there would be no rescue and, if I ever wanted to see my home again, I would have to make my own way to the emergency escape hatch, a naturally occurring phenomenon next slated to take place on the Mediterranean coast of Egypt, near the Nile delta, in 266 Z.E.[9] In the meantime, I was stranded in this ancient era.

All had proceeded more or less as I'd expected. I had the benefit of having read, in preparation for my trip,

---

[8] Virtual Chronoportation Simulator
[9] Zoroaster Era, calculated from Zoroaster's purported date of birth

all that was known about this place and time in our history books and the travelogues of my forerunners. As a result, I had a working knowledge at least about the major personalities and events that I would encounter along my way to the escape hatch. Unfortunately, I had no recollection of ever reading anything about some obscure soothsayer named Aristandros.

The Battle of Granikos was a major event I remembered clearly from my studies. Therefore, I had known exactly what the outcome would be, including the death of the Macedonian leader Alexandros and the annihilation of his forces, and had made my plans accordingly. I had even scoffed when Aristandros had read the entrails and predicted a Macedonian victory. *What a fool*, I'd thought. The fact that this was the first instance of a forecast by Aristandros that contradicted what I knew from the history books didn't seem significant at the time.

When it turned out that the history books were wrong, that Alexandros didn't get killed, and that the Macedonians actually won the Battle of Granikos, I felt physically nauseous, suffering from a kind of time sickness. My moorings had come loose and I had yet to recover my orientation in space-time. Although I refused to think about it, somewhere deep within my subconscious mind, I realized that an impulsive and thoughtless act, in which I had indulged shortly after my arrival, had in fact violated the Prime Directive. As a result, I had evidently altered the future, which explained the failure of the portal to appear and which also explained the unexpected outcome of the Battle of Granikos. But I was not yet prepared to think about any of that. All I knew for sure was that I had lost my ability to see the future, which I suppose was the reason why Aristandros's off hand comment cut me to the quick.

I ran after him, tripping over a body in the dim moonlight. He waited while I regained my footing and caught up to him, an indulgent smile on his face. "As I said, blind as a bat."

"What do you want from me?"

"I want you to disappear, my friend." He steepled his hands. "You're a bad influence on Alexandros, trying to undermine his faith and all. And besides, you don't belong here."

"I belong here as much as you do." I let my peevishness get the better of me. "And I'm sticking around until I'm good and ready to go home. I'm certainly not letting any goat-turd-stirrer like you tell me what I can or can't do."

"I couldn't care less, Metoikos, what you do or where you go, as long as you stay out of my way. But I can tell you one thing for sure. You're never going home again."

Chapter 2 – The Day After

I dreamt of Aphrodite. She was in her chambers, attended by naiads, getting ready for a date. Zeus, forced by Hera to sleep in the stables once again after Aphrodite tricked him into ravishing yet another mortal maiden, decided to pay her back. He beguiled the goddess of love with an irresistible longing to seduce a mortal man. Now, under the vengeful spell of the king of the gods, Aphrodite, desperate to consummate her connubial conjunction, didn't want to leave anything to chance. Despite her divine allure, the goddess was primping, putting on her finest diaphanous gown, dabbing her breasts with provocative perfumes, outlining her eyes with kohl and moistening her lips with her tongue. And the mortal man she chose was me.

Notwithstanding the likely fatal consequences of a liaison with a goddess, I was willing to accommodate Aphrodite's involuntary appetites. In fact, I was feeling rather proud of my manhood even as I found myself on the point of immolation. But then, just on the verge of impalement, she changed her mind.

She was receding from me – an incandescent presence, much too bright to approach – yet I insisted on chasing after her. She never glanced back. I knew, even without seeing her face, that she was leading me astray, but I didn't care. The deeper into darkness we ran, the more determined – and frustrating – my pursuit became.

Soon, I was hopelessly lost. I could still feel her heat, so I knew I was close, but could see nothing. I continued to run, blindly and with my arms outstretched, scared but unable to stop. I sensed a presence directly in front of me, grabbed for it, and found myself clutching a coarse woolen cloak. I yanked at the coat, causing its wearer to turn. It was Aristandros, his face distorted by anger and contempt. Beyond him, far in the distance, I glimpsed the blazing aura of the vanishing goddess, her shoulders shaking with laughter. I let go of the cloak and resumed the chase, leaving a sputtering Aristandros behind.

I ran as fast as I could, leaping over yawning fissures and eluding snarling beasts, narrowing the gap between me and the sultry temptress, only to get snared by some viscid vines, which turned out to be the arms of two of my fellow Companion Cavalry commanders who were particularly ill-disposed toward me. After a brief struggle, I slipped their grip, stamped on some hissing insects, whom I recognized as the soldiers who had captured me years ago, and pressed ahead.

While I was distracted fighting my enemies, the object of my desire disappeared behind a solid wall of vegetation. I was trapped in a maze from which there was no escape. *Who is it this time?* I asked myself, feelings of exasperation welling up in my chest. *There has to be a way out,* I told myself but deep down I knew this adventure wouldn't end well.

Unexpectedly, an opening materialized in front of me. I barged through and caught sight of the glowing goddess once again. I redoubled my speed. She was right there in front of me. I seized her radiant penumbra, spun her toward me, and felt her melt in my arms. A warmth spread in my loins. I rolled over and the warmth turned into a stabbing pain. I looked down and saw Aristandros's knife wedged between the ground and my groin. *So that's where he hid it.* I woke up.

****

There was no knife, of course, just my usual early-morning erection. I sprang to my feet, ready to face (after taking a quick leak) whatever threats the world had in store for me. My conversation with Aristandros was still fresh in my mind. While I had no doubt as to his genuine hostility toward me, his knife attack seemed really out of character. I would have expected him to be a more devious adversary. *I've got to think more clearly*, I told myself.

Flood Tide

I shook my head, trying to clear the cobwebs, but it was no use. Where once I'd enjoyed crystal clear vision, without even realizing what a gift that was, now I was befuddled, frustrated, myopic, unable to discern my place in the world and the best way forward. *Am I surrounded by friends or foes?*

The loyalty of the men in my own squadron was beyond peradventure but there were other soldiers and commanders whose attitudes toward me were more ambiguous. For some reason, perhaps as a result of the dream, I had a feeling that something sinister was afoot. What bothered me much more, however, was the sense of existential vertigo I'd been unable to shake ever since I realized that everything I'd thought I knew about the flow of history might've been an illusion.

Looking at my comrades slowly beginning to rouse around me, it struck me as ironic that, with bands of armed enemy soldiers most likely still roaming the woods and hills nearby, I was worried about men fighting on my side of the conflict. *You're not taking sides*, I reminded myself, *you're just trying to get to the escape hatch in time. Now get your ass in gear!*

Before I had a chance to do anything about my ass or otherwise act on my good intentions, Alexandros came roaring into the tent, trailing a phalanx of aides. He was wearing full armor, which had been polished to its customary state of luster. Instead of a helmet, though, he was still sporting his risible bandage but somehow in the morning light it no longer detracted from his dignity. It was obvious he'd been up and about for some time. I wondered whether he'd gotten any sleep at all.

Parmenion, trotting alongside the king, was once again clearly on the defensive. "I can't explain it, sire. We had them surrounded. There was no way for anyone to get away."

"So where in Haides is he?"

"I don't know, sire. He's not among the captives and we can't find his body. I have personally questioned some of the captured Greek mercenaries but nobody seems to know where he is. He seems to have vanished into thin air."

Alexandros pushed Parmenion out of the way. "Aristandros, get over here!"

The slimy charlatan slithered toward Alexandros. "Here I am, sire."

Alexandros was ready to explode. "That son-of-a-whore Memnon is missing."

"So I see," the slimy seer sibilated. His powers of perception were exceeded only by his dazzling desire to delight.

"I need you to tell us where to find him."

"That will require some work, sire. And it may take a little time. The gods are not always standing by awaiting our inquiries."

"We don't have time, you idiot. While we're chatting, Memnon is getting away."

Aristandros remained unperturbed. "Sire, divination cannot be rushed." You had to admire his gall. "Have your men bring me a white goat and three commanders from Memnon's brigade."

"Where am I going find a white goat?" Alexandros asked, reasonably enough.

"Your majesty, I will need a green river turtle if I have to divine the location of a white goat."

I burst out laughing, which was probably a mistake.

Alexandros reached for his sword, ready to kill someone; it wasn't clear whom. Finally, he relented. "Seleukos found a dog last night. You can have it instead of a goat. And we can certainly bring you three captured mercenaries. You'll just have to manage."

Aristandros, perceptively reading his patron's tone, didn't argue. "The dog will be fine. I'll get my instruments. Please have Seleukos fetch the dog."

"I'm not letting this butcher kill my puppy." Seleukos started to argue but he was silenced by one look at the king. "Yes, sire, I'll be right back."

"Is he also going to examine the entrails of the three Greek captives?" Kleitos inquired innocently. Alexandros ignored him.

We formed a circle just outside the tent. Seleukos returned, carrying a lively brown and black puppy, with a white dickey on its chest and a perpetual smile on its snout, and attempted to hand the dog to Alexandros. "Not me – him!" the king barked.

Aristandros got down on his hands and knees and started to scratch the dog behind its ears, while rubbing noses with the animal and cooing stupidly. The dog wagged its tail. Seleukos cried silently. The rest of us simply stared. Aristandros's "instrument," which turned out to be his butcher knife, materialized from a fold in his long white tunic. *So that's where he hid it.* The dog never noticed the knife at all. Aristandros cut its throat while still cooing softly.

"It's important for the victim to be calm when you cut its throat," he explained. "Otherwise, it will tense its muscles and spoil the signs."

It seemed to me that the muscles of the dog, which was convulsing spasmodically as its life spurted into the dirt, were fairly tense but I refrained from voicing my doubts.

As soon as the bleeding slowed to a trickle, Aristandros proceeded to carve up the poor animal, staining his nice white tunic crimson in the process. The entrails steamed in the cool morning air as he wrestled them out of the tiny abdominal cavity. Blood covered his arms up to his elbows. He peered closely into the intestines, nodding sagely several times. I was sure he was going to dip his nose into the bloody mess. An image of a red-snouted badger crossed my mind.

Aristandros rose to his feet, continuing to nod sagely. I was disappointed to see that his nose hadn't turned into a scarlet beak. "Now, bring me the prisoners," he ordered. All of us in the circle of spectators wondered what he would do next. "One at a time," he clarified.

The first prisoner was dragged in. He was a young man, wearing only a heavily-stained tunic, with unkempt hair and anxious eyes. He was probably not reassured by the approach of a madman drenched in blood and holding a bloody knife.

"I'm not going to hurt you," Aristandros whispered in his ear. "I just need some information." The prisoner was paralyzed, staring at the sanguinary lunatic in terror. "Where is Memnon?"

After a moment, the prisoner regained his power of speech. He tried to make up for lost time by unleashing a defensive torrent of excuses. "I've got no clue. I haven't seen him since yesterday. We were all fighting for our lives. I wasn't keeping an eye on him. I have no idea where he is."

Aristandros raised the bloody knife.

"His orderly was holding his horse behind the lines," the prisoner blurted out. "He must've ridden away."

"We figured that out." Aristandros was patience personified as he raised the knife ever closer to the man's throat. "What we want to know is where he was riding to."

"I have no idea," the prisoner repeated.

A thin red line appeared at the junction of blade and skin.

"But his wife is in Ekbatana."

Aristandros nodded sagely and released the prisoner, who sank to his knees. "Take him away!" He turned to the king. "Memnon is on the Royal Road to Ekbatana, your majesty," he said gravely. "All the signs are in agreement."

Nobody laughed, much to my amazement. Perhaps they believed this charlatan. More likely, Alexandros, who did not appear the least bit amused, petrified them.

Alexandros turned to Philotas, the ranking cavalry commander. "Take two squadrons and chase him down!"

"Send Ptolemaios instead," Aristandros interjected.

"Why?"

"The signs, sire, the signs."

The king didn't even pause. "Ptolemaios, take two squadrons and run down that traitor! I expect to see him standing in front of me – in chains – at the banquet tomorrow."

The entire turn of events was so bizarre, I had no idea what to say. "Yes, your majesty," was the best I could manage.

"Sire, before they go," Parmenion ventured quietly, "we should stop to think for a moment, sire. Is it a good idea to send a small company chasing after stragglers? There are thousands of enemy troops out there. Although most of them are running for their lives, scared out of their wits, a few decent soldiers might still be lurking among them. It's possible they might regroup and ambush a pursuing group. Besides, we've no idea where Memnon might have gone, so we'd be chasing in the dark. Sire, we'll see him again, I'm sure, and we'll kill him when we do, but right now I'm afraid he's managed to slip away."

"I see what you mean." Alexandros sounded almost agreeable. Then, turning his head, he mimicked a look of surprise. "Ptolemaios, why are you still here?"

"But sire," Parmenion started to protest.

"Oh shut up!" Alexandros was suddenly weary. He raised an eyebrow in my direction. I took my cue and left, grabbing Kleitos and Seleukos on my way out.

"This is a suicide mission," Seleukos said as soon as we'd left the tent.

"Plus there's no chance we can catch Memnon. And if we did, he'd fight back," Kleitos added. "We don't even know what he looks like at the moment; he's probably not wearing his usual white-crested helmet."

I dismissed their concerns, striking a tone of optimism I didn't feel. "Let's not worry too much about Memnon. Our primary mission, my friends, is to stay alive. Surely, we can accomplish that much. Now let's get organized." *Can't believe that bastard Aristandros figured out a way to kill me without even working up a sweat*, is what actually flashed through my mind. *But why? All I want to do is go home.* For the past nine years my singular lodestar had been that elusive escape hatch in faraway Egypt that would take me back home. My memories of the people and places I'd left behind were beginning to fade. The only constant was this nagging, gnawing, inarticulate yearning to regain the life I'd lost. I chose not to share my thoughts with my fellow fighters.

Moments later, my squadron, augmented by a couple of dozen men from Kleitos's and Seleukos's commands, was mounted, armed, and ready for combat. We set off across the battlefield in a southwesterly direction, carrying sufficient provisions for a one-day trip only.

Kleitos, Seleukos, and I were riding in the van of our small group. We were, at the time, of roughly equal rank in Alexandros's army, each commanding a squadron of the Companion Cavalry, although there was a strict hierarchy among Alexandros's cavalry commanders. The commander of the first squadron, then Philotas, was deemed hipparchos or the overall commander of the entire Companion Cavalry. The commanders of the first seven squadrons were known as the somatophylakes, or the bodyguards, of Alexandros. I was one of the seven. We outranked the commanders of the remaining squadrons, including Kleitos and Seleukos. There were, of course, other units in Alexandros's army, such as the Silver Shields infantry brigade, the light infantry, the allied cavalry, the allied infantry, and the auxiliaries, and each unit had its own command structure but, at least in our own minds, the Companion Cavalry was the elite division of the entire army.

I had brought Kleitos along because he was my friend. Seleukos was not exactly a friend but at least he was not an antagonist either, which made him unusual among the Companion Cavalry commanders. In addition, he knew more about Persia and the Persians than anyone in Alexandros's army. I figured some local knowledge might prove useful during our wild goose chase after Memnon.

By the time we had managed to pull out, the sun had climbed above the dark blue mountain range to our west, dissipating the last wisps of mist rising from the dense forests mantling its flanks. The plain between the Granikos River and the mountain range we were about to traverse had been, a little more than twenty-four hours earlier, a tranquil sea of green stalks of wheat, undulating gently in the morning breeze. Now, as our horses carefully picked their way toward the foothills, it was a morass of churned mud, trampled vegetation, and bloated corpses. Vultures competed raucously with crows for the tastiest morsels of putrefying flesh.

Living men scurried among the dead, stripping them of arms, armor, clothing, and other valuables, tossing their finds into wagons stationed nearby. Teams of horses dragged chains of human cadavers and equine carcasses toward assembly points, where they were heaped indiscriminately onto large mounds and burned. Huddled upwind from the awful stench of roasting flesh sat the captured prisoners, thousands of them, waiting to be processed by their harried captors.

The survivors of the Greek mercenary brigade that had been commanded by Memnon were penned in a separate enclosure. There weren't supposed to be any survivors of the Greek mercenary brigade. Alexandros, who normally treated defeated adversaries with respect and compassion, had issued specific orders that the Greek mercenaries were to be slaughtered to the last man. He considered their willingness to fight on behalf of the barbarian Persians and against their fellow Greeks an unforgivable sin. In a rare instance of disobedience to orders, Macedonian infantrymen had refused to kill the mercenaries once they had thrown down their weapons and surrendered. Perhaps two thousand Greek mercenaries had survived the battle, out of an original corps of five thousand, much to Alexandros's displeasure.

However, that displeasure was minor compared to Alexandros's rage at the failure of his troops to capture or kill Memnon himself. The Rhodian condottiere had a long history with Alexandros and with the Macedonian high command. When Alexandros's father Philippos dispatched the Macedonian expeditionary corps across the Hellespont, two years earlier, to prepare the ground for the main-force invasion of Asia, the joint commanders of the corps, Parmenion and Attalos, had an easy time of it at first. The Greek-speaking inhabitants of Persian-controlled Ionia welcomed them as liberators; the local satraps, with their contingents of untrained conscripts, were finding it difficult to resist them; and the new Persian emperor Dareios was too distracted solidifying his hold on power to pay any attention to Ionia just then. Eventually, the nuisance of the Macedonian invasion reached the top of Dareios's things-to-do list and he dispatched his most effective commander, Memnon of Rhodos, at the head of a brigade of Greek mercenaries to put a little steel into the weak native contingents and to reestablish order and control. Memnon quickly inflicted several setbacks on the Macedonian expeditionary corps and it was all that Parmenion could do (Attalos had been killed in the meantime) to maintain a beachhead around the Hellespont long enough for the main force, under Alexandros, to land. Unsurprisingly, Memnon was neither Alexandros's nor Parmenion's favorite commander.

But the 46-year-old Memnon's history with the Macedonians went back much further than that. Memnon's father had been a leading oligarch on the Island of Rhodos. When he was killed, during one of the periodic social upheavals on that prosperous but restless island, his two adult sons escaped to Hellespontine Phrygia, where their older sister was one of the wives of the local satrap Artabazos. Hellespontine Phrygia was the most important, and powerful, satrapy guarding the western frontier of the Persian Empire and Artabazos, a grandson of emperor Artaxerxes Deuteros, was one of the salient figures of the Persian nobility.

A man with a keen appreciation for both the marital and martial skills of the Greeks, Artabazos put his newly-arrived brothers-in-law to work training his private army. He also hired thousands of Greek mercenaries as part of an effort to turn his army into a regional force that rivaled the might of the imperial army itself. He eventually put the older brother, Mentor, in command of this growing army and, to cement the relationship, he married his prepubescent daughter Barsine to her uncle Mentor. (Artabazos had twenty-one children, so he could afford to be somewhat profligate in arranging his matrimonial alliances.)

When Artaxerxes Deuteros died under suspicious circumstances in 228 Z.E., his son Ochos became the new emperor, assuming the name Artaxerxes Tritos. Artabazos took advantage of the resultant upheaval to lead a rebellion of satraps against the new emperor. After years of internecine fighting, with Greek mercenaries deployed in large numbers on both sides of the conflict, Ochos ultimately prevailed and Artabazos, along with his entire family, was forced to flee for his life.

In order to escape beyond Ochos's enormous sphere of influence, Artabazos chose to seek asylum at the court of Ochos's most vocal adversary in the Greek world, king Philippos of Macedonia. Artabazos, his wives, his children, and his sons-in-law spent several years living at the royal palace in Pella. King Philippos's young son Alexandros was seven when he first met Artabazos, Mentor, and Memnon. They spent an idle afternoon chatting. The trio, anxious to maintain cordial relations with King Philippos, attempted to regale the young prince with an assortment of Persian fairy tales. Alexandros was not interested in fairy tales. He wanted factual information about the extent, geography, and wealth of Persia, about the military might of the empire, the armaments of the troops, the logistics of moving such large forces through such great distances. Artabazos shook his head at the peculiarity of this child but tried to humor him by telling him, in his broken Greek, more fairy tales. Mentor took Alexandros's inquiries more seriously and attempted to answer some of his questions but kept getting interrupted by Memnon. "You're too young to understand," the 31-year-old Memnon would say or "You're way too handsome to worry your pretty head about stuff like that." Alexandros never forgave him.

Eventually, Mentor grew tired of the provinciality of the Macedonian capital and of his enforced idleness. He returned to Persia, begging Ochos's forgiveness and throwing himself on Ochos's mercy. Mentor explained that he'd been forced to command Artabazos's army because Artabazos held his wife Barsine hostage. Ochos, who'd suffered several defeats at the hands of troops commanded by Mentor, recognized and appreciated military talent. He placed Mentor at the head of a large Persian army and tasked him with reconquering Egypt, which had slipped from Persian control some sixty years earlier. Much to Ochos's amazement and pleasant surprise, Mentor actually succeeded in his assignment. Ochos was crowned pharaoh in Memphis and Egypt once again became a satrapy of the Persian Empire.

Ochos bestowed munificent gifts on this soldier of fortune and appointed him permanent commander of the Greek mercenary brigade. Mentor gratefully accepted the bounty but asked for one additional gift. He sought Ochos's pardon for his family, including of course the entire Artabazos clan. Ochos swallowed hard but granted his victorious general's request, forgiving all and restoring Artabazos as satrap of Hellespontine Phrygia.

And, if this had been a fairy tale, they would have all lived happily ever after. Unfortunately for the Artabazos clan, they lived in Persia. Inevitably, people started to die. Mentor himself, the victorious general, was the first to go. He died (ostensibly of natural causes) three years after welcoming his family back to Persia. As a result, his brother Memnon took over command of the Greek mercenary brigade. By sheer happenstance, Ochos was murdered shortly thereafter and was replaced on the throne by an ineffectual youngster, named Arses, who was in turn murdered and supplanted by a very effective military officer named Kodomannos. The upstart

Kodomannos, whose claim to royal blood was almost certainly entirely fictitious, decided to burnish his credentials, upon ascending to the emperorship, by taking the name Dareios Tritos. Moreover, while his claim to the throne might have been fictitious, his appreciation of military talent was entirely genuine. Accordingly, he confirmed Memnon in his position as commander of the Greek mercenary brigade and, when the Macedonian expeditionary corps crossed the Hellespont, he dispatched Memnon to deal with this nuisance while Dareios fought off various rebellions, usurpation efforts, and attempted assassinations.

Shortly after Mentor died, Memnon also did his duty as the younger brother and married Mentor's wife (and his niece) Barsine, who had fortuitously reached puberty by this stage. Barsine bore him three daughters and a son. Fifteen years after his encounter with the seven-year-old Alexandros in Pella and ten years after his return to Persia, Memnon commanded the Greek mercenaries against Alexandros's army on the left bank of the Granikos River.

As far as Alexandros was concerned, not only was Memnon a Greek fighting for the Persians but also a Greek who had lived for several years as a guest at Philippos's palace and then betrayed his host by joining the enemy. Worst of all, he had treated a young Alexandros with condescension. And now he had slipped through Alexandros's fingers.

Flood Tide

****

"Which way should we go?" I asked Seleukos.

"The Royal Road to Ekbatana is that-a-way." He pointed vaguely in a southerly direction. "At our current pace, we should get there in about a hundred days."

"We've got one. We're expected back in time for the banquet tomorrow."

Seleukos laughed. He understood the absurdity of this mission just as well as I did. "Which is why we're not coming back with Memnon. Assuming we manage to get back at all."

"We'll make it back," Kleitos cheerfully assured us, "'though I have my doubts it'll be with Memnon in tow."

"Memnon is long gone," Seleukos agreed, "and the king knows it. We're out here because some people want you dead, Ptolemaios. And you had to drag Kleitos and me into your mess."

It was impossible to tell whether he was serious or just giving me a hard time; probably both. "Which way do you think Memnon would have gone?" I asked again.

"He got over the mountains through that pass." Seleukos pointed to the southwest. "That would've happened yesterday. By this morning, he's in Daskyleion, where he's currently organizing the local defenses. He's also dispatched a message to Dareios by now, which will arrive in Ekbatana in about ten days."

"I thought you told us it would take about a hundred days," Kleitos interrupted.

"Yes, that's how long it would take us to get there. The emperor's messengers travel somewhat faster than we can. It's about twelve hundred miles to Ekbatana. There are way stations every twenty miles or so, where the messengers can change horses. And of course the point is not to get the messenger to the emperor, only the message. Trust me, the message will be in Dareios's hands within ten days."

Kleitos was having trouble keeping his horse still. "So, let's get across the pass already. Maybe Memnon is injured or his horse is lame; maybe we can still catch him."

Seleukos cut him off. "Hey, gourdhead, stop being so ridiculous. Riding into that pass with our two hundred guys is crazy. There are enemy soldiers behind every tree and every rock on that mountainside. We'd all be dead before we ever reached the pass."

I urged my horse Pandaros into the gap between their mounts. "And yet, that's exactly what we'll do. Seleukos, you're right. But so are you, Kleitos. Riding into that pass is suicide …" Seleukos nodded vigorously. "…

but our orders are to chase down Memnon and bring him back. So we'll ride in the direction of the pass, with all judicious speed, and we'll get through it before nightfall." Now it was Kleitos's turn to smile broadly. "And then we'll make camp on the other side and make sure that we don't get ambushed overnight."

"And then what?" they both asked in unison.

"Then, in the morning, we'll return to Alexandros. And if we happen to run across Memnon during our travels, we'll bring him back with us."

Seleukos nodded. Kleitos shook his head but said nothing. I could tell he was disappointed by my lack of enthusiasm for the mission but I was his friend and I was in command, so he acquiesced.

After we had ridden in silence for a while I turned to Seleukos. "How do you know so much about Persia?" I knew he had crossed the Hellespont two years earlier, as a member of the initial Macedonian expeditionary corps, but so had ten thousand other men, without learning much about the country in which they were operating.

"Parmenion wanted me to act as his liaison to the local populace. I've spent a lot of time speaking to local leaders ... and to ordinary folks."

Kleitos raised his eyebrows. "Do they all speak Greek?"

"Some do, but I've learned to speak Aramaic as well as Persian."

I had heard about Seleukos's linguistic prowess; it was one of the reasons why I had picked him for this mission. "Hey, Kleitos, didn't I always say Seleukos was the smartest kid at Mieza?"

The Precinct of the Nymphs in Mieza, a couple of hours' ride from Pella, was a small, bucolic settlement, clustered around an ancient, two-room temple, hidden amidst an olive grove, that served as the home of a boarding school created by Philippos specifically to further the preparation of his son Alexandros to assume, one day, the kingship of Macedonia. Because Philippos didn't believe in half measures, he hired the foremost thinker in Greece to head the school and staffed it with tough military trainers, progressive teachers, and accomplished artists. He also persuaded the nobility of Macedonia to send their sons of roughly the same age as Alexandros to this school to serve as classmates, playmates, and fellow trainees. Eventually, Alexandros's classmates at Mieza became the core of the command structure of Alexandros's army. Seleukos, a scion of a preeminent noble family from Orestis, in the highlands of Macedonia, and the son of one of Philippos's leading generals, had been one of the students at Mieza. Kleitos and I, although neither one of us was either noble or preeminent or, in my case, even native, had found ourselves at Mieza as well.

"That's not true," Seleukos demurred. "We all know who the smartest kid was at Mieza."

"Well, I know it wasn't me." I grinned. "because I wasn't a kid by the time I arrived there." (I had been twenty-one, Seleukos fifteen, and Kleitos fourteen.)

They both laughed. We agreed that Alexandros had been the smartest kid at Mieza, which might have been true and was certainly the diplomatic position to take.

****

Once we left the carnage of the previous day's battle behind and entered the wooded hillside, we saw nary a human being. I sent scouts to ride ahead, as well as on either side of the path that we were following, in the hope they could warn us of any impending ambush. Fortunately, if there were any fleeing bands of enemy soldiers lurking along our route of travel, they saw us before we saw them and they chose to clear out of our way. The ominous silence of the forest around us was interrupted only by the querulous singing of magpies, the raucous trumpeting of cranes, and the staccato drumming of woodpeckers.

Seleukos gave voice to what we were all thinking. "I don't like this. I can feel people out there."

The trees seemed to be closing in but I continued to urge Pandaros forward. "I don't like it either but let's just get through this pass and out of this forest before we lose the sun. Once we get to the other side, we can find a homestead somewhere, spend the night, and then make our way back."

A mischievous grin crossed Kleitos's face. "What about capturing Memnon?"

"D'you see any Memnons walking around here?"

"No."

"Well then, don't worry about it." I fought hard to keep the irritation out of my voice. "Let's let other people worry about Memnon."

****

One person who was definitely worried about Memnon was his wife Barsine. Even though it would be another ten days, according to Seleukos's calculations, before anyone at the royal palace in Ekbatana received word of the Persian defeat, a nagging, low-grade concern about her husband had taken up regular residence at the back of Barsine's mind, a kind of background brain blight that imperceptibly contaminated all her conscious thoughts.

Flood Tide

At that moment, however, Barsine was in acute distress. She had to pee – badly. For the women and the eunuchs of Dareios's harem, finding an opportunity to exercise normal bodily functions was a daily challenge. Everything the inmates did and thought, from the moment they woke at dawn until the moment they woke again – if they were lucky – at the next dawn, was narrowly prescribed and rigorously enforced. The minutest details, from when they were awakened, what clothes and jewelry they wore, what makeup they applied, what they ate and drank, when they were allowed to wash up in the lavatory, what they did all day, with whom they spoke and about what, to when they went to bed and with whom, were all details dictated by others.

The harem comprised Dareios's mother, his wives, his concubines who aspired to become his wives, young girls who aspired to become his concubines, superannuated hags who had once been concubines, female servants and slaves, the children of all these women, and the eunuchs who guarded them. The person who was unquestionably in charge of all these people was Dareios's first wife, and therefore the empress, Stateira. And at the moment, Stateira was relieving herself in the lavatory, which meant that no one, except the attendants who were there to wipe her, was allowed to approach, despite the fact that the lavatory was a large, marbled affair with many cubicles for urination, defecation, washing, bathing, and sexual activity, which could easily accommodate dozens of people simultaneously.

These extended periods of lavatory unavailability, which could occur at random times throughout the day, were particularly hard on the younger children. As a result, they acquired a tendency to slink off to remote corners of the complex to relieve themselves. The effect was to give a subtle but unmistakable aroma to the complexes in Susa, Persepolis, Ekbatana, and Babylon that housed the harem at different times of the year.

Barsine was beginning to contemplate the possibility of finding a private corner somewhere but decided instead to distract herself by turning her thoughts to other matters. Her position in the harem was different from all the other women. She was not a wife, concubine, aspiring sexual partner, servant, or slave; she and her children were hostages held by Dareios as guarantors for the faithful performance by her husband of his military duties. She allowed herself a hopeful thought, imagining Memnon's return as the victorious hero. The image played in her mind as a cheerful melody, rising above the background noise of her constant worry and the insistent percussion of her overstretched bladder.

An old eunuch poked his head into her cubicle. "You can go in now." He was fat, soft, hunched over, and ugly. Barsine, by contrast, was stunning – a miraculous, exotic amalgam of the sleek, sable beauty of a Persian princess and the radiant intelligence of a Greek goddess. She was the product of a strategic marital alliance between one of the oldest noble houses of Persia and one of the ruling families of Rhodos. As sometimes happens by happy coincidence and random chance, she inherited the best traits, both physical and mental, that the genetic endowment of each family could offer. It was a bountiful legacy that would prove, nonetheless, unequal to the challenges fate had in store for her.

Barsine went off to pee. Her sigh of relief, and the bright tinkling sound of her water hitting the communal sludge below, mingled with the contented sounds and plops of ten other women relieving themselves companionably alongside her. Momentarily, she forgot about Memnon. She washed up, dressed in her daytime tunic, and rejoined her children in the cubicle they all shared.

The lives of the women in the harem were a paradoxical mixture of luxury and privation. The sprawling complex in which they lived consisted of large, airy common rooms, decorated with colorful glazed tiles and intricate mosaics, spectacular apartments for Stateira and her daughters and her mother-in-law, opulent sleeping chambers for Dareios's other wives, comfortable rooms for concubines, and an endless warren of small, windowless, claustrophobic cubicles for everybody else.

Their meals, prepared by slaves and served on silver plates, in a gleaming marble and limestone communal dining room, were healthy, ample, and featured the bounty of the many lands ruled by Persia.

Their clothing, made of linen and wool – soft, colorful, embroidered, and festooned with gold and precious stones – would have been the envy of the most fashionable ladies of Athens. All the wives and concubines owned, and sometimes even wore, great sunbursts of jewelry. There were more oils, unguents, perfumes, cosmetics, incense, and aromatic spices scattered about the washing and bathing rooms of the lavatory than in all of Greece combined. And best of all, wherever it was housed, the inmates of the harem had exclusive use of their own paradeisos, a magical garden filled with flowering trees, berry-bedecked bushes, aromatic plants, babbling streams, fish-filled ponds, chirping robins, strutting peacocks, and flashy pheasants – an oasis of tranquility amidst a hostile, nasty, mean, and violent wilderness.

On the other hand, the women's paradise was also a soul-sapping place of confinement. They were separated from the corrupt but vital world outside by a tall, impenetrable wall. Unless they had children, they had almost nothing useful to do with their time. They spent their days primping, gossiping, abusing the slaves, intriguing against one another, clenching their sphincters, and dreaming of the "call," when they might be summoned into the presence of the emperor to satisfy his sexual needs. They spent their nights being abused by the eunuchs, or by higher ranking women, or simply abusing themselves. And most of them had no realistic hope of ever leaving their ornate prison alive.

Flood Tide

Barsine was one of the lucky ones. She had four children to keep her busy, two servant girls, and a genuine hope of eventually leaving the harem. On the other hand, she had no friends, no privacy, and no books to read. Unlike most of the women in the harem, including Stateira herself, Barsine could read. In fact, she was able to read and write in two languages, Greek and Persian, and could speak in three more. Ironically, although a daughter of a venerable Persian aristocrat, she grew up at the Macedonian court in Pella. She received a surprisingly good education for a girl and possessed a lively, inquiring mind. Her life had been rich in experience, activity, unexpected reversals, and misfortune.

Barsine was three years old when her father was forced to flee to Pella, on the barely-civilized periphery of the Greek world. She enjoyed a happy childhood, mingling with the children of the Macedonian court. She was an occasional playmate of a young boy named Alexandros. When she was twelve, the family returned to Hellespontine Phrygia, thanks to the efforts of Mentor of Rhodos. Her father, wishing to express his gratitude, gave his twelve-year-old daughter in marriage to the 41-year-old soldier of fortune, who also happened to be the younger brother of Barsine's mother. Fortunately for Barsine, her uncle refrained from consummating the marriage for the time being.

Mentor was away on military duty most of the time and the lively young bride, who was rapidly blossoming into a ravishing beauty, attracted the attention of Mentor's younger brother Memnon, who was "only" 36 years old at the time. Memnon decided to do his fraternal duty and consummate Mentor's marriage on behalf of his absent brother. When Barsine became pregnant, a couple of years later, Mentor forestalled any potential intra-family strife by conveniently dying, apparently of natural causes. Of course, in Persia the art of poisoning had reached unprecedented heights and Barsine never knew how natural the causes of Mentor's death actually were. Memnon acted with characteristic dispatch and married the young widow before the child was born. He was 39 and his niece and new mother was 15. The child grew into a beautiful little girl.

Surprisingly, it turned out to be a happy, loving, and fecund marriage. As Barsine sat in her cubicle in Ekbatana, worrying about her husband, she had four children: three girls, aged six, four, and two, plus a brand-new baby boy. She was all of 21 years old.

It was time for the mid-morning communal meal. Barsine left her children in the care of the servant girls and made her way up the covered walkway toward the portico leading to the dining hall. She passed between the stone griffins guarding the entranceway and stepped into a large, light, airy room, whose walls were tiled with a veritable menagerie of enameled terra-cotta lions, bulls, eagles, griffins, sphinxes, and other fantastic animals, sculpted in low relief and glowing with iridescent, luscious, outlandish colors.

She reached her assigned seat on a bench toward the back of the hall in the nick of time, nodding to her companions on either side, but remained standing, as did all the other women in the room. Stateira, trailing her large entourage, swept regally into the hall and seated herself on the raised dais. All the women, including Barsine, threw themselves to the hard, sandstone floor and remained prostrate until given permission to rise by the empress's official crier. Then they sat down and immediately fell into animated conversation with their neighbors. Barsine listened carefully but she rarely participated in these discussions.

The diners were served strictly by rank, with Stateira receiving her food and drink first. Her morning wine, splashing around in an exquisite golden kylix placed on a silver tray, was carried to her by her cupbearer, a beautiful young girl, no more than twelve years old, wearing a sparkling white chiton, reaching to the floor and decorated with bright embroidery.

As the girl made her way up toward the throne, she tripped on a step. She tried to regain her balance, staggered toward the empress, with the cup swaying precariously on her tray, and ended up spilling some of the wine on Stateira's shimmering silk garment. An earsplitting screech issued from the empress's throat. "You stupid boob! Look what you've done."

The mortified girl threw herself down at the empress's feet, her entire, slight body shaking violently, and attempted to apologize.

"Manakes, Oebares," Stateira screamed. Two young, tall eunuchs appeared and prostrated themselves before the empress. "Fifty lashes," she said calmly and resumed eating her breakfast.

The young guards lifted the whimpering girl to her feet and dragged her out of the hall. She had finally found her voice and was loudly begging for mercy. Neither the empress nor the other women in the hall paid her the slightest attention.

The whipping post was in the middle of the yard, not far from the portico. They could all hear the first strike of the whip, followed by a loud scream. It didn't seem to interfere with anyone's appetite. The blows continued at a steady pace, while the shrieks grew louder and more inarticulate. Barsine, in violation of all protocol, rose from her seat and ran to her children. She found them sitting on their bed, hands clapped over their ears. The girl's screams were now more or less continuous, rising and falling with the rhythm of the blows. Barsine's baby began to cry. She picked him up, sat down next to her girls, and tried to comfort them. The animal howling was growing weaker. Barsine's daughters were weeping.

Flood Tide

She watched them, silent tears coursing down her cheeks. Finally, the girl fell silent, although the blows continued methodically for a long time thereafter. Barsine closed her eyes and swore to rescue her children from this hellhole.

****

I was thinking about Memnon, as we emerged from the woods on the other side of the small mountain. With all due respect for Aristandros and his "interrogation" of the prisoner, it was impossible for us to know where Memnon was at that moment and we certainly had no way for us of capturing him. My objective for this mission was to bring all my men back alive.

Yeah, but what's my objective for me? On the surface, this was a simple question. Ever since I'd gotten stranded in this time and place, and ever since I'd accepted the fact that no extraction team was coming to rescue me, I'd set myself three goals: One, stay alive; two, comply with the Prime Directive; three, get back home. In practice, these goals proved to be unexpectedly challenging. Admittedly, I was still alive but clearly, if some people had their way, my state of animation was subject to change at any moment.

As far as the Prime Directive was concerned, I had already failed, as I now realized, but that didn't diminish my determination not to violate it again. For a moment, I'd told myself that, having violated the Prime

Directive and having thus altered the flow of time, I was now free of its strictures. Unfortunately, upon further reflection, it struck me as lightning that just the opposite was true. The only benefit of my inadvertent transgression was to drive home the magnitude of the challenge ahead of me.

The final goal – to get back home – seemed equally daunting. The escape hatch, the portal to my return, was thousands of miles and many years away. *I will make it*, I told myself, with more aspiration than conviction.

We rode through the pass and descended into a narrow valley, bisected by a stream and hemmed in by mountains on all sides. From a military perspective, this topography bore an uncomfortable resemblance to a kill zone, with my company in the role of sitting ducks, even if we were ducks sitting on horses. But we had finally reached flat terrain and my men and their mounts needed a break. I called a halt, told my scouts to fan out, giving the rest of the men a chance to eat and the horses a chance to graze. The stream seemed clean enough, so I let both men and horses quench their thirst, making sure that the horses drank downstream from the men.

I scanned the sky for any trace of smoke, either from the campfires of escaping soldiers or the cooking fires of any nearby homesteaders. My hopeful gaze took in nothing but blue skies, with a diaphanous garnish of cirriform clouds high overhead. What was worse, the sun was just beginning to fade behind the treetops crowning the ridge to our west. I was not looking forward to spending a night out in the open, without much gear to set up camp, cowering in an indefensible position.

Perversely, I was almost hoping to encounter some people. There had to be refugees taking the same route. It would've been preferable to see them, rather than be surprised when we least expected them. It also seemed odd that this fertile, well-irrigated valley apparently lacked any permanent inhabitants. Up to that point, we'd seen nary a soul nor any sign of habitation, not even a trace of cultivation. After a short break we pressed ahead, southward, between two ridgelines.

The shadow line of the setting sun was creeping toward us at an alarming rate when one of our scouts came galloping back. "Smoke ahead, sir." He pointed toward the vanishing point where the mountains seemed to choke off the valley. I couldn't see any smoke but I took his word for it. We proceeded slowly and silently into the gathering twilight.

Soon enough, we could all see the slender strand of smoke trailing off into the darkening sky. Tracing the wisps back to their point of origin led us to a small farmstead, hidden in a birch grove, on the right bank of the creek. A tall wattle-and-daub wall surrounded what appeared to be a fairly sizeable compound. We saw only one opening in the wall, a small gateway completely barred by a pair of stout oaken doors.

Seleukos and I rode up to the gate and dismounted. I hit the double door a few times with the pommel of my sword. No response. Several of my men joined us and started to kick and pound on the wooden panels. They didn't seem to be inflicting much damage on the door but the ruckus they raised was beginning to spook our horses.

Kleitos, tired of watching our futile efforts, maneuvered his horse next to the wall, removed his sword and armor, and threw them on the ground. Then he stood on his stallion's withers and reached up the wall as high as he could. Even when he rose to his toes, though, his fingers fell a little short. Undaunted, he leapt upward, catching the top edge of the wall and then, by pulling, scrambling, and extensive cursing, managed to hoist himself to the top.

Coincidently, at exactly the same moment, a small flap in the door swung open, revealing a pair of wary eyes.

"We come in peace," Seleukos called out in Aramaic and then repeated the sentence in Persian and Greek.

"We've got nothing left," an old man's voice responded in a vaguely Greek dialect. "The soldiers took it all."

"He's lying," Kleitos informed us from above. "I can see chickens in the courtyard."

The old man slammed the flap shut. We could hear his steps retreating from the door.

"What else can you see?" I asked Kleitos.

"The thing I'm standing on is the roof of the gatehouse. There are buildings leaning against the outer wall on all four sides but I don't see any people, except for the old guy who just ran into one of the mud huts. ... Oh, oh. He's back out, carrying his bow and a bunch of arrows. You guys had better break down that door before he manages to shoot me."

"Old man," Seleukos called out. "We're Macedonians. We're not going to hurt you but you've got to open up right now. If we have to break the door down, we will kill everybody inside."

An arrow came whistling over the wall.

"Can you jump down and open the gate from the inside?" I asked Kleitos.

"Nah, it's too high; I'd probably break a leg. Plus, this geezer is gonna shoot me while I'm in the air. Just hurry up and break down the door."

"Here." I tossed a bow up to him, followed by an arrow. "Take the guy out."

"I missed," Kleitos said after a moment. "Toss me another one."

The next thing we heard was the scraping sound of the two halves of the door being pulled apart. We saw a hunched but wiry old man, bald head, scraggly white beard, and blazing eyes. "Take what you want," he spat. "Just leave us alone."

"We'll pay for anything we take." I kept my voice low and even. "Mostly, we need shelter for the night. We have our own food, which we're glad to share with your family."

He shrugged, whether with doubt or resignation, I couldn't tell. "Haven't got much room." My men pushed him aside and poured in through the gate. "But I'll do my duty as your host."

A number of buildings lined the perimeter wall but none large enough to hold all my men. Having little choice, we made ourselves comfortable in the courtyard, around an improvised campfire, and put the horses in the two empty stables, in the gatehouse, in the reception room, in the large dining hall, in any space that could hold them. It turned out some of those spaces held people within. They came pouring into the courtyard, squawking like the chickens we had scattered a moment earlier.

Mostly, they were women, a score of them, ranging in age from ancient to bursting with youth, plus dozens of kids, plus a few old men. There were no men of military age. The old man, who was evidently the head of this community, tried to herd them back into whatever rooms had been left unoccupied by our horses but it was a futile task.

"Let them join us for our meal." I patted the ground next to me. Eventually, the old men and the children sat down among us, while women went off to the cookhouse.

The old man started to talk, without looking at me. "My name is ..."

He was interrupted by a voice from above. "What about me? Get me down from here!"

We had forgotten about Kleitos. He was standing on the flat roof of the gatehouse, waving down to us. He looked rather forlorn. The men started to laugh and heckle. "Jump, Kleitos, jump!"

"C'mon guys, get me a ladder."

"You'd better grow a pair of wings, Kleitos," someone yelled. "Jump on those old guys. They'll cushion your fall," somebody else suggested. "No, wait a minute," another voice called out, "those guys are too bony. I'll go get one of those nice plump girls for you to land on. You won't feel a thing."

Just then one of those plump young girls came out of the cookhouse, carrying two flagons of wine. The men instantly forgot about Kleitos and surrounded the girl, holding their helmets out to her, which she proceeded to fill with wine.

Some of the men decided to help her, by supporting her arms, circling her waist, patting her rear.

"Get your hands off of her," I yelled. "If anybody touches one of these women tonight, I will chop his hand off. And if you try to screw one of them, whether she agrees or not, I'll cut your dick off too. Is that understood?" The men let go of the girl with the flagons.

"My name is Harmodios," the old man resumed, "and we really don't have much food. The Persians cleaned us out marching to battle and then they cleaned us out again last night and this morning, running away. They also took our men away."

His last comment caused me to whip my head around. "Are there any left hiding in here?"

"Nah, they saw you coming and ran away."

I turned to Seleukos. "Search every room in this compound!"

A plaintive voice rang out from above. "What about me, fellas?"

"Here, have some bread." One of the men tossed him a hunk.

"C'mon guys, it's not funny."

That was the cue for everyone to start laughing again. I nodded to a couple of men and they fetched a ladder. Kleitos descended briskly but, once safely down on the ground, he joined in the general merriment. The men handed him some wine, slapped him on the back, and were soon playfully wrestling in the dirt.

After the meal, I set the watches and made sure we had vigilant sentries on the roofs throughout the night. The rest of us bedded down for a comfortable night's sleep, right there amidst the chickenshit. *Nothing bad happened today*, was my last thought. *So much for the predictive power of dreams.*

Little did I know.

Chapter 3 – Delusions of Salvation

After what seemed like five minutes of sleep, I was awakened by a general commotion. "Incoming!" somebody yelled, followed shortly by the distinctive ping of arrows striking mudbrick walls.

I must have slept more than five minutes, though, because dawn was breaking. Silhouetted against a pinkish lavender sky, sporadic arrows came arching in over the eastern wall, the one with the gate in it.

"Attack coming," a sentry yelled, somewhat superfluously.

I scrambled up to the flat roof of the gatehouse to assess the situation. "Take cover in the lee of the gate-side wall," I ordered.

There were a dozen men milling about in the clearing in front of the gate but only two of them had bows and none wore armor. The two men with bows were attempting to hit the sentries standing atop the roofs. The archers were barely within the effective range of their bows and didn't strike me as accomplished bowmen. Their missiles continued to fall harmlessly into the courtyard.

More worrisome were the small bands of men descending from the hillsides and starting to converge on the clearing. It was difficult to estimate numbers, because new groups kept emerging from among the trees, but it seemed likely that soon our only escape route would be blocked by several hundred men. Some, but not many, of the newly-arriving men wore armor; a few were equipped with Persian-style curved swords; most were carrying short pikes; the rest were armed with farm implements. About half of the men still had their large, wicker shields.

I was confident we could break through a cordon of these amateurs but we'd likely incur some casualties in the process. The prospect of casualties struck me as rather irksome. *I wish I'd brought some bowmen with me,* I thought, but of course elite cavalry soldiers didn't mix with lowly Kretan archers. We did have half a dozen bows with us and I ordered the men carrying them up to the roof. I pointed to the two bowmen below. "Kill those two bastards!"

Unfortunately, my horsemen were as accomplished with a bow and arrow as the two tyros outside. I'd never witnessed a more ineffectual display of archery.

Seleukos joined me on the roof. "It's like watching two virgins trying to have sex."

We laughed but the crowd gathering outside the wall continued to grow. "Who are these people?"

Seleukos shrugged. "Looks like refugees from the battle, reinforced by locals."

"Let's go down and talk to them."

We left Kleitos behind, with orders to get all the men and horses ready to go. "After Seleukos and I get out there, have the men amble through the gate, with their horses in tow, two or three at a time, in armor and ready to mount, but very casually. Don't want to trigger a premature attack. Just keep pouring out until they suddenly realize there are too many of us to attack."

"Boil them like frogs," Seleukos put it.

Kleitos gave him an uncomprehending look.

"Just keep pouring out until we scare the shit out of them," I resumed. "If that doesn't work, we'll have to charge them. But don't do that until Seleukos and I have come back to join you. And keep the noise down. Let's save a surprise or two for these fellas. Got it?"

Kleitos nodded and quietly went about organizing the troops.

Seleukos and I walked out of the gate. We were wearing our armor but carrying our helmets under our arms. We were unarmed. The nearest enemy soldiers were only a couple of hundred feet away. We walked briskly toward them. *I hope our bowmen have enough sense to stop shooting.* The enemy fighters, once they saw us, stopped milling about. There must've been at least forty of them by now. A tall soldier, wearing good armor, shouted out some orders. His men began to fall in. *Native infantry,* I thought.

"They look like conscripts," I muttered to Seleukos under my breath.

Seleukos laughed. "Yeah, conscripts who threw away most of their weapons as they ran from the field the other day."

We stopped ten steps from the tall soldier. "Ask him where they're from."

There was a brief, hostile sounding exchange between Seleukos and the tall soldier. "He says they're from Phrygia. They seem determined to take some measure of solace after their rout."

"Tell him we're from Macedonia. If they put down their weapons and surrender by the time our men come out of the gate, we will spare their lives. And don't bother waiting for his response. Just turn around and follow me." And I started to walk, very slowly, back to the gate, relieved to see that most of our men were already outside.

Seleukos caught up with me. "Do you think it'll work?"

"Let's hope it slows them down at least."

I wonder whether they'll charge after us, I worried. *If they do, they'll cut us to ribbons before we get a chance to fart.* "Don't turn around," I told Seleukos. "Just keep walking."

We reached Kleitos, who was holding our horses and arms, as well as his own. The last of our troopers were casually filtering out, as instructed, leading their horses by their reins.

"What are they doing?" I asked Kleitos.

"They seem to be conferring. And waiting for more of their buddies to join them."

"How many are there now?"

"Close to three hundred."

"All right, men." I kept my voice low. "Let's pick it up and get everybody out here!"

Slowly, I turned around. The enemy line continued to grow but it had not advanced.

I leaned in toward Seleukos. "These guys are wusses." Then, more loudly to my men: "On my signal, everybody mount up. I want everybody to mount simultaneously. Let's pretend we're on the parade grounds. Ready? Now!"

Flood Tide

The sound of two hundred men in armor mounting their horses simultaneously was music to my ears. One measure; three beats: The vault off the ground; the thud onto the animals' backs; the clatter of swords against greaves. And then, an ominous silence.

I looked at the enemy. Maybe it was my imagination but their line seemed to waver. They were chattering, which was encouraging, given the evident imminence of a clash. A line getting ready to fight should be screaming defiantly at the enemy or, better yet, should be singing or, hardest of all, should maintain an absolute, menacing silence. These men were chattering.

"Form a wedge," I yelled out, "on my point." I let my mount, Pandaros, trot out a few steps, confident that my squadron would fall in behind me with military precision.

Much to my disappointment, the enemy line was still there and now it spanned the entire width of the clearing. Normally, it's foolhardy for cavalry to charge an organized phalanx; that's the job of the infantry, while the cavalry seeks to outflank the enemy line and hit it from the rear. Unfortunately, we had no infantry at our disposal that morning. Nor was a flanking maneuver a viable alternative, since it would have required our riding through the thicket surrounding the clearing, with each shrub, bush, and tree enlisted in the service of the enemy.

On the positive side, this bunch of Phrygian soldiers was neither organized nor a phalanx. Their line was likely to cave at the first sign of pressure. Still, I hated to attack them head-on. If we charged them, we would lose some horses and perhaps even a couple of men.

Perversely, I was not anxious to kill too many enemy soldiers either. I'd long since given up my initial resolution not to kill anyone, made in the naive hope that by avoiding bloodshed I'd also avoid any inadvertent violations of the Prime Directive. True, as far as I could tell, I'd yet to kill anyone with my own hands (not for lack of trying, mind you) but soldiers under my command had certainly killed people. The fact was that a soldier determined never to kill an enemy was likely to have a short life span; more to the point, a commander determined not to kill enemy troops was likely to kill his own men instead. *This commander dodge isn't easy,* I thought, *and flying blind only makes it harder.* I missed the days when I thought I knew what the future held in store.

We might have been able to ride away, behind the compound and through the thicket, and perhaps avoided any bloodshed. Of course, had I ordered a craven flight, the resultant loss of face would've inevitably proven to be fatal – probably sooner, rather than later – not only to me but most likely to many of my men as well.

"Follow me!" I screamed and took off, hoping the rest of my squadron was galloping behind me.

Flood Tide

With a light touch on the reins, using mostly my knees, I guided Pandaros straight at the tall enemy commander. He stood in the center of the front rank of the opposing line, where the men stood shoulder to shoulder, their shields smartly overlapping, and their pikes pointing threateningly ahead. On the other hand, I'd noticed previously that there were not too many ranks behind the front one and the men filling them had no shields, no pikes, and very little discipline.

As we approached the enemy, I did something truly foolish: I urged Pandaros into a jump, which of course exposed his belly to all those pikes pointed at us. I was afraid he would shy away at the last instant. My steed proved to be more of a trooper than the men opposing us. While they scattered out of the way, forgetting to use their pikes, we soared through the front line and landed amidst a bunch of scared, disorganized, and mostly unarmed youngsters. I kept riding, hoping to get out of the way of any of my men who might wish to emulate my maneuver. Only a few of them did but it didn't matter. Once we had landed behind the front line, all semblance of organization among the enemy vanished. Some men were getting trampled by our horses; some were being struck by our swords; many were backing away, looking for safety; more of my men came flying over; soon, the enemy youngsters were throwing down their arms and running away. In a few minutes, all organized resistance vanished.

The tall commander found himself standing alone, still facing forward, holding his pike, trying to poke at my men, who were careful to stay out of his range. Silently, I prodded Pandaros back and bopped the helmet of the tall man with the flat of my sword. He twirled around, flailing wildly with his pike. One of my men rode up behind him, ready to separate his head from his shoulders. I made a calming gesture with my left hand, indicating to the enemy commander to drop his weapon and to my trooper to stay his stroke. Miraculously, they both obeyed.

As I looked up, I saw enemy soldiers running pell-mell for the woods, pursued by a few of my men. Most of my company had retained its shape and stayed massed in the middle of the clearing, awaiting further orders. "Stop," I yelled at the pursuing men. "Back to me!"

Reluctantly, they broke off pursuit, turned their horses around, and sheathed their swords. "Parade formation," I called out. With a minimum of grumbling, the men urged their mounts into a well-ordered column and we set off at a stately trot. "We captured enough prisoners the other day," I called over my shoulder. "We don't need any more. We just need to get back to camp safely." Nobody made any comment, at least not aloud. Seleukos and Kleitos joined me at the head of the column. As far as I could tell, not a single soldier, from either side, had been killed during the brief clash.

"Why didn't we capture some of those guys?" Seleukos asked me after a while. "At least their commander?"

"Did he look like Memnon to you?"

Seleukos smiled. "There was a passing resemblance but no, that was no Memnon."

"Well then, our mission was to capture Memnon. Since we didn't see him, we couldn't capture him. And now, we're going to ride back to camp. We don't want to miss the festivities."

"Aye aye, sir," he answered smartly.

****

The trip back over the pass was just as hazardous as the trip in the opposite direction had been the day before but somehow it seemed much safer. Perhaps all the refugees of the battle had cleared out by then or perhaps we knew our way better or maybe we had just gotten cockier. Whatever the explanation, we made our way back to camp – cheerfully, swiftly, and uneventfully – by midafternoon.

We surmounted the last ridge and started to descend into the Granikos Valley. The victory games were in full swing. The competition was taking place at the inflection point between the mountain and the plain. The contestants raced and battled on level ground at the bottom of the hillside, with spectators standing ten deep around the hastily created arena and with many others spread out way up the adjoining slope. Could've been twenty thousand people crowded in there and some of them could actually see something. Most enjoyed the atmosphere (a mixture of the clean mountain air, the sickening stench of putrefying flesh, and the smoky bouquet of funeral pyres), the camaraderie, and the imperfect narration of the competition provided by the crowd noise. They reminded me of the captives watching shadows cast on the wall of a cave, in Platon's famous parable, and mistaking it for the real thing.

On the far side of the improvised stadion, immediately behind the teeming crowd of spectators, Alexandros and his friends had commandeered a captured Persian baggage train and were now standing atop the overturned wagons, enjoying an up-close, unobstructed view of the competition.

Farther out in the plain, beyond the upside-down wagons and beyond the heaped bales of metallic junk, cooks, orderlies, grooms, and assorted servants were busy with preparations for the evening feast. We could see the temporary altar, on which choice cuts of beef were still going up in smoke, but happily plenty of fine meat remained on the spitted bull carcasses roasting over sizzling flames.

Flood Tide

"Too bad we missed the sacrifices," I said to Seleukos and Kleitos, hoping not to let too much sarcasm creep into my voice.

"Hard to believe Alexandros managed to finish his thanksgiving before nightfall," Kleitos observed, without missing a beat.

Seleukos maintained a diplomatic silence.

We descended into the valley, carefully skirting the crowd. We could see that all of the footraces and many of the other contests had already concluded but the best part of the games, as far as my men were concerned, still remained.

After some quick instructions to Seleukos and Kleitos, I gave my men leave to disband and attempted to make my way, still aboard Pandaros, toward Alexandros. It quickly became apparent that, unless I was willing to trample scores of people, I'd never get there. I dismounted and waded into the throng, pulling my horse behind me. My progress was incredibly slow but it didn't matter. I was basking in my anonymity amidst people who had no designs on my life. Laboring under the delusion that the danger had been on the far side of the mountain, I actually laughed with relief. *So much for people trying to kill me.*

Chapter 4 – Death in the Shadows

My anonymity didn't last for long. Perdikkas, my fellow commander and rival, emerged from the crowd, trailing half a dozen lieutenants. "Alexandros wants to see you – now!" I couldn't tell whether his peremptory tone was part of the original message or a helpful embellishment by Perdikkas himself. "Leave your horse and follow me!"

Perdikkas son of Orontes was from Orestis but that alone didn't explain his abrasive personality. Seleukos, after all, was from Orestis as well and he was a master at getting along with people. Perdikkas, on the other hand, never tired of telling us that he was descended from that canton's royal house. Never mind that Orestis, situated mostly on desolate mountains halfway between the fertile plains of lower Macedonia and the rugged coastal kingdom of Epiros, had long since been conquered and absorbed by the kings of Macedonia. Somehow, that fact did nothing to reduce the size of the chip Perdikkas perennially carried on his shoulder.

Flood Tide

It didn't diminish Perdikkas's self-esteem that, when Alexandros's father Philippos was organizing the elite school for the education of his heir apparent, Orontes of Orestis was one of the first noblemen whom he asked to send his son to the academy at Mieza. Perdikkas was sixteen at the time, three years older than Alexandros, and one of the oldest boys at the school. (I was twenty one, but I was not a student; I was an instructor.) He took the young prince under his wing, not that Alexandros, even at age thirteen, required, or tolerated, much mentoring by anyone. But Alexandros appreciated the gesture.

Once Alexandros became king, Perdikkas quickly rose in the ranks. He specialized in risky, dangerous assignments, both in the infantry and the cavalry, and proved himself a capable, brave, almost reckless commander, which only raised him further in Alexandros's esteem. He didn't spend as much time cultivating the esteem of people below his rank.

I turned toward Perdikkas as we pushed our way through the crowd. "How are the games going?"

"I've got more important things to worry about than games," he replied. We refrained from further chitchat.

Finally, we reached the overturned wagons. I clambered aboard, secure in the knowledge that no threat against me could possibly lurk on this elevated platform. There was a pause in the games just then, as the makeshift arena was reconfigured for the combat sports. Judges marked out a large circle, using small logs and tree branches to demarcate the extent of the fighting field. Inside the zone, soldiers were picking up debris, raking the ground, and pouring a layer of sand on top. Outside the boundary, spectators pushed and shoved one another in their rush to secure the best vantage points around the circuit.

While waiting for the games to resume, Alexandros was busy dictating correspondence and cracking jokes. Kallisthenes the Historian was tasked with the unenviable responsibility of separating what was meant to be written down from what was meant only to amuse the assembled posse of the king's friends and hangers-on.

"Two days after the battle was concluded, Ptolemaios succeeded in capturing Memnon," Alexandros solemnly recited upon noticing my arrival. "Don't write that, you fool," he yelled when Kallisthenes dutifully started to scratch his reed across the papyrus sheet. "Am I right, Ptolemaios?"

"I am sorry, sire. We didn't succeed in capturing Memnon."

A shadow passed over Alexandros's sunny mien but it didn't last. "We'll catch up to him yet." He turned his back on me. "We urgently require additional men if we are to make good on our promise to liberate the Greek cities of Ionia from Persian captivity – why aren't you writing?"

Flood Tide

Poor Kallisthenes got busy again, while I carefully edged as far away from the king as I could manage without falling over the side. Kallisthenes was unique in our ranks. In fact, he was unique in the history of warfare, as far as I knew. He was a pale, pudgy young man, whose complexion betrayed an aversion to sunshine and whose physique testified to a lifelong abstinence from physical exercise. Surrounded by men raised from childhood to endure the rigors of war, Kallisthenes fit in like an earthworm crawling on a porcupine. He was from Athens, which made him only slightly less of an outsider in this camp than I was, but he spoke such a highfalutin, refined Greek that my heavily accented Macedonian dialect made me one of the boys by comparison. But what made him truly unique was his commission in Alexandros's army – he was the official campaign historian.

Before Alexandros, it had never occurred to a military leader about to launch an audacious invasion of the greatest empire on Earth that what the expeditionary force really needed was a noncombatant intellectual, incapable of defending himself against an attacking mouse, whose primary function was to keep contemporaneous written records of the campaign, so that an accurate chronicle of the military leader's deeds could be bequeathed to posterity after his inevitable triumph. In fairness, Kallisthenes had other functions as well: He was responsible for committing to written form Alexandros's correspondence and his propaganda, to the extent there was a discernable difference between the two.

At the moment, the king was evidently writing a letter to Antipatros, his regent back in Pella, to request reinforcements. He was interrupted in his dictation when a sleek youngster, dressed only in a perspiration-soaked tunic, sprang up to our jury-rigged platform. His appearance elicited much cheering among the tussling crowd below, which he acknowledged with a smile and a wave.

"Gorgias," Alexandros called out, "magnificent race. You practically flew above the ground. Even if I'd had a chance to run today, you might have beaten me."

Gorgias shook his head. "Never, sire."

Alexandros obviously knew this contestant by name and the contestant obviously knew Alexandros's proclivities by heart.

As if on cue, Hephaistion materialized from among the clutch of people surrounding Alexandros and Gorgias. "It'd be too boring if we had to keep crowning you the winner after every race, sire," he observed as he handed a wreath to Alexandros. The young king laughed, clearly pleased. I couldn't tell whether he was enjoying the subtle mockery of the conceit of his being a great runner or simply accepting the acknowledgement of his purported running prowess. He ceremoniously placed the wreath on Gorgias's head, provoking a fresh round of cheers among the spectators. "Go see Parmenion over there about your prize money."

Flood Tide

A beaming Gorgias made his way across our platform, accepting congratulations as he went. Perdikkas patted him on the back, carefully maintaining a discreet distance from his sweaty torso. Kleitos, by contrast, showed no hesitation in exchanging a warm embrace with the victorious runner. Philotas, whom we used to call Fast Philotas in Mieza, seemed genuinely pleased to meet someone clearly faster than he. He grabbed Gorgias by the arm, punched him in the opposite shoulder, and indulged in a bit of good-natured ribbing. Aristandros the Seer, cleverly anticipating the perspiring runner's approach, carefully stepped to the other side of the platform before Gorgias could reach him. Eventually, Gorgias made his way to Parmenion, who regretfully informed him that he carried no coins on his person but advised him to see Harpalos the Purser to claim his prize. While all this was going on, Alexandros turned back to Kallisthenes and resumed his dictation, except now he seemed to be writing to his mother, Olympias, who had also remained back at the palace in Pella.

"It's not nice to eavesdrop on other people's correspondence," someone whispered into my ear. I whirled on my heels, almost punching the whisperer in the nose. When I saw it was Aristandros, I wished I had. I laced my fingers to keep them from balling into fists. "Get out of my face, before I find an excuse to knock you off this wagon." Aristandros favored me with one of his malevolent smiles before silently gliding away.

Everyone's attention turned to the three judges who were marching ostentatiously across the field toward us, wearing long, flowing robes. Each judge carried a freshly-cut switch. They were followed by five extremely large, naked men, walking jauntily, single-file, swinging their arms and other appendages, acknowledging the shouts of their supporters among the crowd. Illustrating the diversity of Alexandros's army, three were clearly highland Macedonians, one looked to be some sort of Thrakian, judging by his war paint, and one was an Agrianian. The wrestling competition was about to begin.

Alexandros administered the oath to the judges. The wrestlers spread olive oil on their bodies, rubbed sand on one another's arms and backs for a better grip, and infibulated their penises. *That's not something I could ever do,* I thought as I watched the men pull down their foreskins, tie leather thongs around them, and then fasten their penises against their abdomens.

The head judge set up a silver urn and placed five small lots into it. The wrestlers lined up in front of the urn. Whether by happenstance or design, they ended up standing in size order. The smallest contestant, standing at the head of the line, was twice as large as I was. Not twice as tall (he was shorter than I) but twice as thick and probably three times as heavy. His neck was as thick as his head; his arms as thick as my legs; his legs as thick as my torso; and his torso as thick as a barrel - a short, stout barrel.

Flood Tide

His thick hand reached into the urn and emerged clutching a lot. At least we all assumed it was clutching a lot because nothing was visible amidst those massive fingers. "Beta," Mr. Thick announced loudly and showed the small tile to the head judge, who nodded his agreement. His supporters – presumably his phalanx mates – shouted their approval, even though they had no way of knowing whether beta would turn out to be a favorable draw.

The next contestant, the Agrianian, was slightly taller and somewhat thinner, although certainly solidly built. His most distinguishing feature was his face. I could easily believe he won most of his matches by scaring his opponents to death. To say he was ugly, while accurate, would miss the essence of his countenance. He looked like a man who enjoyed breaking things. In fact, he gave the impression of someone who couldn't wait to start breaking his opponent's bones.

Mr. Scary reached into the urn. I was surprised he didn't shatter the little pottery shard in the process of extracting it. "Alpha," he called out, which was duly confirmed by the judge. He ambled over to Mr. Thick and glared at him in a ravenous sort of way. Mr. Thick ignored him, continuing to stretch his legs, arms, and fingers.

The third contestant, sporting the blue battle paint favored by some of the Thrakian tribes, was a fairly tall youngster, perhaps eighteen years old, and thin as a rail. I couldn't imagine what he was doing in this lineup because he looked intelligent enough to realize he was sure to get killed in short order.

Mr. Lucky drew a gamma. He was delighted, dancing a jig in the dirt and waving his arms jubilantly. The other contestants, and the crowd, studiously ignored him since he was a gamma. Undeterred, in skipped his way to the wrestlers' tent.

The tension in the arena rose by an order of magnitude. People stopped their screaming. Everyone stared intently at the silver urn. The next lot would determine everything.

The fourth man was seriously large, in every dimension. But what was more surprising was his agility, especially in a big man. He did everything nimbly and fast. He ran into the arena on cat's paws; he tied up his massive penis in a flash; he oiled himself more adroitly than Aristandros buttering up his next mark; and now he ran up to the urn and jabbed in his hand like a frog flicking his tongue at a fly, emerging with the penultimate lot in his fingers. "Beta," Mr. Quick cried out, showing the scrap of baked clay to the head judge. He, and his supporters (he was another heavy infantry man) seemed pleased enough.

Mr. Quick ran over to Mr. Thick, the other beta, and they engaged in a brief, animated conversation. Then together they made their way out of the rink, Mr. Quick jogging and Mr. Thick trying his best to keep up. When they reached the boundary of the rink, the crowd parted respectfully to let them pass and they disappeared into the wrestlers' tent.

The last contestant walked up to the urn. To me, he looked like a man from the Macedonian mountains; he was certainly a mountain of a man. His size caught your eye but his physique sucked your breath out. To watch him walk was to observe a dynamic work of art. With every step, his glutes clenched, his pecs rippled, and his abs danced under his gleaming skin. It was like watching a marble statue of Herakles, sculpted by a masterful albeit overexuberant artist, come to life. His muscles didn't move; they flowed, the way a swollen river flows over the cataracts.

Although there was no suspense left, the crowd was buzzing. Mr. Muscles reached in and drew out the last tile, which had to be the other alpha. Impassively he walked over to Mr. Scary, the first alpha, and offered him his hand. Mr. Scary slapped it away.

"Let the betas go first," Alexandros called out. The crowd picked up his call. The head judge frowned but then conferred with his two colleagues. The two alphas were sent to the wrestlers' tent and an attendant was dispatched to recall the two betas.

Messrs. Thick and Quick ambled back onto the fighting field. They were handed cups of wine; made their libations; said their prayers; and saluted their king. They rubbed more dirt onto each other. They circled each other warily, trying to get the sun in the other's eyes. They slapped each other across the arms and shoulders. Mr. Thick tried to grab Mr. Quick's hand but was too slow. Mr. Thick slapped Mr. Quick across the face, hard. This maneuver earned him a prompt lash of the assistant judge's switch. "No punching," the judge admonished. More circling, slapping, and unsuccessful grabbing ensued.

Suddenly, Mr. Quick lunged to one knee and grabbed Mr. Thick behind his right ankle, pulling vigorously. Mr. Thick hopped awkwardly a couple of times on his left foot but couldn't maintain his balance and toppled. He managed to turn his body in the air, keeping his back and shoulders from hitting the ground and using his hands to cushion his landing but his left hip brushed the dirt.

"One fall," the head judge called out.

Both men regained their feet and the match resumed. This time, Mr. Quick didn't wait. He immediately lunged for his opponent's leg, grabbing him behind the knee. Mr. Thick, however, was ready for the attack. He hunched forward, tensed his muscles, and refused to budge. Try as he might, Mr. Quick couldn't unbalance him. Instead, Mr. Thick placed his hands on Mr. Quick's shoulders and started to push down. Mr. Quick, who was down on one knee, tried to rise back to his feet but Mr. Thick was too strong. After a few moments, during which there was no apparent movement but during which both men were evidently exerting tremendous effort, Mr. Quick sank, ever so slowly, to his knees.

"Two knees," the head judge called out. "One fall each."

The match resumed without a pause. The next fall would decide the outcome. Mr. Thick kept trying to grab his opponent's hand, wrist, or arm and Mr. Quick kept eluding his grasp. Finally, Mr. Thick managed to latch onto Mr. Quick's left hand and they held onto each other, their fingers intertwined. Mr. Thick, whose fingers were short and thick, in keeping with all other aspects of his body, tried to bend Mr. Quick's fingers back. Mr. Quick, using his right hand, grabbed Mr. Thick's right arm and tried desperately to free his left hand but Mr. Thick was just too strong. Mr. Quick's fingers started to bend back. It was clear that in a moment, his fingers would start breaking, one by one. Mr. Quick let out an anguished yell and raised his right arm, conceding the fall and thus conceding the match.

As soon as Mr. Quick raised his arm, the head judge immediately jumped between the fighters and separated them, hitting Mr. Thick with his switch for good measure. Mr. Thick let go of his opponent's hand and started jumping for joy. It was amazing to see how high such a short and heavy man could jump. The members of Mr. Thick's company were screaming their heads off. The remainder of the crowd rewarded him with polite applause. Mr. Quick hung his head in shame and disappeared.

Messrs. Scary and Muscles now made their way onto the fighting field. They also made their libations, said their prayers, and saluted their king. The match started but neither man seemed to be in any hurry. Mr. Scary didn't seem to mind when he ended up looking into the sun, presumably pleased at not having any shadows detracting from the natural ugliness of his countenance. He must have done some boxing in his time because his ears were flattened and his nose unnaturally contorted. More importantly, he must have partaken in an armed conflict or two because a long scar curved from below his left eye to the corner of his jaw below his left ear. A thick, purple rope of cicatricial tissue ringed his neck like a collar. Innumerable little blotches, bruises, and blemishes adorned his face and body. And then there was that blood-curdling leer.

Mr. Muscles didn't seem intimidated. He walked up to Mr. Scary, placed one hand on his opponent's arm and the other around his neck, and started to pull. Mr. Scary took no umbrage at the familiarity of the embrace and reciprocated his adversary's gesture. Then they pulled and pushed, snorted and grunted, waltzed and curtsied, as best of friends. Except in a few minutes Mr. Scary's knees buckled and he sank to his knees.

When the match resumed, Mr. Scary tried to run and evade but that strategy proved short-lived as well. Mr. Muscles cut off the ring, trapped him against the boundary sticks, embraced him in a bear hug, lifted him high in the air, squeezed the living daylights out of him, and threw him into the dirt.

"Karanos son of Pandrosos is the winner," the head judge announced, "two falls to none." Karanos's comrades started to cheer. "Akoniti," the head judge added over the noise, "dust-free." The appellation was picked up and amplified by the crowd. "Karanos Akonitos, Karanos Akonitos," they chanted.

The three remaining contestants gathered once again in front of the silver urn. This time Mr. Lucky went first. He drew a beta and couldn't contain his happiness. His cheer infected the crowd, which found the unlikely turn of events amusing. The other two contestants, Messrs. Thick and Muscles, didn't appreciate the humor of the situation. They dutifully reached into the urn, each emerging with the inevitable alpha in his hand, and grimly proceed to prepare for their match. Mr. Lucky disappeared once again into the wrestlers' tent.

The bout between the short but incredibly strong Mr. Thick and the extremely large and amazingly built Mr. Muscles proved to be somewhat anticlimactic. The two men latched onto each other and danced, neither able to uproot the other, notwithstanding the expenditure of prodigious amounts of energy. Eventually, neither man had any strength left. At the end, they remained on their feet only because they were holding each other up. Mr. Muscles finally let go and Mr. Thick sank to his knees.

Although he had suffered only one fall, Mr. Thick declined (or was unable) to continue and Mr. Muscles was declared the winner of the bout.

Mr. Lucky now returned for the final match. It was no contest. The skinny, tall, blue-tinted kid from Thrake ran around the ponderous and exhausted mountain man from Macedonia, spotted an opening, dove in, and felled the huge man with a single lunge. Mr. Muscles rose laboriously to his feet and tried gamely to even the match but he had no chance. The speed, agility, and especially the freshness of Mr. Lucky were too much to overcome. After some desultory slaps and attempted grabs, Mr. Muscles meekly succumbed when Mr. Lucky moved in for the victorious throw.

"Asteropaios son of Pyraichmes is the winner," the head judge announced, "two falls to none, dust-free."

There was noise in the crowd but it was more buzzing than acclamation. Of course, Mr. Lucky's fellow Thrakians were overjoyed but the rest of the spectators, with some justification, felt that the outcome of the competition had been determined by the luck of the draw, rather than the merits of the competitors.

"Well, that was not a satisfying outcome," Parmenion observed.

"Yeah, it sucked," Kleitos agreed.

Flood Tide

Alexandros didn't say anything; however, when Asteropaios climbed up to our platform to accept his victory wreath, the king clapped him cheerfully on the shoulder. "No such thing as luck," he told the young man. "It just means the gods are smiling on you. Next battle, make sure you're at the spearpoint of our attack, so they can smile on us all."

The winning wrestler beamed from ear to ear. "I will, sire, I will." From the sound of it, I was sure he meant it.

"Now, let's bring on the boxers!" Alexandros called out.

After a brief pause, three new judges walked in, followed by a lone competitor. The crowd looked at him in stunned silence.

"Who is that?" I whispered to Kleitos.

"Oh, that's Demophon. He's actually from the next village over from mine. He's pretty famous. He's won lots of boxing competitions."

"He looks like he's lost most of them."

"Oh no, no. He never loses. He's as tough as they come. It's actually an interesting story. His father was the richest man in the village but because Demophon was the second son, he was not going to inherit the farm, so he had to make his own way in the world."

"That's true of everybody in this army, isn't it?"

"Yeah, pretty much. But anyway, Demophon decided to make his fortune by becoming a boxer. You can see that he has the build for it."

And indeed, Demophon was large, well-proportioned, and heavily muscled. "But look at his face," I said.

Kleitos shrugged. "Yeah, well, that's what happens when you become a professional boxer. He used to have a nose, chin, forehead, ears, and eyelids. But here is the funny part. After he had been boxing for a few years, his older brother died. So Demophon returned home to claim his inheritance. But the number three brother objected, claiming that his number two brother had died and that this man was an imposter. Eventually, there was a trial in Pella. The brother produced a picture of Demophon from before he had left to become a boxer. The judges agreed that Demophon couldn't possibly be the man in the sketch and awarded the estate to the number three brother. So here he is, in Alexandros's army. But I thought he had retired from boxing."

"This is not really boxing," Perdikkas, who had overheard our conversation, chimed in. "This is just a friendly, amateur contest."

"Except, there's not going be a contest," Parmenion observed, "because nobody wants to fight him. All the other contestants dropped out when he entered."

"I'll double the prize for the winner," Alexandros announced loudly. "And all you have to do is win one bout. There will be no preliminary rounds."

Nobody stepped forward.

"How about you, Asteropaios?" Alexandros asked Mr. Lucky, who was still standing just below our platform, surrounded by his fellow tribesmen, accepting their plaudits.

At first, Asteropaios didn't understand the question. He looked up at the king, his eyes sparkling amid the smeared blue battle paint.

"You know how to box, don't you?"

"I don't know about boxing, sire. I have certainly had my share of fights but wrestling is my thing."

"Nothing to it, my boy. Just stay out of that ugly mug's reach until he gets tired and then you can put him away with one punch. Do it for me."

"Yes, sire," Asteropaios said.

Alexandros gave him a winning smile. "And now, going for a rare double win, here's our friend Asteropaios," he announced loudly, "who will take on the formidable Demophon. May the gods aid them both. Now, let's have a clean contest."

The crowd cheered as the fighters prepared for their bout. Asteropaios carefully removed his winner's wreath and placed it on the ground. His friends spiffed up his war paint. Demophon quietly worked on his "sharp gloves," a complicated affair of stiff leather panels, designed to protect the knuckles while striking the opponent's head, and flexible leather strips, used to keep the panels in place and to turn the hands into armored clubs. A set of "sharp gloves" was produced for Asteropaios's use as well and one of the judges helped him strap them on.

When the fighters were ready, Alexandros administered the oath, the fighters made their libations, asked the gods for their aid, saluted the king, and started to fight. Or more accurately, Demophon started to stalk Asteropaios. The old (he must have been close to thirty), disfigured boxer lumbered after the eighteen-year-old, tall, skinny, luminescent Thrakian, who did his best to stay away from the Macedonian's armored battering rams. Demophon kept his guard up, peeking between his raised fists, looking for an opportunity to strike, while Asteropaios, his arms dangling by his side, danced away, keeping safely out of striking range.

No punches were landed, or even attempted, by either fighter for a good long time. Finally, Asteropaios, sensing an opportunity, launched a wild, looping swing at Demophon's head. The old boxer easily caught the punch on his left forearm and continued to plod ahead. Asteropaios started to throw more punches but none of them could penetrate the experienced boxer's guard.

"Punch straight," somebody in the crowd called out, presumably to Asteropaios. "Short, straight jabs," another voice suggested helpfully. "Right between his fists." Advice was raining down on the contestants' heads, in sharp contradistinction to the dearth of actual landed blows.

Demophon continued his impassive pursuit of his quarry. Eventually, his persistence paid off. Asteropaios launched another long, looping, hopeful shot and Demophon stepped into it, parrying the punch with his left forearm while simultaneously delivering a devastating right jab into Asteropaios's face.

Asteropaios crumpled to the ground, unconscious, blood pouring from his nose. "Get up, get up," the crowd yelled. One of the assistant judges knelt next to the motionless youngster who, miraculously, began to stir. "Take your time, son," the judge said quietly as the Thrakian struggled back to one knee. "There's no rush."

Demophon approached, hulking menacingly above his kneeling opponent. The head judge stepped in and pushed him away, restraining him while Asteropaios rose to his feet. "Give him a chance, will you."

"I'm fine," Asteropaios called out, dancing a little jig on wobbly legs. The head judge let Demophon go. The veteran fighter moved with surprising speed, pressing his advantage, hoping to finish the bout, but the wiry Thrakian surprised him, and the rest of us, by his powers of recuperation. Before long, he was once again dancing and launching the occasional, ineffectual roundhouse shots, while Demophon continued to pepper him with a steady dose of straight, stiff jabs to the face and body.

A cut opened below Asteropaios's left eye and he was spitting blood but he was not slowing down. On the contrary, it was Demophon who seemed to be tiring. Every once in a while now, Asteropaios even succeeded in landing a punch and, although Demophon didn't deign to notice any of these blows, his face, already disfigured by a career in boxing, was slowly turning the color of an angry eggplant.

"This is going to end soon," Parmenion observed to Alexandros.

"True. But which one will win?"

"Isn't it obvious? The youngster is unable to hurt that bull, so it's only a matter of time before the bull gores him."

Alexandros shook his head. "I wouldn't be so sure. That youngster has the gods on his side." Turning to Hephaistion, he asked: "Who do we have lined up for the pankration competition? We should tell them to get ready."

Flood Tide

"It doesn't look like there's going to be a pankration competition, sire. We can't find anybody willing to take Iolkos on."

"You're kidding me. Another unopposed victor? What's everybody scared of?"

"In all fairness, sire, Iolkos is a lot scarier than Demophon ever was."

There was a sudden uproar in the crowd. Demophon had stopped chasing and was standing impassively in the center of the rink, although his guard was still up. Asteropaios ran up to him and started poking him, tentatively at first, then with more speed and precision. Every once in a while, his punches even got through, eliciting a loud roar each time. Until Demophon grew tired of the exercise and unleashed another devastating blow against Asteropaios's left temple.

Alexandros grimaced, whether in sympathy or dismay was hard to tell. "Well, that's that, I guess. Now let's get somebody to fight against Iolkos."

"We've tried, sire, we've tried. But nobody wants to get killed. Remember, unlike in boxing, there are no rules in pankration."

"That's bullcrap. There are rules in pankration: You can't bite, you can't gouge your opponent's eyes, and you can always stop the fight by simply raising your hand.

Nobody's getting killed. In fact, I think pankration is safer than boxing because they don't get to wear those ridiculous sharp gloves. If anything, I think boxing is more dangerous. Just look at that guy's face."

At the moment, that guy's face was exultant as he glared at his supine opponent. Asteropaios wasn't moving. "Can he continue?" the head judge asked. His assistant shrugged. They, and the crowd, waited. Finally, Asteropaios began to stir. The head judge leaned in. "Do you want to stop, son?" Asteropaios shook his head, sending droplets of blood flying in all directions. "I'm not hurt," he insisted as he spat out a large glob of bloody sputum and started to get up.

"Let him rest," somebody in the crowd called out. "Give him some water."

The head judge ignored the suggestions. "Can you continue or not?"

"Yes, I can," Asteropaios insisted. "I'm fine."

The head judge arched his eyebrows. "Are you sure?"

Asteropaios responded by jumping to his feet and waving his arms triumphantly. The fact he could still raise his arms at all surprised most everybody there.

The head judge shrugged. "Proceed!" He unleashed Demophon, who didn't dance and didn't wave his arms, concentrating instead on delivering the coup de grace. Asteropaios continued to elude him and Demophon continued to get more tired.

Alexandros turned back toward us. "All right then. Who's going fight against Iolkos?"

"I don't know," Hephaistion admitted.

"How about Ptolemaios here?" I looked up, startled. *Who said that?* "He can take on Iolkos. Wasn't he your hand-to-hand combat instructor in Mieza?" I should have recognized the slimy tones of Aristandros.

Kleitos, recognizing the danger, jumped in. "We don't fight the enlisted men."

Perdikkas, equally aware of the threat to me but presumably enjoying the prospect, was almost as quick off the mark. "Who says we don't?"

"That's true." Hephaistion pursed his lips and nodded. "Alexandros is willing to race against anyone."

"Well, actually, I'm not." Alexandros was smiling. "But the fact is, Ptolemaios, you could beat any two or three guys at a time in Mieza, without any weapons, and without ever suffering a defeat. So how about it? Won't you show this Iolkos how it's done?"

My hackles rose to attention. "I'm honored, sire, but those were boys and that was training. And it was nine years ago."

"So, that means you're stronger now, and more experienced. You're not scared, are you?"

"Buck, buck, buck – chicken," Perdikkas interjected, to great general merriment.

I shrugged, reconciling myself to my fate. "I'll do it, sire."

"What, are you insane?" Kleitos hissed.

"Good," Alexandros said. "Get down there and get ready. We'll start your bout as soon as the boxing is finished. This is dragging out a little longer than I'd expected."

Hephaistion patted me helpfully on the back. "So finish Iolkos off as quickly as you can. We're getting hungry."

"Or let him finish you, if you can't." Aristandros leered at me from behind Hephaistion's back. *I should've known this had been his plan all along.*

Kleitos and I jumped off the platform. "What did you do?" Kleitos demanded. Seleukos joined us. "That was really stupid," he observed. "Thanks, fellas. I appreciate your vote of confidence," I said.

Flood Tide

We stood in front of the crowd, watching the boxing match. Demophon continued to press ahead and Asteropaios continued to evade him. Perhaps they were both moving a little more slowly but their stalemate persisted.

After a while, I stopped watching them. The truth was, aside from watching a few matches, I knew very little about pankration. And the only thing I knew about Iolkos was that he had previously killed at least three of his opponents. *Am I going to be number four?*

It was getting dark. It was hard to see the contestants. Alexandros ordered torches to be brought in. A few were set up on poles at the back of the crowd but they didn't help much. If anything, the flickering play of light and shadow only made it more difficult for us to see the contestants and for them to see each other.

"We're getting hungry," somebody called out. "Finish him off, Asteropaios," somebody else yelled. "Kill him, Demophon," answered another voice.

"Let's bring some food in," Alexandros ordered. "We can eat and drink while we're watching the fights."

Walking up to the edge of the platform, he yelled to the men: "The food and wine are ready. You can go and help yourselves, if you're not worried about missing the end of the fight. But at least make sure to be back for the pankration. We have a very special match arranged for you."

There was not much action in the rink. The spectators meandered away and then gradually they meandered back, having eaten and drunk and carrying more food and wine with them.

"Want me to get you something to eat?" Kleitos asked. I shook my head. "At least have some wine," Seleukos suggested. "I don't need anything, thanks," I said. "But you two go ahead." They refused to leave, so we stood there, watching the boxing match.

I loosened up a little, while mentally reviewing all my moves and countermoves. *You won't get hurt*, I told myself, *much less lose the match*. It didn't matter who my opponent was. After all, I had been a hand-to-hand combat instructor once.

"You're gonna be okay," Kleitos said, as if reading my thoughts, but it was clear he had his doubts.

"We're here for you," Seleukos added, in tones usually reserved for addressing the widow at a wake.

The moon rose but its thin crescent reflected very little light. The torches were spluttering. The faces of the two fighters were dark, shapeless masses but whether as a result of the pounding they had absorbed or the lack of illumination was impossible to tell. They circled each other in slow motion, in the dark shadows, as if in a caliginous dream.

"Call it a draw," somebody yelled out. "Bring on the pankratiasts." "No, let them finish." "This is ridiculous."

I could see Alexandros conferring with the others on the platform. Then he called the head judge over.

"Stop," Alexandros called out as the head judge ran back and separated the two fighters.

"No!" the people in the crowd protested. "We want a winner."

Alexandros motioned the two contestants over to the wagon and crouched down to talk with them. After a brief discussion, both men nodded and Alexandros rose back up.

"You will get your winner," he announced. "This is what we'll do: First, one man will take a clean shot at the other. If he survives the blow, then he's going to get a clean shot in return. Whichever man is still standing after that, he'll be the winner."

"What if both men are still standing?" somebody asked.

"That won't happen," Alexandros said, "but if it does, then they'll both be winners."

There was a hastily arranged drawing of lots. Asteropaios the Lucky won, which meant he would deliver the first blow. The two men stood in the center of the ring, Demophon hiding behind his fists, Asteropaios contemplating the best place to hit him and gathering his strength. His tribesmen were cheering him on, willing him to victory. Asteropaios smiled and waved. He even attempted his patented little jig but was too tired to pull it off. Then he grew serious, drew a deep breath, and delivered a tremendous punch to Demophon's head, putting his entire skinny body into the blow. Demophon absorbed most of the energy of the blow on his hand, which he had held protectively in front of his face, but enough force was transmitted to his skull to knock him off his feet and render him momentarily unconscious. He recovered fairly quickly, though, and rose laboriously to his feet.

Asteropaios stood in front of him, facing him fearlessly, confident in the favor of the gods. "Get your guard up," someone yelled and Asteropaios dutifully raised his fists in front of his head.

Demophon took one step forward and, with the fingers of his right hand rigidly extended, struck Asteropaios just below the sternum, his bound fingertips penetrating the abdominal wall, his hand sinking in almost to the wrist. He quickly withdrew his now closed hand, wrenching a fistful of viscera out through the gaping wound, followed by a cascade of blood and offal.

Flood Tide

There was absolutely no sound. Asteropaios's body twitched silently on the moist ground as judges and spectators rushed up to him. Philippos the Physician tried to stuff his intestines back and stem the explosion of blood, peritoneal fluid, and fecal matter but Asteropaios was dead within minutes. Demophon wearily raised his bloody hand in victory.

There was no celebration, only angry shouts. "That's not right," people yelled. "You're a murderer." "He was only eighteen."

Alexandros pushed his way through to the lifeless body. It was clear from his expression that he was deeply agitated. Whether it was because a young man whom he liked had been gruesomely killed or because the gods had failed to protect someone he had supposed to have been their favorite or because there was something fundamentally unfair about the outcome of the bout, it was impossible to tell. "Demophon, you're disqualified." His usually loud and steady voice quaked.

Demophon stood impassively, saying nothing in his own defense. Even he looked crestfallen and ashamed, seeing the results of his handiwork.

Alexandros struggled to control his emotions ... and to find a rationale for the disqualification. "That was not one blow," he finally said, "but a series of assaults." Only silence greeted his words. "Now get out of my camp!" he screamed. "You have disgraced yourself."

Demophon, maintaining his sepulchral silence, spun on his heels and walked away. Alexandros picked up the victory wreath doffed by Asteropaios prior to the start of the bout and placed it on the pale, pulverized, startled face of the once handsome youngster. The festivities were over. No one mentioned any pankration match."

Chapter 5 – Crossroads

We were wasting valuable time but Alexandros – normally a swift and incisive leader – refused to budge. Orpheus was covered in shit. Even his lyre sported a coating of guano. The little shrine, meant to protect him, had fallen into disrepair eons ago. There was nothing left of the roof and two of the three walls had mostly tumbled to the ground. He had become the favorite roosting place for seagulls, herons, and egrets. Our invincible commander was appalled.

"What's the meaning of this?" Alexandros demanded to know. Poor Aristandros was hard pressed to come up with an answer.

There were cult statues, shrines, and altars at most major crossroads in the ancient world, designed to accommodate the religious needs of travelers anxious to propitiate the local deities. The more dangerous the road, the more frequent these monuments seemed to become. This particular shrine, which stood at the intersection of two major roads, one hugging the coast to Ephesos and then on to Miletos, the two principal ports at the southern end of Ionia, the other leading farther inland toward Sardeis, the capital of Lydia, had evidently been erected by Greek colonists to celebrate the mythical, semi-divine singer from Thrake, who was willing to descend to Haides to recover his beloved. Alas, the perception of Orpheus's mystical powers, or perhaps the appreciation of his musical talents, must have declined over time, at least locally, because no one had made any effort to maintain his abode for many years.

Alexandros would rarely forego an opportunity to pay homage to a deity, or even to a singer with mixed reviews, on most days but, in this case, the Orpheus legend happened to be one of his favorite childhood stories. He remained rooted to the spot until we all got busy cleaning up the mess, after which he insisted on observing the usual proprieties and offering a suitable sacrifice.

Aristandros's difficulty was of an entirely different order. Alexandros, who was nothing if not superstitious, considered Orpheus's dilapidated state a bad omen, especially at this moment, when he was trying to decide which road to take. He wished to receive his seer's reassurance concerning the meaning of the omen and his interpretation as to the direction of travel favored by the gods. Aristandros was unable to answer the latter question, though, because he couldn't figure out which way Alexandros wanted to go.

Flood Tide

The great soothsayer forged ahead gamely. "The state of this shrine, when you arrived here, great king, was truly deplorable. This can only mean one thing: The great Orpheus has been waiting, patiently, for the man who would restore him to his rightful splendor, just as the oppressed Greek cities of Ionia have been waiting, lo these many years, for the man who would restore their liberty. The message of the gods is unmistakable, sire. You are the man who will free our Greek brethren from the yoke of Persian oppression."

Alexandros was beaming. "Thank you, Aristandros." He sounded genuinely relieved. "Only one more question: To achieve our great victory, should we march toward Sardeis or toward Ephesos?"

And now Aristandros was stuck. I could see the terror in his face. He had no clue what his patron wanted to hear, which was severely crimping his oracular panache. He temporized. "The answer is clear, sire. The birds that defecate on gods do not know what they do. Similarly, men must choose their path through life by letting their instincts guide their steps. Birds are going to fly and men are going to march, free as the wind."

"Just as long as they don't step where the birds flew," I added. I couldn't help myself. Aristandros didn't seem to appreciate my assistance.

Alexandros didn't press the point. Too many people were listening and he didn't wish to discuss his quandary within earshot of his men.

****

Until the previous night, Alexandros had been clear in his own mind about his immediate plans. His next objective was going to be Sardeis, which had once been the home of legendary King Kroisos, reputed to have been the richest man in the history of the world. Now, two hundred years later, Sardeis was still the capital of one of the richest satrapies in the Persian Empire and the site of one of Dareios's regional treasuries. Alexandros's need for money was growing desperate. Since crossing the Hellespont, his men had received only sporadic pay. Alexandros had promptly distributed any loot, ransom payments, or taxes collected since his arrival in Asia but all such income fell woefully short of the cost of keeping the army in the field. My guess was that Alexandros needed perhaps 250 talents of silver per month simply to pay his men. I doubted that Harpalos the Purser had, at that point, more than a couple of talents left in his treasury. This was enough money to make one person comfortably rich for life but not nearly sufficient to pay an army for even a day. The soldiers understood that their pay depended on their success in the field but they were under the impression that the spoils captured from the Persians after the victory at Granikos, especially when added to the loot taken from the cities occupied prior to Granikos and to the ransom payments received from other cities in the Troad seeking to avoid being plundered, was more than enough to cover their regular wages, plus a little bonus on top. Alexandros did not wish to disabuse them of their misimpression, which was the reason why he was anxious to get to Sardeis and replenish the army's coffers with all possible dispatch.

Alexandros's clarity of purpose changed overnight, however, when a Greek defector from Ephesos, named Helbidios, stealthily entered his tent. Helbidios brought startling intelligence: Memnon had turned up in Ephesos. What was more, the Rhodian condottiere did not arrive as some furtive fugitive from the Battle of Granikos. Somehow, Memnon had managed to accomplish the impossible. Not only had he escaped Dareios's wrath as one of the commanders responsible for the stinging Persian defeat, he had actually convinced the emperor that the reason for the debacle was the failure of the other Persian commanders to listen to his advice prior to the battle. The fact that Memnon's assertion happened to be true did not lessen the miraculous nature of Dareios's response.

Persian tradition, dating back hundreds of years, would have dictated the immediate execution of Memnon, if only to deflect any possible taint of defeat from becoming attached to Dareios himself. Instead of killing Memnon, however, Dareios had listened to his analysis of the causes of the defeat, which included the failure of the Persian cavalry to kill Alexandros when it had the chance and the failure of the conscript infantry to put up any resistance at all. The solution, according to Memnon, was for Persia to utilize its overwhelming advantages in the fight against Alexandros. It was still a contest between an elephant and a mouse but the elephant had to become more agile, if it was going to succeed in squashing the mouse.

Memnon proposed a two-pronged approach. He advocated continued resistance to the invading pan-Hellenic army but at times and places of Persia's choosing, coupled with an invasion of Greece and Macedonia by a Persian expeditionary force. He pointed out that Persia could mobilize more than enough troops to field an army in Ionia that far outnumbered Alexandros's expeditionary force, while at the same time assembling a second, equally large army to invade the Greek homeland. In addition, he reminded Dareios that Persia enjoyed substantial naval superiority in the Aegean, which meant that it could attack the Greek homeland at will. "Let's see how long the allies in Alexandros's pan-Hellenic army stick with him, once their home cities come under threat. And for that matter, let's see how long Alexandros can keep even his own Macedonian troops in the field here, once Macedonia itself comes under attack."

Finally, Memnon suggested, as diplomatically as he could, that Persia needed to recruit every available mercenary in the Greek world, both to stiffen the native, conscript forces and to weaken the military capabilities of the Greeks. Certainly, Persia had the resources to outbid the Greeks for the services of any mercenary.

Flood Tide

Dareios, who was a capable soldier, immediately grasped the strategic brilliance of Memnon's proposals. Instead of killing Memnon, he appointed him supreme military commander, charged with the responsibility of repelling the Hellenic invasion and, more importantly, consolidating Persian hegemony on both sides of the Aegean. The emperor and his new commander in chief agreed that the first point of Persian resistance would be Ephesos, a strategically located port on the western coast of Anatolia, with stout walls, a strong akropolis, and a fine harbor. What's more, if the Persian navy could keep the sea lanes to Ephesos open, then the chances of a successful siege of the city by Alexandros would be greatly diminished. And if Ephesos did eventually succumb to the invaders, the Persians would fall back to Miletos, with its own strong walls, formidable akropolis, and easily defensible harbor. And if, by some mischance, Miletos too should fall, then there was always impregnable Halikarnassos, farther down the Anatolian coast. And while Alexandros was occupied trying to sack Ephesos and Miletos and then, if necessary, Halikarnassos, the Persians would be busy putting together their two armies for the return engagement that would destroy the pan-Hellenic expeditionary force once and for all and that would carry the conflict to the Greek mainland. Never again would the upstart Greeks threaten the mighty Persian Empire.

Orders were dispatched that same day to the naval forces of Phoenicia and the subject islands of the eastern Aegean to sail for Ionia with all possible speed; to all garrison commanders in Karia to place their forces at Memnon's disposal forthwith; and to all the satraps throughout Anatolia, specifying the numbers of fully equipped and trained troops each had to supply to the imperial armies by next spring. In addition, in the course of the next few days, recruiters, heavily laden with treasure, fanned out across the Persian and Greek worlds, with the urgent mission of recruiting every brigand, pirate, cutthroat, and soldier of fortune willing to enlist with the imperial armies. Memnon himself made his way to Ephesos to take over the defenses of the city. Meanwhile, Dareios set out for Damaskos in order to be closer to the action while he oversaw the war effort. No longer was Dareios taking anything for granted.

When Memnon arrived in Ephesos, he commandeered one of the finest private residences in the city as his headquarters. It happened to be Helbidios's house. The ethnic Greek merchant, whose family had been among the leading citizens of Ephesos for generations, entertained his uninvited guest and his entourage lavishly, loosened their tongues spirituously, and made his way to Alexandros's camp expeditiously.

Alexandros spent half the night interrogating Helbidios. He spent the other half issuing orders. He sent Parmenion, with a small detachment, to occupy nearby Daskyleion. He appointed Parmenion's son Nikanoros as commander of the small pan-Hellenic navy, comprised mostly of vessels contributed by Athens and manned by allied sailors (Macedonians were no mariners) and ordered them to establish a blockade of Ephesos. He appointed Alexandros of Lynkestis commander of allied cavalry and instructed him to remain behind and maintain control of Hellespontine Phrygia. The only thing he couldn't decide was whether to march on Sardeis first, and then on to Ephesos, which was the rational course, or march directly against Ephesos, which was the lion-hearted route. And Aristandros was of no help at all.

****

On another royal road, heading west south west out of Ekbatana, Dareios's harem was also on the move. Barsine, carrying her son strapped to her back, and surrounded by her three little girls, was trudging along on the dusty, uneven, and unyielding surface of the highway, keeping a weather eye out for the piles of excrement left behind by assorted beasts of burden (including the two-legged kind) marching ahead of them; for the callously whistling whips of slave drivers urging the procession along; for the flying fists of officious eunuchs pounding back and forth on their mules; for sudden rain squalls and unexpected sandstorms; and for that elusive glimmer of deliverance.

Dareios, his court, and his bodyguard of ten thousand Immortals had left only a day before the harem's departure but the emperor's caravan had quickly outdistanced the women's procession. Dareios's endless column of dignitaries, knights, infantrymen, servants, and slaves, traveling on foot, by horse, and in all manner of wheeled vehicle, and accompanied by horse-drawn wagons, camels, innumerable other pack animals, and human porters, carrying the emperor's and his retinue's weapons, armor, baggage, and treasury, moved at a stately but steady pace, covering twenty miles or more each day.

By contrast, the women's procession – consisting of palanquins, which were more like small, portable, human-borne houses, for the emperor's mother and his wives; smaller litters and sedan chairs for the concubines; carts for the decrepit and the exceptionally concupiscent; mules for the eunuchs; perambulation for all the rest; and a baggage train that rivaled in length the emperor's own entourage but was powered mostly by oxen, mules, and donkeys – was lucky if it advanced five miles in a day.

They were all headed for a small town in Lowland Assyria[10], near the eastern tip of the Mediterranean, which Dareios had chosen as his administrative seat for the duration of the campaign against Alexandros. He wanted to be near the action in Anatolia but not too near. His lines of communication with Memnon would be relatively short but at the same time his court, his harem, and his treasury would be safely out of harm's way. At his current pace,

---

[10] The Assyrian Empire had long since fallen to the combined assault of the Babylonians, Medes, and Persians. It was eventually absorbed into the Persian Empire. Two Persian satrapies, however, continued to use the name.

Flood Tide

Dareios expected to arrive at the dusty, sleepy town of Damaskos in about forty days. It would take the harem four times as long to get there but there was no rush. Although Dareios was confident of the ultimate success of the plan that he and Memnon had devised, he realized that it might well take months, perhaps even a year, before Alexandros and his army were totally eradicated and even longer before Persia succeeded in establishing its control over the Greek mainland. While wishing to exercise close supervision over the upcoming military operations, Dareios saw no need to deprive himself of the usual comforts of court, including ready access to his harem. And, being as cautious as he was hedonistic, he made sure that Memnon's family remained in captivity and close to hand, a precaution that was not lost on Memnon.

Barsine was only vaguely aware of the progress of the war. No one ever bothered to update the inmates of the harem on current developments in the outside world and, in truth, many of the women couldn't have cared less. They lived in a severely circumscribed universe, where the only things that mattered were the emperor's satisfaction with his sexual encounter or encounters of the previous night, the current stage of each woman's menstrual cycle (through some strange magic, their cycles tended to synchronize over time), their devoutly hoped for parturiency, and their resultant standing in the rigid pecking order of the harem.

Some of the women did manage to retain a vestigial interest in life beyond the walls. A favored few were able to glean occasional tidbits of gossip from the eunuchs, while submitting, whether willingly or otherwise, to their nocturnal attentions, which morsels of information they then traded as precious currency during their daytime gabfests. They understood that some savages from Greece had invaded the Ionian coast of Anatolia but, except for the handful of women from that corner of the empire, they wasted absolutely no mental energy worrying about the outcome of that localized conflict. They had much more important concerns: One of the concubines had missed her menses for the second month in a row.

Barsine knew, from a terse, coded note smuggled to her from Memnon, that there had been a battle and that her husband had survived. She also understood that more battles would be coming. Memnon promised her that, after the Greek invaders had been defeated, she and their children would be released from the harem and they could once again live together as a family. She spent her time, as they plodded along mile after endless mile, daydreaming of the moment when their captivity would end. She also spent considerable time plotting their escape.

Their confinement was necessarily less secure while on the road. Barsine believed that it should be possible for her and the children to disappear during some moonless night. No tall walls surrounded them and the eunuchs had to spend at least as much time worrying about external threats as they did maintaining the absolute separation between the inmates of the harem and the outside world.

The farther west they marched, the closer they came to her father's ancestral lands. In two nights, it would be the new moon and they would be very near Adhorbaigan. If she was ever going to make good their escape, that would be her chance.

But then, she had second thoughts. Did the Phraortes family still occupy their homestead? Would they be willing to shelter Artabazos's daughter and Memnon's wife? What would the eunuchs do to her, and to her children, if they were caught? What would Dareios do to her husband if his family disappeared from the harem? She had two days to make up her mind.

****

In Pella, Olympias was peering idly into the courtyard from the second story gallery that served as the entranceway to the women's quarter of the royal palace. She had been spending a lot of time standing and staring in the weeks since her son's departure for Asia. This particular afternoon, her persistence was rewarded by the appearance of a dust-covered rider in the gatehouse. She recognized the man as one of Alexandros's soldiers and her heart skipped a beat. She tried to read the messenger's expression – for she had correctly surmised his mission – as she ran down the stairs leading into the courtyard. The man's name flashed into her mind: Iphitos. He seemed downcast as he alighted from his lather-covered mount and handed the reins to one of the guards but she couldn't tell whether he was dejected or simply tired.

Her emotions seesawed wildly between dispirited foreboding and exhilarated anticipation. She occupied an ambiguous position at court since her son's departure. On the one hand, she was the mother of a popular king and a formidable figure in her own right; on the other hand, she had little doubt that, if her son ceased to be king, her own fortunes were likely to decline precipitously. Her chief antagonist was the man chosen by her son to act as regent in his absence, Antipatros, and the regent's malign son, Kassandros, but in truth she had managed to turn almost everybody at court into an enemy.

"Iphitos, what news?" she yelled as she ran around the ornamental pool in the center of the courtyard.

Iphitos reached into a satchel fastened over his shoulder and extracted two rolls. After examining them both, he handed one to Olympias. "From Alexandros, queen mother."

"Tell me!" she urged as she struggled to break the seal. "Is he alive?"

"Rejoice, your highness, and read the letter."

Olympias let loose a wild shriek at the word 'rejoice' and thus didn't hear the rest of Iphitos's sentence. She continued to struggle with the letter, her shaking hands proving unequal to the task of unrolling the balky papyrus. Iphitos took pity on her, retrieved the letter from her hands, unrolled it, and handed it back.

Olympias drank in the words like a parched wayfarer handed a jug of water after crossing a wide, desolate desert. Her frosty pale blue eyes, usually cold and hard, melted into tears. Her narrow, gaunt, haunted face softened into a smile. Her angular, arrogant cheekbones grew more rounded and approachable. Dimples broke the haughty cast of her cheeks. At forty-three, she was still a strikingly beautiful woman.

"I knew it," she said softly, fighting back sobs, when she had finished reading. "He's destiny's darling, beloved of the gods." She paused, struggling to regain her composure. "And he's my son," she added, wonder mingling with triumph in her voice.

"Yes, ma'am. He's that."

"I knew it. I felt it in my heart all along. The gods love him," Olympias shook her head as she reread the letter. Then she reached for the second roll. "Here, give me the other one!"

"That one's for Antipatros, ma'am."

"Yes, I know. I'll give it to him."

"I was told to place it directly in the regent's hand."

"Listen, Iphitos ..."

"... by your son."

"Exactly. So let's have it."

"I'm sorry, ma'am."

"You think you're sorry now." Olympias laughed. The dimples disappeared; her eyes regained their chill. Fortunately for the messenger, several men emerged from the reception hall and the queen mother chose to desist. Iphitos was escorted into the armory, where Antipatros and Kassandros were engaged in an animated conversation. Olympias entered close on the messenger's heels.

Antipatros looked up and quickly assessed the situation. He accepted the proffered roll and motioned with his head and eyebrows toward Olympias. Three guards, stationed by the door, approached the queen mother and attempted to usher her out of the room. They knew better than to touch her, though, and she refused to budge.

Antipatros shrugged and turned his attention to the letter. In his sixty-four years, he'd seen it all before. The tall, bearded, aristocratic regent was already one of King Philippos's trusted generals when a twenty-year-old Olympias first arrived at the Macedonian court as Philippos's fourth wife. He rose to become Philippos's foremost diplomat, one of his two (along with Parmenion) most trusted generals, and occasional regent. When

Philippos was assassinated, Antipatros smoothly transferred his allegiance to Alexandros and was rewarded for his loyalty by maintaining his position as regent of the realm when Alexandros departed for Asia. He had been dealing with Olympias for twenty-three years. He took another skirmish with her in his stride.

Alexandros's letter, on the other hand, was creating a more difficult dilemma for Antipatros. The young king wanted more troops, oblivious to reports recently received by Antipatros that clearly indicated rising discontent among Macedonia's ostensible allies in the Hellenic League. Sparta, which was not a member of the League, was wasting little time, now that Alexandros had crossed the Hellespont, trying to foment uprisings among the allies.

"What's he say?" Olympias wanted to know.

"He wants more troops."

"Then he shall have them. All these soldiers lolling about Pella are not doing us any good."

"It's not that simple, madam," Antipatros replied. "Here, read this." He handed her the document he had been discussing with his son when Iphitos delivered the letter from Alexandros. It was a decoded version of a report received from one of their spies in Sparta. It made for bracing reading.

"Doesn't matter." Olympias shrugged, having reviewed the report. "My son wants more troops; we will send more troops."

"*We* will not do anything, madam. *I* will consider the situation and *I* will advise you what I have decided to do. Now, perhaps madam would consider letting me get on with my work."

Olympias walked out of the room, chin disdainfully upturned, accompanied by a couple of the guards. "Once my son is back, that old bastard will get his comeuppance," she muttered under her breath, not particularly concerned who might overhear her comment.

When the door to the armory closed, Antipatros turned to his son. "Don't worry, when Alexandros is gone, she'll get her just deserts. Now, what shall we do about this request?"

****

I was sitting in the weeds at the margin of the road, waiting – with some empathy – for Alexandros to make up his mind. In a sense, I was at a crossroads as well.

Kleitos sat down next to me. "Which way d'ya think we'll go?"

"Your guess is as good as mine."

"I'm sure he'll decide to go straight for Ephesos," Kleitos ventured after a moment.

"Why?"

"Didn't he send us, the day after Granikos, on that wild goose chase after Memnon? He was livid that the traitor got away. Now that we know where he is, he's got to go get him."

"He didn't go get him last time, did he? He sent us to get him. And besides, that mission was not about getting Memnon. It was mostly about getting me killed."

"Now you're starting to sound paranoid."

"You could be right."

I left it at that. How could I explain to my friend the weight of isolation and uncertainty that were my daily companions? I had spent nine years cut off from the place where I grew up, from my friends and family, from my own time, from any sense of belonging. And now I'd somehow acquired a malignant enemy to boot. All I wanted to do was go home.

According to an adage I'd learned at my mother's knee, time heals all wounds. Yet, somehow it didn't work in my case. Instead of a balm, for me, time was a barrier. As the days and weeks of my exile turned into months and years, my memories of what I'd left behind didn't fade. Like

Zeus's eagles, the ordinary challenges of survival pecked away at my reveries each day but, like Prometheus's liver, my longing for home seemed to regenerate every night. No matter where I woke, a sense of loss greeted me each morning. As my recollections decreased in definition and nuance over time, the pain of loss became sharper, more persistent, and more torturous. In my case, the saying "absence makes the heart grow fonder" might have been more apt.

I resolved anew to continue to struggle, to strive, to live for that elusive dream of repatriation. Alas, if all went well, it would be another fourteen years before I could return home. What made it worse was that, for most of the past nine years, I'd had a clear plan for getting to the escape hatch and thence back home. The unexpected outcome of the Battle of Granikos had knocked my plans into a cocked hat. *I should have been in the Persian world by now, slowly making my way toward Egypt*, I thought, *instead of being stuck in the middle of this pointless campaign to "liberate the Greek cities of Ionia."*

How could I tell my friend that I was sitting there, just then, contemplating the possibility of deserting to the other side? But the inescapable truth was that Persia controlled Egypt and therefore, if I wanted to get to Egypt, I would have to enter Persia sooner or later. *Timing is everything*, I reminded myself ruefully.

"How long does it take?" Kleitos asked, as if reading my mind. "We've been sitting here since dawn."

I shrugged. "It's a tough decision." I wasn't sure whether I was answering Kleitos's question or my own thoughts. "There may be reasons why he might need to go to Sardeis first."

"What reasons?"

Based on some thought process known only to him, perhaps having to do with my status as an outsider, Alexandros had chosen to confide in me from time to time. As a result, I was aware of his financial straits and Kleitos, along with the rest of the army, was not. I was not inclined to betray the confidences that Alexandros had reposed in me. "I have no idea," I said.

"So what the hell are you talking about, then?"

"Oh, I'm just talking." A new thought struck me: *Deserting Alexandros's army is worse than betraying his confidences, isn't it?* "You have to weigh the arguments on both sides," I added after a moment.

"What arguments? We want to capture or kill Memnon. Memnon is in Ephesos. We go to Ephesos. End of argument."

I said nothing. I was busy weighing the pros and cons in my own mind. There was no rush to do anything; I had fourteen years to get to Egypt. On the other hand, the trip was long and uncertain. The sooner I got going, the better my odds of being in the right place at the right time. Besides, getting bogged down in this conflict in faraway Anatolia could have unforeseeable consequences. *It's a lot easier inadvertently to violate the Prime Directive as a soldier caught up in a war than as an inconspicuous pilgrim traveling anonymously through a placid, slumbering land.* On the other hand, I hated to betray my friends and comrades. *But they're trying to kill you,* I objected. *Not all of them.*

My objectives floated to the forefront of my mind: Stay alive; comply with the Prime Directive; get back home. These had been my goals since the day I realized I was marooned and would need to get back on my own. In a way, my quest had almost settled into a routine. Unfortunately, the unexpected turn of events at Granikos had upset not only the patterns of my quotidian activities but my subconscious thinking as well. I still had plenty of enemies and was certainly still an outsider but now I had friends and comrades and new allegiances. My perspective on the Prime Directive was changing somehow. And I was slowly getting a little more used to the daily uncertainties of a violent and competitive world, even if I still found the notion that I had no idea of what would come next quite disconcerting.

It's all very confusing, I thought. The only rational course was to defect at the earliest opportunity and get as far from this war, and as close to Egypt, as I could. But I had gotten to know these people and even liked some of them. I didn't know anybody in the entire Persian Empire and what I had heard about them was not flattering. And then there was the wait, the interminable wait. *Will it still be 'home' by the time I get back?* I found this last thought particularly depressing.

⊹⋆⋆⋆⋇⋇

My musings were interrupted by a sharp command from Alexandros. "We're marching on Sardeis."

"Exactly what the auguries indicate, sire," Aristandros hastened to put in.[11]

---

[11] For maps of locations mentioned in this book, visit AlexanderGeiger.com.

Chapter 6 – Liberation

Alexandros rode in the van as usual. Aristandros somehow ended up riding right next to him. As a result, most of us in the king's personal bodyguard found ourselves in a loose formation around both of them.

I maneuvered my horse between Kleitos and Seleukos, riding just behind our leader and his seer. "Since when did we become the protection detail for that charlatan?" I muttered under my breath, perhaps more loudly than necessary.

Everyone within earshot of my stage whisper pretended not to have heard, except for the charlatan himself. For an old man he had remarkably good hearing. He didn't say anything but brought his mount to a stop, causing the three of us to overtake him.

When we were abreast, he smiled at me amiably. "Is this better, Metoikos? Now you're not protecting me. Instead, all four of us are protecting the king."

Flood Tide

I looked the other way.

Aristandros continued undaunted. "Beautiful day for a ride, isn't it?"

I couldn't ignore him any further. "Don't you have to check with the king first, before making such a bold pronouncement?"

The soothsayer laughed. "Now, now. Let's pretend to be friends, shall we?"

"Or at least butcher a couple of goats before going out on a limb?"

Seleukos, being a lot more sensible than I, jumped in before I made a complete fool of myself. "Yes, it is. And the air is so fresh."

He was joined in his rescue mission by Kleitos. "It must be the sea breeze. How far are we from the coast?"

"It's just beyond those hills," Seleukos assured him.

Aristandros took a deep breath. "Ah, the Greek sea." I thought I detected a note of sarcasm in his voice but it was probably just my imagination. "Homeros called the Aegean the wine-faced sea," he continued.

"But it's blue," Kleitos objected.

"Well, he was blind." I was still in a peevish mood.

"It depends on the weather and the depth of the water," Seleukos said. "Sometimes it seems blue and sometimes it's turquoise and sometimes, if the wind picks up, it turns a deep, angry, foaming purple, embellished with racing whitecaps."

Aristandros patted his mare to keep her in step with our steeds. "Homeros's eyes might have been sightless but he more than made up for it with his second sight." All I could do was groan, which the seer pointedly ignored. "In his mind's eye, the brilliant cerulean splendor of the Greek sea reminded him of the savory oxblood of fine Pramnian wine. Or perhaps he was simply alluding to the deep, luxurious sensory delight triggered by both."

"Why do you keep calling it the Greek sea?" Kleitos interrupted. "I thought it was the Aegean."

The great soothsayer nodded his head, relaxed in his seat, and smiled sagely. "Greek-speaking peoples have been sailing the Aegean for thousands of years. Long before the Trojan War, hordes of Sea People, speaking various Mycenaean dialects, washed up, like the incoming tide, on the shores of Anatolia, the Levant, Egypt, Greece, and all the islands in between, clashing against the native Hittites, Assyrians, Phoenicians, Egyptians, and all the rest. In the most fertile, and therefore most densely inhabited, areas of the eastern Mediterranean, their settlements ebbed, under the weight of armed resistance, and eventually disappeared. But on the rocky, inhospitable shores of mainland Greece and on some of the Aegean islands, their strongholds took root and grew into established hamlets, ports, and principalities."

Kleitos shook his head in amazement. "How do you know all this?"

I was as astonished as my friend. The old goat certainly knew his stuff but I was damned if I was going to let him trump me. So I jumped in, heedless of the consequences. "That's all true, Aristandros, but there was one area of the Aegean basin where, despite the determined opposition of the native kings and potentates, the Mycenaean migrants clung tenaciously to a narrow strip of land along the seashore. This patch of contested land comprised the western shore of Anatolia, which is where we happen to be marching right now. In this region, no matter how often their settlements were attacked, and even destroyed, they returned again and again, driven by the unrelenting demographic dynamo of their ancestral Central Asian homeland. It was here, on the western coast of Anatolia, near the Hellespont, that the Mycenaeans fought the Trojans in a long, costly, epic war. Despite that war, and many others, their settlements on the coast of Anatolia survived, prospered, and grew into established cities."

The contented, satisfied grin on Aristandros's face should have stopped me then and there. But I, as is my wont, obliviously forged ahead.

"Perhaps a century after the Trojan War, new waves of marauding seafarers came, speaking a different, Dorian dialect. To the Mycenaeans, these uninvited and unwelcome cousins seemed to be primitive savages. However, they were vigorous, desperate savages, and they displaced the earlier immigrants, plunging the Greek world into a temporary dark age. The Greek-speaking cities on the Anatolian coast declined, lost their cultural attainments, changed their dialect, and reverted to primitive village life, but mostly they survived."

By now, Kleitos was rolling his eyes but that didn't stop me either.

"When the light of civilization dawned once again across the Hellenic firmament, a couple of hundred years later, it found the Greeks still plying the wine-faced sea. One group, speaking what came to be known as the Ionian dialect, sailed in the opposite direction, from the Greek mainland eastward, across the Aegean, toward Anatolia. They returned to this thin sliver of land, located in the middle of the western coast of Anatolia, a couple hundred miles to the south of where Troy had once stood. They co-opted the Greek-speaking primitive villages, raised them into prosperity once again, and turned them into enlightened beacons of progress. They called their new homeland Ionia."

Aristandros clapped his hands. "Amazing, Metoikos! For an ignorant foreigner, you sure weave a pretty tale. Please tell us more."

"Is this true? How do you know this?" For once, Seleukos was as dumbfounded as Kleitos.

And I sat there, gritting my teeth, thunderstruck. *How could I have fallen into this trap?*

"Don't stop now!" Aristandros was beaming. "Please finish your story."

"No, that's all I know. It's a story a drunk sailor told me once when I visited Athens with Alexandros. This is as far as he got before a passing porne got her claws into him." I knew it was too late but I wished I could've stuffed my words back down my throat.

Seleukos, perhaps because he wanted to help or, more likely, because he wanted to show that he was almost as well-informed as Aristandros and I, decided to dive into the deepening silence. "Well, in that case, let me tell you a story a middle-aged merchant told me the last time we occupied Ephesos. According to him, a long time before Athens reached its pinnacle of culture and learning, the leading intellectual centers of the Greek world were the city-states of Ionia. Herakleitos, famous for his observation that, 'No man ever steps into the same river twice,' came from Ephesos; the island of Samios claimed Pythagoras, the great mathematician and mystic, as a native son; Miletos gave birth to Thales, one of the Seven Sages of Greece and recognized as the first true lover of wisdom, or philosopher, by Aristoteles himself; and Anaximandros and Anaximenes, two other well-known, early philosophers, carried on Thales's work in Miletos. Herodotos the Historian came from nearby Halikarnassos."

I interrupted. "You do know that Halikarnassos, although situated close to Miletos and possessing a large Greek-speaking minority, is in Karia and not considered a part of Ionia." My rush to self-unmasking, and consequent self-destruction, was pathetic.

Seleukos pretended he hadn't been interrupted. "As I was saying, according to this well-educated, native-born merchant, the Ionian League of Greek Settlements, as it came to be known, consisted of twelve city-states, including the two adjoining islands of Samios and Chios. They were modest in size and population but strategically located athwart the juncture of overland trade routes from Anatolia, Mesopotamia, Persia, India, and points beyond and the sea lanes leading to Cyprus, Krete, Egypt, Greece, Sicily, Italy, and the western Mediterranean. In the fullness of time, the Ionian city-states succeeded in transmuting their strategic location into enormous wealth."

"That's exactly right." I jumped in again. "But did you know that it was this wealth which, on the one hand, provided people like Thales, Pythagoras, and Herodotos with the leisure to pursue their interests in philosophy, mathematics, and history, but which, on the other hand, led to never-ending envy, enmity, and attack from their less fortunate but more populous neighbors? After a brief period of independence, following the collapse of the Hittite Empire, there came an endless succession of occupiers, including the Assyrians, Phrygians, Medes, Lydians, and Persians. By the time the Macedonian expeditionary force arrived on the scene, some two years ago, Ionian Greeks had spent the preceding two hundred plus years as subjects of the Persian Empire, despite repeated revolts and short stretches of freedom."

"Yes, I did know that." Seleukos's voice was flat. "You forget I was part of that expeditionary force. Unlike you Johnny-come-latelies."

Aristandros was trying hard not to look like the cat that swallowed the canary. "Now, now boys. Let's not fight. You're both very well informed. Although I can't fathom how this foreign fart came to know so much about our business."

Kleitos shook his head. "I don't know either. It's like I never met you before, Ptolemaios. Who are you?"

"What are you talking about? Everybody knows the liberation of the Ionian Greeks and the unification of all Greek-speaking people around the Aegean Sea had been the dream of ambitious Greek leaders since at least the time of Perikles of Athens."

"I didn't know that. Who's Perikles?"

I forged ahead. "And our old king, Philippos Deuteros of Macedonia, had spent a good portion of his reign chasing that dream. Unfortunately, he died on the eve of leading our pan-Hellenic invasion of Anatolia. But now, his son is finally ready to launch the decisive and permanent liberation of Ionia. Unfortunately, he has to make a short detour to Sardeis first, for a much-needed replenishment of his treasury."

"Whoever called him Philippos Deuteros of Macedonia?"

"What do you mean, 'a much-needed replenishment of his treasury'?"

"Enjoy it, Metoikos. You'll never recover from this."

I finally shut up, long after the horses had bolted from the stable. Aristandros the Seer was right – I'd never recover from this. It was way too late to undo the harm. *What possessed you to do that?* I asked myself.

******

"Ouch, that hurts," Kallisthenes cried out as another load of coins cascaded down on his head.

Flood Tide

"Next time, put your helmet on." Hephaistion laughed as he picked up another strong box and proceeded to empty its contents over the hapless scribe.

"Does he even have a helmet?" Aristandros inquired with his typical sneer.

"Do you?" Kleitos rounded on the seer and splashed fistfuls of coins directly into his face.

Alexandros intervened. "Boys, boys, we're supposed to be counting the loot, not playing in it." But then he undermined his words by diving into the large pile of coins, gold and silver bars, precious stones and jewelry that was slowly accumulating on the floor of the treasury, as we emptied more and more of the wooden and clay containers.

"Watch your head," Hephaistion cautioned. "Your wound is still fresh."

"Good point. Give me that shield!" Alexandros lay down on the floor, placed the shield over his head, and ordered us to cover him in gold. "Feels heavy," he observed.

"Like two fat whores on top of you at the same time," Kleitos contributed.

Alexandros laughed. "But even more luxurious. Keep piling it on!"

"It's like watching a bunch of kids at a grape-pressing party," Philotas observed.

"You're a lot like your father, you know." Alexandros sat up and shook off the coins. "Go outside and see to the guard. We don't want anybody interrupting us in here."

As soon as Philotas was out of the hall, Alexandros resumed splashing around in his jumble of riches. "C'mon boys, dive in! We're swimming in gold!"

Hephaistion got down on his knees and started to build a fortress, made of gold darics, Milesian staters, Ephesian tetradrachmas, and whatever other coins came to hand. His walls collapsed before he got very far.

"Who would've thought," Perdikkas marveled, "when I seized this city, there was so much treasure here?"

We all stopped our tally and looked up at him. "You seized it?" Seleukos asked.

Alexandros stood up. "Enough goofing around. Let's get back to counting. Hephaistion, you take charge; I've got some other matters to attend to. The rest of you boys help him out. Perdikkas, you come with me."

Alexandros left the treasury, but not without regret and not before calling back, "and no souvenirs," over his shoulder. "Aristandros is keeping an eye on each one of you."

Hephaistion was not much of a warrior but he was an efficient administrator. There were about thirty of us in the large, windowless, sparsely furnished room and he had us working late into the evening sorting, counting, and re-packing the loot. We were all racing to get out in time to make it to the banquet that night (all the food and most of the wine was gone by the time we got there) but he made each of us strip naked before letting us leave the antechamber, then carefully checked our clothes and body cavities, before returning our gear. "It's not that I don't trust each and every one of you," he said with a smile, "but gold can get so sticky."

All told, there were more than two million silver coins in the treasury, of various weights and denominations, minted at cities throughout Persia and Greece, with some coins from Egypt and the Aegean islands thrown in. Even without counting the eighty talents of gold, the jewelry, and the precious stones, there was more than enough silver to cover the wages of each soldier in our army, from the time we crossed the Hellespont to the day we conquered Sardeis.

Of course, we didn't really conquer Sardeis. It was more a case of Sardeis being handed over to us. Reports of Alexandros's triumph at Granikos, coupled with a restive population of ethnic Greeks within the city walls, had persuaded the Persian commander of the garrison, a dandified courtier named Mithrines, that his future lay in collaboration with the Macedonians. Hence, when we approached the city walls of the Lydian capital, Mithrines led out a delegation of local citizens and turned the city over to us.

Alexandros invited the delegation to dine with us and negotiated the terms of surrender over a few cups of wine. The surrender was unconditional. Not only the city and its inhabitants, but also the akropolis, with its Persian garrison and its Persian treasury, were to be turned over to us, without any resistance. In return, Alexandros promised nothing. He dispatched Perdikkas, with a few squadrons of infantry, to take control of the city, to disarm any soldiers within, and to secure the Persian treasury. In the meantime, he kept Mithrines and his delegation of leading citizens hostage, just in cases there was any trouble. There was none. Perdikkas was in complete control of Sardeis in a matter of hours. Alexandros and his staff took up residence atop the akropolis the next day, while the rank and file settled in throughout the city.

"We are an army of liberation," Alexandros reminded the troops before letting them loose on the city. "So, we don't want to destroy what we already own. Plus, we want to set an example to the cities of Ionia: If they surrender, we won't harm them. Don't kill anybody, unless they're trying to kill you, and don't take anything, unless you pay for it first. And that includes the women," he added to some laughter.

Flood Tide

The troops showed exemplary discipline. There was no looting or mayhem. It helped that Alexandros promptly distributed the contents of the Persian treasury among the troops, covering not only their overdue wages but also adding a generous bonus.

Next, Alexandros reorganized the administration of Sardeis and of Lydia, setting a template for future arrangements for the governance of liberated cities and satrapies. He appointed Parmenion's brother Asandros satrap of Lydia. (The office was vacant, because the previous incumbent, Spithridates, had been killed at Granikos.) In a departure from established custom, however, Alexandros separated financial affairs from the remaining duties of a satrap and assigned control of Lydia's vast income to a trusted Macedonian nobleman named Nikias. He installed a company of Argives, one of the Greek contingents of our pan-Hellenic army, as garrison on the akropolis, but placed them under the command of a Macedonian cavalry commander named Pausanias. (He was known as Short Pausanias, to distinguish him from the many other Pausaniases in our ranks.)

Beyond making these three key appointments, Alexandros retained all of the existing local administrators in their positions. Presumably, Asandros, Nikias, and Pausanias would keep an eye on them, as well as on one another. Alexandros also maintained all tax and tribute payments unchanged, except for redirecting their flow from the Persian to the Macedonian treasury. The liberated inhabitants of Sardeis could have been forgiven for failing to notice much change from their prior status as vassals of the Persian Empire.

******

Barsine, too, was ready for liberation, but despaired of Dareios's ever relinquishing the control over her husband Memnon that keeping her and their children hostage gave him. Accordingly, she decided to propitiate the Fates, take charge of her life, and make good her escape from the harem. Just at that moment, though, she could have used an extra hand.

It was pitch dark and they couldn't see a thing. The children had been wonderful, not uttering a sound. The little one was always a sound sleeper but she gave him a drop of wine at the last feeding, just to be on the safe side. He was sleeping contentedly on her back. And the girls were brave little angels, terrified but quiet and obedient. She was holding the two-year-old and the four-year-old by the hand. Unfortunately, this left no hand over for the six-year-old, who arguably needed it the most, because she was old enough to glimpse the stakes at issue.

As they crept along in the darkness, Barsine fought to suppress her trepidation. She was under no illusions as to the treatment she could expect if they were caught but she hoped their captors would at least hesitate before harming the children of the commander of the Persian army. Of course, she knew better. Nobody was ever safe in Persia. Yet, she kept trying to convince herself otherwise.

She knew it was a mistake to walk on the road. Still, in the obscurity of the night, sticking to the well-trodden path gave them their best chance of making any headway before dawn. It was imperative that they be as far from the camp as possible when the first light of the new day revealed their absence. So, they continued to stumble along in the middle of the roadway.

She thought she'd heard something. She paused. There was definitely somebody or something behind them. She herded the kids into the glowering gloom beyond the fringe of the road. The six-year-old tripped and fell but didn't cry out. She wanted to gather the little girl into her arms; there was no time. They plunged deeper into the unfathomable blackness. Thorns tore their skin, vines grabbed their feet, and rough branches pummeled their arms. The quiet, timid sound of rustling leaves caught up to them and then passed within an arm's length. It was just a deer.

She dragged the children back to the road. Even though they didn't utter any complaint, she could tell from the rhythm of their breathing that they were all crying. She wanted to stop for a moment in order to kiss away their tears but decided to redouble their speed instead. She thought she had detected the first glimmers of dawn ahead. Turned out, it was only her tired eyes playing tricks on her.

She definitely heard something. This time it was no illusion. She heard the beating of hooves. It was getting louder, almost loud enough to drown out the pounding of her heart. They dove back into the thorns, vines, and pugilistic branches. A rider clattered by. All of them, except the baby, were frozen in fear. The peaceful, regular breathing of the baby sounded as loud as the bellows of a furnace in her ears. She was sure the rider would stop and peer into the underbrush. He rode on instead, not even slackening his pace. It might have been one of the eunuchs from the harem but how could she possibly tell in the dark?

The only reason why anyone would have ridden out of the camp in the middle of the night was because their absence had been discovered, of that she was certain. She wondered whether others would follow. She also wondered whether the first one would turn around and return. She was paralyzed by indecision.

"Mommy, I have to pee," the six-year-old whispered.

Barsine laughed. "Go ahead, dear. This is the perfect place to pee."

When all the girls were done, they resumed their walk down the road. After a while, she thought she could see a dim, solitary light far in the distance. Perhaps a torch kept aflame by a fellow denizen of the dark. She hoped it marked the location of the homestead she had seen from the road during the previous day's march. Would they grant her shelter? She didn't know.

Chapter 7 – Ephesos

It took Alexandros eight days to complete the liberation of Sardeis and to implement the transfer of power over the entire Lydian satrapy from Persia to Macedonia. At dawn of our ninth day in Sardeis, we were off once again, this time intent on liberating the great Ionian port city of Ephesos. We brought Mithrines with us, to provide intelligence and to teach us about Persian tactics, according to Alexandros. I had my doubts as to the real reasons why this turncoat accompanied us. The renegade himself didn't seem overly taxed by his change of allegiance and spent most of his time, as far as I could tell, fawning over Alexandros.

The trip from Sardeis to Ephesos seemed more a recreational jaunt than a military march. Although the men's purses were heavy with all the back pay they had received and their legs exhausted from all the whoring in which they had indulged, they strode along sprightly, singing as they went. The army covered the seventy miles to the coast in less than four days. It helped that it was a mostly downhill march on one of the emperor's wide, well-maintained royal roads.

We crested the heights over Ephesos just as the sun was sinking into the sparkling blue waters of the Aegean, casting a golden glow over the magnificent metropolis spread out below our feet. I had been to Athens and had sampled its grandeur but Athens was a dowdy old matron, admittedly still beautiful and lavishly accoutered with pearly edifices and precious temples, but showing her age nevertheless, compared to the youthful vigor, salubrious sensuality, and joyful sparkle of Ephesos. Athens, which housed perhaps twice as many inhabitants as Ephesos, had grown up organically over the centuries, with a couple of broad, curvaceous roadways leading from its gates to the large agora, but in-between these ancient thoroughfares lay a tangled maze of narrow, winding alleys, teeming with people, animals, and vermin. Ephesos, by contrast, thanks in part to having been repeatedly conquered, destroyed, and then totally rebuilt once again, had straight, broad avenues, intersected at right angles by narrower, but equally straight streets, with small back alleys further subdividing the regular blocks of private dwellings and municipal facilities. Most of the residential buildings were covered in glistening white stucco, with burnt-sienna-colored tiled roofs. The public edifices – temples, gymnasia, theaters, government offices, and market stalls – were scattered strategically throughout the city. Only on the far side, down by the harbor, did weathered, utilitarian, wooden warehouses, wharves, and piers fall short of the resplendent perfection of the city. But those structures were almost invisible in the shimmering luster of the setting sun.

The central avenue, which bisected the city, ran all the way from the harbor to a small hill, just beyond the city walls. Built at the foot of the hill was a large, sumptuous amphitheater but our eyes were drawn further up the hill, beyond the city walls, and to our right. There, atop a high plateau, gleamed the crowning jewel of the city, the still unfinished Temple of Artemis. (Artemis, a somewhat conflicted deity, was the goddess of wild animals and of hunting, of virginity and of childbirth, of the pure state of nature and of the man-made cities of Ionia, including of course the city of Ephesos.)

The building we saw was actually the third incarnation of the temple. The original version, according to legend, was built by the Amazons, who roamed Anatolia in the mythical days of Troy and who considered Artemis a kindred spirit. That temple was destroyed by a violent storm, allegedly unleashed as a result of a family spat between Zeus, who was Artemis's father, and his wife Hera, who was definitely not her mother.

The second version of the temple was built by Ionian Greeks, during that initial flowering of prosperity that also gave the world the first crop of Ionian philosophers. That version was underwritten by Kroisos of Lydia, who lived in nearby Sardeis and could well afford to pay. It was built under the supervision of a Kretan architect named Chersiphron and completed perhaps a hundred years before the construction of the Athenian Parthenon. It was the first Greek temple constructed entirely of marble and it was huge, much larger than the Parthenon, with many more and much taller columns. While not as finely wrought as the exquisite Parthenon, the Artemision remained, throughout its existence, the biggest and arguably most impressive temple in the Greek world. It was universally acknowledged as one of the Seven Wonders of the World.

Tragically, this second iteration of the temple was destroyed in 230 Z.E., burned to the ground by a lunatic named Herostratos, who sought to achieve immortality by his heinous act of cultural vandalism. The Ephesians not only executed him, as one would have expected them to do, but also passed a law that made it a capital crime to write or utter his name. Yet, in one of history's typical, wanton jests, everybody in the Greek world knew the name of the temple's arsonist but very few people remembered the name of its architect. As soon as Herostratos had been killed (but not forgotten), the Ephesians started once again to rebuild the temple.

As it happened, 230 Z.E. was also the year in which Alexandros was born.[12] Word of the destruction of the Artemision reached Pella a few weeks after Alexandros's birth. When Aristandros heard the news, he did a quick calculation and concluded that the temple must have been destroyed the same night as Olympias gave birth to her prophesied son. He pronounced the coincidence a portentous omen of Alexandros's future greatness. (I was not there, so I don't know how he reached that conclusion but I could make a shrewd guess.)

By the time Alexandros's father, King Philippos Deuteros, dispatched the initial expeditionary corps across the Hellespont, twenty years later, to prepare the ground for the main-force invasion of Asia, the Temple of Artemis had been more or less completely rebuilt. The columns, walls, and roof were back, standing as tall, proud, and dazzling as they had before the great fire; only some of the architectural details, decorations, and furnishings were still in the process of being completed. When the Macedonian expeditionary corps, commanded by Parmenion and Attalos, stormed Ephesos, almost exactly two years prior to our arrival, they were welcomed by the Ephesians as liberators. The Persian garrison was forced to flee, the ruling oligarchs were expelled, and a new, populist government was installed. In fact, so grateful were the citizens of Ephesos for their liberation

---

[12] 356 B.C.E.

that they installed, at their own cost, a statue of King Philippos in the Artemision, standing in the naos, right next to the goddess herself. Even though Philippos's likeness was considerably smaller than Artemis's cult figure, the Ephesians' gesture was an unprecedented honor, verging dangerously close to blasphemy.

Eventually, Dareios deigned to take notice of the Macedonian invasion of Ionia and dispatched his top commander to clean up the mess. Memnon successfully reconquered all of the Ionian cities liberated by Parmenion and Attalos. In Ephesos, Memnon's troops killed the leaders of the populist government, installed a government of oligarchic Persian collaborators, and smashed the statue of Philippos in the Artemision.

Memnon went on to put out other fires on behalf of his emperor, continuing from victory to victory, until that fateful encounter against Alexandros at the Granikos River, where he was not in overall command and where his troops were roundly defeated and massacred. Now, he was back in Ephesos (as far as we knew), organizing the city's defenses against an assault by Alexandros's army.

****

We continued to stare at the Artemision as darkness gradually enveloped Ephesos. The city seemed strangely deserted. I could see occasional groups of men running down streets and disappearing into houses; otherwise, all seemed eerily quiet. We were standing too far above the city to hear any sounds emanating from the streets but it appeared, from where we stood, that there was nothing to hear, even if we had been standing in the middle of the agora. Then, as we watched, a flame flared up in one of the houses.

It's like watching stars twinkling into existence, one by one, in the darkening sky, I thought. First, one house started to burn, then another, then another. Pretty soon, there were dozens of buildings burning throughout the city. And the streets were now full of running people, some chasing, some fleeing. When the chasers caught up to the fleers, the fleers invariably ended up lying motionless in the streets while the chasers set off in pursuit of other prey.

"What in Haides is going on?" Alexandros wanted to know. "Mithrines, get down there and find out! I want an answer by dawn. And don't you dare double-cross me, you double-crossing scum. If you do, we'll find you and we'll squash you like the toad that you are."

Mithrines took no offense. "Sire, why would I wish to double-cross your highness? It would be like finding myself warmed by the rays of the Sun and choosing to run away to the comforts of a cold rock. Trust me, your majesty; I'm your faithful servant for life."

Alexandros didn't seem entirely convinced by this effluence of eyewash. "Just get down there and be back before dawn!"

Flood Tide

The rest of us dug in and made a fortified camp in the heights, in case any Ephesian defenders decided to sally out of the city overnight.

Mithrines was back well before dawn. "The democrats are slaughtering the oligarchs," he reported breathlessly.

Alexandros didn't appear too terribly upset by this turn of events. "What happened to the Persian garrison?" he wanted to know.

"They withdrew to Miletos, sire, when they got wind of your approach, sire."

"And what about Memnon?"

"Oh, he withdrew along with the garrison, I imagine."

"So there's no one left to oppose us, is that what you're telling me?"

"On the contrary, your majesty, the population is anxiously awaiting your arrival."

"For once, the oligarchs might be more anxious to welcome us than the democrats," Hephaistion observed.

"Are those the guys who've been helping the Persians for the past two years?" Alexandros asked innocently.

"The very same," Mithrines affirmed.

"Well, we'll be down as soon as it's safe for us to come in."

The young Macedonian king, already renowned for his fearlessness and speed of action, then took two days to prepare us for an unopposed, one-mile march into the undefended city. The oligarchs were mostly dead by the time we arrived. The surviving population seemed happy enough to see us, although their enthusiasm was probably mitigated somewhat by the knowledge they had been liberated by another Macedonian army just two years earlier, only to find the liberators hastily withdrawing a few weeks later, to be replaced by the returning Persian occupiers. Now, the Persian occupiers had withdrawn and the Macedonian liberators were back. Unsurprisingly, there was a dearth of local leaders willing to step forward to lead the welcoming cheers.

Alexandros made a beeline for the Artemision, to which he felt an understandable, congenital tie. He organized and then took a leading role in elaborate sacrifices and thanksgiving services conducted at the outdoor altar situated just to the side of the temple. Afterward, he toured the unfinished edifice, trailed by a phalanx of fluttering priests, and donated some captured shields and armor for display in the completed sanctuary. Returning to the front steps, he explained to the priests the close connection that existed between his family and the goddess. He offered to cover the costs of completing the rebuilding of the temple and asked for nothing more in return than a modest epigraph at the entrance recording his contribution to the reconstruction effort. The priests politely but firmly refused his offer, perhaps because of their unfortunate experience with the statue of his father or perhaps because they had (well-founded) doubts about the state of his treasury, which was, at that moment, once again nearly empty.

We were finally leaving Artemis's sacred precinct when Alexandros discovered that Apelles, one of the most famous painters of the era, happened to be in Ephesos at that moment. "Have him at headquarters tomorrow morning, with his brushes, paints, and assistants," he ordered. Then, he set off in search of a suitable place to establish his headquarters.

****

Barsine and the children reached the site of the solitary light shortly after dawn. It was in the middle of a roadside clearing. There was no homestead; there was no torch; there was no torchbearer. All they found were the glowing embers of a camp fire someone had used to keep warm during the night. The solitary sojourner (she saw only one set of footprints and one set of hoofprints) was gone by the time they arrived. On further reflection, it was perhaps for the best that the traveler was gone.

They hid in a stand of poplars beyond the far side of the clearing and rested. While the children slept, Barsine hunted for food. She didn't have far to go. Following her nose and her ears, she discovered a small, clear, cool stream tinkling nearby. After slaking her thirst, she picked lotus leaves and fashioned them into cornucopias, which she filled with ripe, juicy blackberries, sweet wheatgrass shoots, and wild asparagus spears. She added a sprinkling of mashed night crawlers to each and brought them back to her sleeping children. She breastfed her youngest and fell asleep with the baby curled in her arms. When she awoke, she found the rest of her children munching on the lotus leaves, having consumed all of the nature's bounty their mother had packed inside. The children continued to nibble, sip, and doze for the rest of the day, while Barsine continued to worry.

They resumed their eastward trek shortly after sundown. Although it was still daylight, Barsine couldn't wait any longer. She dreaded another night stumbling along in the dark and she was afraid they'd walk right by the hoped-for homestead without ever realizing it. As it turned out, their destination was only another hour away. The walled compound was impossible to miss, even in the dying dusk of the fast-fading day. It loomed like a huge, squat monster, crouching on a rise, beyond a thick fringe of trees, up a narrow, meandering path from the road. No light was visible from within.

She knocked on the gate, timidly at first. Engendering no response, she gradually increased the vehemence of her pounding but to no avail. Perhaps the place was deserted, although someone had carefully barred the door before leaving and there was no evidence of a conflagration or a sack.

She continued to hammer her fists against the hard wood for a long time, driven on by stubbornness and despair. Finally, she slumped to the ground. "Why have you forsaken me?" she cried out, then immediately clamped a hand over her mouth in terror. They were still close enough to the road for any passerby to have heard her.

Someone had heard her inside the homestead. "Who are you?" a gruff voice asked in Aramaic.

She tried to convince herself that the voice sounded familiar. "Phraortes, is that you?"

"They were all killed years ago," the voice answered, dashing her hopes. "But not by us," the voice hastened to add, rekindling a spark of optimism. "This place was vacant when Emperor Dareios gave it to my master in return for services rendered." So much for any chance of salvation.

Barsine fought off the seductive embrace of resignation. Drawing a deep breath, she pleaded. "Please give us shelter. My children are starving."

"Wait there," she was told.

After what seemed like an eternity, a head appeared in an opening in the wall high above the gate. "The master says we can't admit anyone in the middle of the night."

"We'll wait till the morning."

"I wouldn't do that," the voice advised. "The master also gave orders to kill you and your brats if you're still here at daybreak."

"But that's crazy," she protested. "Even if your master doesn't believe in his duty of hospitality, he should at least want to take us captive. We might have some value to him."

"Exactly. He's doing you a kindness by not enslaving you."

Barsine was speechless.

"And he did send some food. Just promise you'll be gone before dawn."

"I promise." Barsine wearily watched as a basket slowly descended from the crack in the wall. It was full of bread, olives, and dates. There was even some olive oil and a jug of water.

"Thank you. And please thank your master."

The grizzled old head bobbed happily in the opening high up on the wall. "Where will you go?" he asked as she distributed the food among the children.

"I have no idea."

"Go west," the old man advised. "There is a village half-a-day's walk from here. Well, maybe a full day with those little ones. But be careful. You'll come across an official government station before you get to the village. You might want to get off the road and skirt around that station. I don't think they take kindly to people using the road without an imperial pass."

Barsine nodded, too busy eating to answer aloud.

"There is a common house in the village," the old man continued. "They'll take you in, especially if you can afford to pay."

Barsine nodded again, sending the empty basket back up.

"Just be sure you're gone from here before dawn."

And they were.

169

****

"You must keep still, your majesty," Apelles implored, not for the first time. "Otherwise, the painting will not do you justice."

We were all munching on figs and cucumbers and sipping the local wine, sprawled across couches in the dining hall of a recently deceased oligarch, whose former home had become our headquarters in Ephesos. Alexandros, sitting atop Boukephalas in the middle of the room, in full armor, with his helmet under one arm and brandishing a sword with the other, was getting tired, hot, and impatient. "How long can this possibly take?" he wanted to know.

"Great art takes time, sire," Apelles assured him.

"Even Boukephalas could paint a good picture," Alexandros snorted, "given enough time. It's speed of execution that differentiates the master from the hack." He gave a barely perceptible nudge to Boukephalas's ribs and the horse neighed its assent.

All of us, including Apelles, broke into laughter at the animal's timely interjection.

"See, even my horse thinks you're too slow," Alexandros observed with mock seriousness. "Now, who's next?"

Flood Tide

"The ambassadors from Tralles and Magnesia are waiting outside," Hephaistion announced. "They're here to offer the surrender of their cities."

"See, now that's fast," Alexandros observed. "Not only are these Ionian cities beautiful but they can surrender faster than Apelles here can paint."

Hephaistion concurred. "I guess that makes them great surrenderers."

"And here I thought Parmenion did a great job conquering them the first time around."

"Sire, I never claimed personal credit for our victories in Ionia," protested Parmenion, rising to the bait, as usual.

"Just kidding, Parmenion. Calm down. You've been a great commander for many years. All you have to do now is develop a sense of humor."

"Yes, sire – sorry."

"I actually have another assignment for you but let's hear from these ambassadors first."

Two fearful men were shown in. They were both physically large, elegantly dressed noblemen but it was obvious they weren't impressive people. Upon entering, they prostrated themselves at the feet of Boukephalas and didn't rise until told to do so by Hephaistion.

They handed over the gifts they had brought, including official dispatches from their respective ruling cliques. Hephaistion bid them to read the dispatches out loud, which they proceeded to do, in flawless Greek. After an endless string of greetings and salutations, each letter described in effusive terms the pleasure of the citizens of Tralles and Magnesia at their forthcoming liberation and each professed eternal allegiance to Alexandros and the Argead dynasty.

"Our welcome to you, exalted ruler, is heartfelt and unconditional," the Magnesian ambassador added, after he finished reading. "All we ask is a remission of the oppressive tribute that has been imposed on us by the Persian emperor, which he uses to buy more mercenaries to oppose you and to oppress us."

"Thank you, honored ambassadors, for your gifts," Alexandros said, from on high. (Boukephalas was a very large horse.) "And we welcome your cities into our Hellenic League. It's high time the cities of Ionia rejoined the family of the Greek cities of the mainland whose offspring they are. We gather you into our bosom as a parent would embrace a long-lost child. You'll forgive me if I don't get off my horse to give you an actual embrace but Apelles over there would be very cross with me if I did."

"Of course, your royal highness. Thank you, your majesty. We're humbled by your graciousness." The ambassadors couldn't stop bowing and scraping.

"There are only a couple of minor details that we'll need to attend to," Alexandros continued. "As you know, we don't tolerate tyrants, autocrats, or oligarchic cliques. My soldiers will visit your cities soon to supervise the creation of democratically elected governments."

The two ambassadors blanched but said nothing.

Seeing their discomfiture, Alexandros hastened to reassure them. "There will be no purges, once my soldiers take control of your cities. So, all you need to do is hang on for dear life till we get there." He laughed at his own joke.

The ambassadors didn't join in the general merriment.

"And as far as the tribute is concerned, you're absolutely right. From this moment forward, not an obol will go to the Persian emperor. And of course, we Macedonians do not ever extort tribute from our fellow Greeks. So, your days of paying tribute are over."

The ambassadors nodded, pleased to have achieved at least this one concession.

"How much was each of your cities paying in tribute, by the way?"

The ambassadors told him, exaggerating a little perhaps, to emphasize their former plight.

Hearing the two figures, Alexandros lit up with pleasure. "What an absolutely marvelous coincidence! As you both must appreciate, all member cities must pay dues to the Hellenic League. The benefits of League protection don't come free but, trust me, they're well worth the cost. As luck would have it, the dues that your cities will have to pay from this moment forward are almost exactly equal to the tribute you've had to bear so patiently heretofore."

The ambassadors stared at him numbly.

"And now, if you'll excuse me, I have some other matters I must see to. And again, I am sorry I can't get down to give you a proper welcoming hug."

Hephaistion put a hand on each of their shoulders. The two ambassadors, recovering themselves, bowed deeply and backed out of the room.

"Well, that went well," Alexandros laughed when they were gone. "Who's next?"

"We have no further ambassadors waiting at the moment," Hephaistion informed him.

"In that case, let's get out there and round some up. Parmenion, this is where you come in. Take the Thessalian cavalry, plus two brigades of allied infantry, but leave all of our Macedonians with me. I'll need them soon enough at Miletos. Your job is to liberate all the remaining cities of Ionia, aside from Miletos. If they come over voluntarily, great. If they don't, it's your job to persuade them to change their minds. I don't want any massacres and I don't want any purges. We don't want to destroy our own property. But, most important, we don't want Ionia reverting to the Persians by next spring. Got that?"

"Yes, sire."

"And in the meantime, we need all the treasure you can seize. The boys and I are going on to Miletos as soon as we're finished here. And if necessary, we'll move on from there to Halikarnassos. So, let's keep in contact. I can send you reinforcements if you need them and I want you and your men available, if we run into trouble at Miletos or Halikarnassos. Any questions?"

"No, sire. I understand. I know what we're trying to accomplish and I'll carry out your instructions to the letter. And thank you for reposing your confidence in me."

"I know you'll do a great job, Parmenion. Because if you don't, I'll find somebody else who will."

"But sire," Parmenion started to protest.

"Just a joke, old man. Relax. May Tyche look kindly on your endeavors. And send me frequent updates. I want to know everything that's going on, every step of the way. And don't forget to forward all tribute and treasure you collect as soon as possible."

"I understand, sire. Same as always."

"And one more thing. Get a message out to the fleet in the harbor. I need to speak with your son."

"I'm here already," Nikanoros spoke up from one of the couches. "I figured the fleet could manage without me for a day or two, once it was obvious the Persian garrison had run away."

"Sorry, Nikanoros; didn't see you there. This posing is getting to be a pain in the ass. Hey, Apelles, how is that picture coming?"

"We're getting there, sire. Just sit still, please."

At that Alexandros jumped off his horse. "Enough already. Let me see what you've got."

We all crowded around the easel. The painting was unfinished but the central figure of Alexandros, sitting on his steed, was done. It was a remarkably good likeness, especially in light of the speed with which the artist had executed it.

176

Flood Tide

"I don't like it," Alexandros announced, as soon as he laid eyes on the unfinished picture. He snatched it off the easel and started waving it around. "Does anybody like it?" No one was willing to venture an opinion, except Boukephalas, who whinnied.

"Your horse is a better art critic than you are, sire," Apelles quickly noted.

For a moment, I wasn't sure what would happen next but Alexandros broke into boisterous laughter. The rest of the company quickly joined in.

Alexandros struggled to catch his breath. "Well, in the case, you'd better ask Boukephalas to pay your fee." He finally stopped laughing. "If you expect *me* to pay, you'd better redo this picture."

An extended conference between the painter and his subject ensued, during which the subject clarified his expectations. The painter assured him that he now understood the subject's wishes and the subject resumed his seat on the art critic's back.

"Nikanoros, I've received new intelligence this morning from our friends down the coast. The Persian fleet has been observed sailing north, presumably toward Miletos. You have to get your ships down there, fast! We've gotta beat them to the harbor and then maintain a blockade of the city. Otherwise, our siege of Miletos's got no chance."

"But sire, the Persians have three times as many warships as we do," a voice spoke up from the room.

"Parmenion, are you still here? I thought I'd sent you to organize your forces."

Parmenion only shook his head. He was finally beginning to realize there was no talking sense into his young king, once the king had made up his mind.

Nikanoros came to his father's rescue. "We can do it, your majesty. Come on, father, let's get going." And with that, they were both out of the room.

Many other details required attention. It was getting late in the afternoon by the time Alexandros had finished appointing (or reappointing) officials to administer Ephesos once we were gone and mapping out our strategy for the coming days.

The next time he alighted from his horse, the painting was done. When Apelles handed him the second version of the portrait, Alexandros would not let go of it. "It's perfect," he cried. "A masterpiece."

I couldn't wait to see it for myself. It was indeed an extremely workmanlike portrait. Alexandros was still seated on Boukephalas but now he was no longer wearing armor. Instead, he was clothed in the flowing robes of Zeus. The helmet under his left arm had been replaced by a chubby, wiggly baby Hermes and the sword in his right hand had become a lightning bolt.

"It's perfect," Alexandros repeated. "Hephaistion, pay the man his fee!"

Hephaistion nodded, not bothering to ask where the money was supposed to come from.

******

I felt a nudge in my ribs. "You're needed outside," a voice whispered from behind. "Follow me!"

By the time I turned to see who it was, the man was already walking briskly toward the door. He wore the standard armor of a cavalry officer and, although I didn't recognize him from the back, I shrugged and followed. Just then, Alexandros cracked another joke at poor Apelles's expense, causing a momentary uptick in the already boisterous hubbub enveloping the large room, making it unlikely that anyone noted my departure. *I wonder, what is it now?*

No sooner had I cleared the doorway than the world turned dark and dusty, as a result of a filthy feedbag being thrown over my head. Simultaneously, a number of hands grabbed my arms and torso. Someone embraced me from behind, placing the edge of a dagger against my carotid artery just below the Adam's apple. "You'll bleed out like a sacrificial lamb if you make a fuss." The timbre, the cadence, the sibilance were unmistakable.

"Aristandros, my old friend!" I tried unsuccessfully to keep my voice light and jovial. "I knew you'd pull something like this."

"Well, in that case your powers of clairvoyance are almost as good as mine. What do you think will happen next?"

Chapter 8 – Milctos

They must have bonked me on the head because the next thing I remember was awakening, underground, with a tremendous headache. *The bastards buried me alive.* My first reaction was surprise. Greeks didn't bury people alive, even people they were trying to kill. I was also surprised to be breathing; laboriously but gloriously breathing. *Must be an air pocket.*

I tried to claw my way out. That's when I realized I was all tied up. A thick, coarse rope wound its way all the way up my legs, binding them together, and then continuing up my arms and torso, pinning my arms against my body. I could wiggle my fingers, though, and the dirt in which I was entombed felt funny, more straw than soil. A then something truly scary happened – my grave moved.

In fact, once it started to move, my grave kept bouncing and lurching along, shifting the burden pressing down on my chest from side to side. There were also the usual sounds associated with a heavy wagon making its way down a rutted path. *Hey, I'm not buried alive! I'm just being shipped along, trussed up like a pig ready for roasting, covered by a big load of hay.* It was the happiest thought I'd had since I realized I wouldn't be getting killed in a pankration match.

A short while later, we stopped and I could feel people scrambling atop the hay pile, trying to dig me out. Eventually, I was disinterred and carried up some steps into a nice, cool, echoingly quiet building, where I was unceremoniously dumped on a rock-hard surface. *Too bad more of that straw didn't stick to my butt.*

Someone raised me to a sitting position and pulled the feedback off my head. I found myself looking at the crotch and skinny legs of an enrobed old man. I shifted my gaze upward. Aristandros's viperous visage came swimming into sight. He smiled at me brightly. "I trust you found your transport comfortable enough, Metoikos. We certainly meant you no harm but we couldn't afford to make a scene with all those people around. It's much more private here."

I glanced around. I was sitting in the naos of a small, plain temple, facing the entryway, which was also apparently the only source of illumination. Two armed men, with their backs to me, stood guard, making sure no inconvenient worshipers intruded. A dozen additional soldiers lined the walls, facing me. I recognized most of them. They were fellow cavalrymen, although none had served directly under me.

I wonder whose temple this is? The cult figure must have been positioned directly behind me, so I had no clue. *C'mon, focus!* I forced myself to look back at Aristandros. "Get me to my feet, you charlatan, so I can spit in your eyes!"

"Now, now. Let's try to be civil. These men simply want to hear one of your historical disquisitions. I told them that you, despite being a foreign fart, know more Greek history than any man alive."

One of the cavalrymen leaning against the wall bestirred himself. "Yeah, how come you know so much?"

"I know you, don't I? What's your name, soldier?"

Aristandros, worried about losing control, took over. "You're here to answer our questions, not the other way around. We know you're a Persian spy. We're just trying to find out your accomplices before we put an end to your snooping."

"Why would you think I was Persian?"

"There he goes again, responding to a question with a question," Aristandros said. "Definitely a spy."

"Because Persians have all that book learning and stuff," another cavalryman interjected. "That's why they're such lousy fighters."

I laughed. "They are lousy fighters, that's for sure. But don't be so damn insecure. They don't know any more history than you do. Just the opposite. There's no Persian Homeros or Herodotos or Xenophon. They're barbarians, remember?"

"Who in Haides are those people?" This from another soldier. "I've heard of Homeros but the other two?"

Aristandros stepped in again. "Enough chit-chat. Are you ready to tell us your fellow traitors in the ranks or should we start breaking bones right now?"

I tried to get to my feet but the ropes made it impossible. "Listen, you overgrown sphincter! If there's a traitor in this room, we all know it's you. The rest of us have been fighting and risking our lives since this war began. What have you been doing? Slaughtering defenseless animals and poking around in offal."

That's when he kicked me in the jaw. For an old man, he had surprisingly good balance and plenty of power left in his leg. "That's enough! He's just playing for time. He'll never reveal anything. Let's kill him right now."

His blow had caused me to topple onto the stone floor. Before I could gather myself, the slimy seer pounced, butcher knife in hand, ready to cut my throat. I managed to roll to my side, throwing him off temporarily.

Aristandros scrambled to regain his perch on top of me. "C'mon, men. Hold him steady! The gods prefer us to finish our sacrificial animals with a clean cut."

Finally, I'd had enough. "I'm not an animal!" I roared. "I am the king's bodyguard! The next man who touches me will die by the king's own hand – I guarantee it."

None of the men moved.

"What's the matter with you? You gonna let this old charlatan bamboozle you?"

"He's not a charlatan," a hesitant voice rose from a corner. "He's brought us victory after victory."

"He's brought us diddlyshit. It's your arms and your valor that's brought us victory. Now, get this maniac off of me and untie me right now!"

The men hesitated. Aristandros, in the meantime, grabbed my hair and yanked my head back to give himself space to operate.

"Cavalry squadron coming!" one of the guards standing at the door called out.

"If you free me now, I give you my word no one will ever find out what happened. We'll chalk it up to horseplay."

The men physically lifted the aging soothsayer from my torso, stood me up, untied me, and brushed off the remaining straw. And I kept my word. No one ever found out what had almost happened. On the other hand, I also resolved to prevent Aristandros from ever attempting to do it again.

****

Not all the cities of Ionia welcomed liberation as eagerly as Ephesos, Tralles, and Magnesia had done. In Priene, for example, the citizenry voted to lock the city gates and keep them locked as long as there were any elements of the pan-Hellenic army roaming the countryside. Presumably, they counted on their town being too insignificant to warrant a detour by Alexandros. And indeed, Alexandros didn't take the time to besiege Priene; however, he did order Parmenion to do so. The old general carried out his orders. The city walls were breached; all visible opposition hunted down and destroyed; and a Macedonia garrison left behind. Priene became a part of the Hellenic League and its voluntary contribution was set at a level significantly higher than the tribute it had been obliged to pay to Dareios. On the other hand, Parmenion also managed to restrain his troops, so there was no generalized pillage, rapine, or slaughter. (Perhaps a small touch of looting may have taken place.) Finally, when Parmenion's report mentioned a shrine to Athena under construction in the city, Alexandros dispatched some captured Persian armor for display in the sanctuary, a small donation to the building fund, and one additional order: When the citizens came to visit their newly constructed temple, they were greeted by an inscription on a column flanking the entrance that read: "King Alexandros built this temple to Athena Polias." This time, Alexandros hadn't asked the temple priests for their consent.

And then there was the case of Telmessos, where the citizens, relying on a small but well-armed Persian garrison, securely entrenched on the akropolis, refused to negotiate with the Macedonian envoys.

Alexandros took a particular delight in the obstinance of this small city. "I should've known," he said to Aristandros, upon receiving his envoys' report. It's exactly what I would've expected from your home town. Aristandros, you're a worthy native son of Telmessos."

Aristandros was mortified, which made Alexandros amused and the rest of us delighted. *I hope he nails the old charlatan's ass to one of his divination rods*, I thought but kept my mouth shut.

"I'm so sorry, sire," the old seer protested. "My fellow Telmessians are incredibly blind to the will of the gods but I think I have a way to make them see the light."

"This I've gotta see," Kleitos muttered.

Aristandros ignored the interruption. "I still have friends in town. Leave it to me, your majesty. I'll have the problem solved by dawn. Just have a small commando unit ready to go upon my signal."

This was too much gall for Philatos. "Nobody's going anywhere on a diviner's signal. We still have military officers in charge of this army, last I heard."

Alexandros clapped a calming hand on his shoulder. "Just hold your horses. Let me talk to Aristandros in private."

In the event, Perdikkas was put in charge of the commando unit, which captured the Telmessos akropolis shortly after dawn. Perdikkas had received his signal from Alexandros, who had acted as soon as Aristandros gave him the nod. And Aristandros had nodded as soon as he saw the beacon flare up on the akropolis. The signal beacon had been lit by one of the dancing girls hired by Aristandros.

The dancing girls had made their way up to the akropolis the previous evening, claiming it was their religious duty to celebrate some festival or other on the hilltop that night. The Persian commander rescinded his standing order against admitting any outsiders to the akropolis upon learning the celebrations included not only feasting, drinking, music, dancing, and chanting, but also a round of ritual coupling. In fact, believing it would be good for morale, he encouraged his soldiers to participate in the festivities. The soldiers didn't need to be told twice.

In due course, after all the food was eaten, and all the wine imbibed, and all the dancing completed, and all the women's garments removed, and all the soldiers paired off with the worshippers, the commander chose the comeliest celebrant for himself. At which point, the women tugged apart their flutes to reveal hidden stiletto blades, which they used to stab the soldiers repeatedly, aiming their thrusts, acolytes of Eros that they were, for the hearts of their partners. After their work was completed, one of the dancing girls lit the beacon to send a signal to Aristandros. Perdikkas's commandos didn't encounter any resistance when they reached the akropolis. And the rest of us learned another important lesson about the visionary powers of Aristandros the Seer.

****

Barsine and the girls were reaching the limits of their endurance. Skirting the government station proved to be more easily said than done. After lurching alongside the road, from grove to thicket to outcrop to bramble, for the better part of the day, and after diving for cover every time they heard the sounds of some approaching traveler, they could barely move. Yet, Barsine urged them on, watching with concern as the walls of the valley they were traversing closed in on them. Finally, at the point where the cliffs on either side left barely enough room for the imperial road and a babbling brook, Barsine spotted the government station. Its location at that particular site was probably not an accident. No one was going to pass by the station without alerting the guards inside.

Barsine decided to wait until nightfall. She herded the girls under a weeping willow growing by the creek, which hid them from the road. She gathered some food, fed the baby, told the girls to eat and rest, and promptly fell asleep herself. She was awakened, in the semidarkness of the approaching night, by a hand across her mouth. "Don't scream or you'll wake the kids," a strange, high-pitched voice whispered in her ear. She nodded. What would have been the point of screaming in any case?

Still lying with her back to her captor, she felt a loosening of the constricting embrace and cautiously turned her head. The sight that met her eyes caused her to shudder. Long, dark, oily, perfumed tresses, framing a fat face; loose jowls; leering eyes; thick lips pulled back in a triumphant sneer; a mouth full of black voids and a few rotten teeth. "Kobad, is that you?"

His laugh was silent, mirthless, and effeminate. "Who else, my lovely." Grabbing her shoulders, he forced her to roll over and face him. "You didn't think I'd let you get away, did you? You know I love you too much to ever let that happen."

Flood Tide

She tried to push him away and get up but he straddled her and kept her down. He was heavy, sweaty, smarmy, disgusting. "You've always been so kind to me, Kobad," she lied. "Please let me go."

"You know I can't do that." He sounded almost regretful.

A small spark of hope kindled in her chest. She told herself that, among the eunuchs of the harem, he had been relatively humane. "I can pay you. My husband's an important man."

He shifted his weight and crushed any remaining hope. "I know who your husband is," he taunted, "and he may be important today but will he still be important tomorrow? Besides, what good is money to me?"

"I can make your life easier."

"That you can." A lecherous sneer distorted his face.

"Please," she pleaded, "be kind. Your kindness will be repaid a hundredfold."

"Oh, I'm always kind." He laughed as he cupped her breast in his paw. "The question is whether you're willing to be kind to me."

"You're a eunuch, for crying out loud."

"Eunuch have needs too, my dear Barsine, and you're the most beautiful woman in the harem. I've been admiring you since the day you arrived."

"I can't, Kobad, please."

"Sure you can. And by the way, I can too. So the choice is yours. You can give me what I want and I can sneak you back into the harem, with no one the wiser. Or I can turn you in and they'll make you watch as they torture your kids to death, after which they'll keep you alive much longer than you'd think possible. So, what do you say? Yes or no?"

The oldest girl stirred. "Mommy, who is that on top of you?"

"Oh, it's just Kobad. You remember him, don't you? He's keeping me warm. Now go back to sleep."

She lowered her voice to a whisper. "I can't do it here. Let's move away from the children."

He complied with surprising agility, getting off her and lifting her to her feet. "After you, madam." His strange, high-pitched voice was pitiless and mocking.

She considered hitting him and running away but realized she couldn't overpower him and she couldn't leave her children behind. "Just this one time, right Kobad?"

"Of course. All I need is one short trip to paradise to make me forget I'm not quite a man. After that, I can die contented."

She knew he was lying but what choice did she have. Besides, he was a eunuch. What could he possibly do?

It turned out that, notwithstanding the absence of a scrotum, he could do most things that an intact man could do; only, it took an inordinate amount of effort and patience on her part to get him to the point where he could do it.

He was alternatively cajoling and rapacious, repulsive and relentless, predatory and pitiless, as he forced her to carry on. "That's right, dear. You're on the right track. They only cut off our balls, you know. We have to be able to piss somehow. Just keep going."

When he was finally able, he entered her from behind, pounding away brutally. He kept it up for a long time, all to no apparent effect. Then he tossed her down, crying and bleeding. "Go get your brats. We've got to get going."

She was glad he insisted on keeping the mule for himself; she preferred to walk. And she was in no hurry to catch up to the women's caravan.

******

When Aristandros and his henchmen returned me to Alexandros's headquarters, the festivities were still in full swing. No one had noticed my absence. They were all too busy admiring Apelles's latest masterpiece.

Two days later, we marched on Miletos, in pursuit of the elusive Memnon. When we arrived, no surrender delegation came out to greet us. On the contrary, the city gates were locked and its walls bristled with defenders. We were on a winning streak and therefore confident that Miletos would turn out to be our next conquest but this would be no cakewalk. Alexandros relished the opportunity for a real fight. He was tired of chasing after Memnon and desperately needed a decisive victory to persuade the wavering Ionians that this time their liberation from the Persian Empire would last longer than a passing summer squall.

Miletos was situated near the delta of the Maiandros River, at the foot of Mount Grion.[13] It enjoyed a fine harbor on a finger of the Aegean Sea called, understandably enough, Miletos Bay. The harbor itself was further protected by a small island in the bay, called Lade, which sat directly across from the port of Miletos. Alexandros's first order of business, upon arriving at the outskirts of Miletos, was to send observers to the top of Mount Grion to determine why the pan-Hellenic fleet,

---

[13] See Map 5 at AlexanderGeiger.com

under the command of Nikanoros, was not yet in the Bay of Miletos.

Upon seeing the frantic signaling of the observers, Alexandros, trailed by his usual phalanx of aides, scrambled up the mountainside to assess the situation for himself. He, along with the rest of us, was treated to a dramatic maritime regatta. Just to the north of Miletos Bay, in the straits between Samios Island and Mount Mykale on the Ionian mainland, we could see the 160 ships of our fleet, sails fully deployed, oars churning the blue sea, sprinting toward the bay. Looking over our shoulders toward the south, we could see the 400 ships of the Persian naval armada, stretched out in a long line around the Grion Peninsula, bending every effort to reach Miletos Bay first. We all understood what was at stake: Unless Nikanoros reached the bay first, our upcoming siege of Miletos would have little likelihood of success.

Although there was no chance that the sailors down below could possibly hear us, we all started to cheer and jump up and down. Because of the distances involved, the progress of the ships was imperceptibly slow and we soon tired of jumping but no one was willing to sit down. The wind was freshening, blowing from north to south – a good sign for us. On the other hand, the lead ships of the Persian line were almost at the mouth of the bay – they were going to make it into the bay first.

The pan-Hellenic fleet, sailing perhaps ten ships abreast, finally reached the bay. However, instead of tacking toward Miletos, they continued to run ahead of the wind, straight toward the vanguard of the Persian ships. (Actually, they were Phoenician ships. The Persians themselves couldn't sail across a fishing pond but they controlled all the great seafaring nations, cities, and islands of the eastern Mediterranean.) As we watched in astonishment, the Phoenicians stopped rowing, then turned around and ran toward their confederates farther down the line. This time, I was sure our mariners could hear our cheering all the way down in the bay.

As soon as the outcome of the race was clear, Alexandros plunged back down to our camp and started issuing orders. Commandeering some fishing vessels, he dispatched two battalions of infantry to take control of Lade Island. Then, turning to Philotas, he ordered him to patrol the coast as far south and north of Miletos Bay as he could feasibly manage. "Use the entire Companion Cavalry, if necessary, but I don't want those bastards landing anywhere near Miletos." And then he boarded a small fishing boat and made his way out to Nikanoros's ship to offer his congratulations in person and to conduct an impromptu thanksgiving to Poseidon and the local deities.

It turned out we had a terrific defensive position. Our fleet, with the effective support of the troops on Lade Island, controlled the Bay of Miletos. Philotas's cavalry prevented the Persian navy from landing foraging parties anywhere near Miletos. Their ships were forced to anchor offshore, without fresh provisions and without fresh water, exposed to the ravages of weather on the open sea. Our infantry surrounded the city, preventing any of the inhabitants from getting out. The only problem was that Alexandros didn't want to be in a terrific defensive position; he wanted to be on offense.

Parmenion and his troops, having pacified the rest of Ionia, joined us under the walls of Miletos. The siege engines, which had been sitting on barges since we had crossed the Hellespont, trailing our progress down the coast of Anatolia, were finally offloaded near the Miletos harbor. There was, for the moment at least, even some surplus coinage in the treasury from the spoils, ransom payments, and "voluntary" contributions collected from the liberated cities of Ionia. Our foraging parties had no difficulty bringing in sufficient supplies from the surrounding countryside, which was in the middle of the harvest season. We were ready to settle in for a long siege. Alexandros, on the other hand, was eager to breach the walls, defeat the garrison, conquer Miletos, and kill Memnon.

While the siege engines were being assembled and rolled into position, Alexandros held a council of war. The first item on the agenda was a decision on attacking the Persian fleet. Nikanoros wanted to attack, despite his inferior numbers. He reasoned that we had nothing to lose. As things stood, Persia, using the combined fleets of all its subject nations, cities, and islands, enjoyed almost complete control of the Aegean sea lanes. While the pan-Hellenic fleet was able to enforce a blockade of Miletos, it was in turn trapped in the Bay of Miletos and therefore practically useless beyond its immediate objective. Nearchos the Kretan, who knew something about naval warfare, was opposed to an attack, pointing out that not only did the pan-Hellenic fleet have greatly inferior numbers but the crews supplied (under some duress) by the member cities of the Hellenic League were also not yet sufficiently trained and possibly of suspect loyalties. Everyone had heard about the rumored invasion of the Greek mainland by Dareios and Memnon and these crews were likely to feel stronger allegiance to their home cities than they did to Alexandros's army. Uncharacteristically, Parmenion found himself on the side of those urging aggressive action, perhaps swayed by the fact that Nikanoros was his son. Hephaistion pointed out that, while it could be argued that the pan-Hellenic fleet had nothing to lose, Alexandros did have something at stake; namely, his reputation for invincibility. Alexandros decided that the pan-Hellenic fleet would not attack and ordered Nikanoros to maintain a defensive position, enforce the blockade, and otherwise do nothing.

There was much less debate about the advisability of attacking Miletos itself. Alexandros wanted to attack and that was that. He assigned a company of sappers to undermine the watchtowers that anchored Miletos's walls, three companies of light infantry to man our own siege towers and rain destruction down on the enemy soldiers stationed within, separate companies of heavy infantry to wield the battering rams against each of the city gates, and a company of engineers to operate the catapults lobbing stones, flaming barrels, and other missiles into the city.

While we were busy laying out detailed plans for the capture of the city, word arrived that the Milesians were abandoning the city walls and leaving the city gates unguarded. Alexandros immediately dispatched Perdikkas, with a company of heavy infantry and a battering ram to break down the nearest city gate, with the rest of us, on horses, following immediately behind. The Milesians, seeing the approach of the battering ram, decided to preserve the gate by opening it. Our troops poured in but there was no wild stampede. Alexandros enforced rigid discipline. We proceeded building by building, street by street, and neighborhood by neighborhood, seizing all weapons and armor we found, confiscating all items of significant value, occupying every building, and arresting all men of military age. But there was no wholesale destruction. Miletos would not become another Thebes.

Finally, we reached the akropolis, which had its own set of walls, gates, and towers. The akropolis was garrisoned by Greek mercenaries, presumably under Memnon's personal command. They welcomed our arrival with a hail of imprecations, bolts, boulders, javelins, arrows, and missiles of every description. Evidently, they were not quite ready to surrender.

A small, residual force of Macedonians could have kept the akropolis surrounded and could have starved the Greek mercenaries out in a matter of weeks, while the rest of us collected our spoils and moved on. But Alexandros had other ideas, especially because he believed Memnon was trapped with his men inside the akropolis. He ordered the siege engines to be brought into the city, set the sappers to work, and massed his forces under the akropolis walls.

The siege of the Milesian akropolis turned out to be a useful training exercise for Alexandros's army, which, up to that point in our Anatolian adventure, had not been required to execute the seizure of a single walled fortress. It took a few days to undermine the watchtowers and breach the walls, to kill or capture the defenders, and to determine that Memnon had once again slipped through our fingers.

It was interesting to watch Alexandros's reaction to the news. He raged, of course, at our failure to kill or capture Memnon but it was a controlled rage. His dispositions for the captured men and materiel were equally measured. All captured foreigners were sold into slavery; all Milesians were set free. The captured Greek mercenaries were not summarily executed, as might have been expected. Instead, they were offered an opportunity to enlist in Alexandros's army, provided they agreed to swear allegiance to the pan-Hellenic cause and to Alexandros personally. The valuables seized from private homes were returned but all public treasure, whether Persian or Milesian, was expropriated. Alexandros put a "democratic" government (selected by him) in charge of the city, under the supervision of a Macedonian commander and the protection of a Macedonian garrison. Miletos was enrolled in the Hellenic League and assessed a heavy membership contribution.

Alexandros took a tour of the city in the company of the leading citizens who had been formerly in charge. They proudly showed him their extensive sculpture gardens, featuring dozens of statues of Milesian athletes who had prevailed at the Pythian and the Olympic games.

"And where were the men of such physiques when Miletos was being enslaved by the Persians?" he asked. He was too tactful to mention their similar absence during our recent liberation of Miletos.

The Persian navy, growing hungry, thirsty, and seasick in the choppy waters of the Aegean, withdrew to Dareios's next line of defense, at Halikarnassos. In response, Alexandros surprised us all. He disbanded his own navy, sending all the allied ships and their crews back to their home cities, except the Athenian ships, which he kept, allegedly for transportation needs. (I suspected he also considered them useful hostages in case the leading city of the Greek mainland decided to give him trouble.)

"Why would he do that?" I asked Seleukos, regarding Alexandros's decision to disband his own navy.

"I think it bothered him a lot more than he let on when Hephaistion told him they threatened his reputation for invincibility."

"But now we have no navy."

"They would've been destroyed sooner or later anyway. And they certainly wouldn't have been able to blockade Halikarnassos the way they did Miletos, since the enemy ships are at Halikarnassos already."

I raised my eyebrows. "You realize that, without a navy, if we lose a battle against Dareios, there'll be no way to evacuate the men back to our side of the Hellespont."

"Exactly," Seleukos said.

Chapter 9 – Halikarnassos

In the end, the occupation of Miletos proved to be easier than appeared likely at our first approach to the city. On the other hand, the decisive showdown that Alexandros desired hadn't materialize either. Most annoying of all was Memnon's ability to inflict delays, costs, and losses on our forces and then move on, eluding death or capture.

The next big city, only two or three days' march down the coast, was the capital of Karia, Halikarnassos.[14] Clearly, that's where Memnon was headed and that's where our next fight would take place. But Alexandros didn't have us march directly down the coast; he had a more circuitous approach in mind.

Alexandros had had some previous history with Karia, which was a small kingdom squeezed in between the larger satrapies of Ionia, Pisidia, and Phrygia. Although always under the domination and thumb of

---

[14] See Map 6 at AlexanderGeiger.com

Persia, until recently it had retained a semblance of autonomy under the Hekatomnid dynasty, founded by a local Karian of uncertain origins, named Hekatomnos. This soldier and adventurer managed to pick the right side in one of Persia's civil wars and was subsequently rewarded for his acumen by being named satrap of his home region, a singular honor for a non-Persian. Hekatomnos ruled Karia for some seventeen years and managed to transform his position from being an appointed satrap of Karia to becoming the hereditary king and ruler of his small kingdom.

Hekatomnos had three sons and two daughters: Mausolos, Artemisia, Idrieos, Pixodaros, and Ada. To keep things in the family, Mausolos married his sister Artemisia and Idrieos married Ada. (There being no sister left for him, the third son, Pixodaros, was forced to marry a cousin.)

When Hekatomnos died (in 209 Z.E.), Mausolos and Artemisia became king and queen of Karia. They decided to move their seat of government to a sleepy port on the Aegean coast, named Halikarnassos, and turn it into a naval base for their rapidly expanding maritime empire. They dredged and enlarged the small harbor and built two fortresses to protect it. One, called King's Castle, was built on a small island in the harbor; the other one, named after the naiad Salmakis, was situated on a promontory jutting into the harbor. They also rebuilt and greatly enlarged the original fortress located farther inland, on the akropolis. Then they surrounded their burgeoning city with tall, impregnable walls, punctuated at regular intervals by forbidding watchtowers and by fortified, easily defensible gates.

After seeing to security arrangements, Mausolos and Artemisia embarked on a spectacular building program, turning the small, albeit venerable, town into the greatest and most magnificent city on the coast of Anatolia. For their residence, they built themselves a huge, gleaming, marble-clad palace, with beautiful decorations inside and out. The palace adjoined Salmakis Fortress and took up the rest of the space on the promontory overlooking the harbor.

Between the harbor and the akropolis, they laid out a rectilinear grid of wide, paved streets, lined with homes for ordinary people, temples for the gods, agoras, colonnades, and porticoes for the merchants, stoas for the artists, theaters and circuses for entertainment, palaistrai and gymnasia for physical culture, and assorted public buildings and spaces for the exercise of government functions. Many of the intersections, squares, porticoes, theaters, temples, and public buildings were adorned with colorful statuary and paintings of gods, heroes, athletes, and wealthy patrons.

When Mausolos died, after twenty-four years of joint rule, Artemisia built a tomb for him that became the crowning architectural achievement of their reign. It was built on an artificial, stepped terrace in the heart of the city, next to the thoroughfare that connected the western and eastern gates. It was not a very large building, perhaps an eighth of the size of the Artemision in Ephesos, but much taller. With its raised stylobate, tall walls, and a steep, pyramidal roof, topped by a massive horse-drawn chariot at its apex, it towered above the city and was visible to mariners long before they reached the harbor. Its four external marble walls were completely covered by brightly painted sculptural reliefs of such striking beauty, balance, and harmony that the building instantly became another of the Seven Wonders of the World.

Mausolos's resting place was called the Mausoleion and the name stuck, even after Artemisia was laid next to her husband after ruling over Karia for two years on her own. (It was said that she died of a broken heart. However, considering the avidity with which her successors took up her vacated post, there may be room for skepticism concerning the purported etiology of her demise.) Thanks to the magnificent sepulcher built for him by his wife, Mausolos's name has survived to this day; Artemisia's name has been largely forgotten.

Artemisia was succeeded by her brother Idrieos and sister Ada as co-rulers of Karia. After they had reigned for seven years, Idrieos died. Ada hung on for four more years, at which point the third brother, Pixodaros, grew tired of waiting for his turn. He overthrew and exiled his sister. Ada took up residence in a mountain fastness in the interior of Karia, called Alinda.

Pixodaros had several daughters and, in keeping with the usual practice, he decided to use them to cement his position on the Karian throne. He married off his eldest daughter to a well-connected Persian nobleman named Orontobates, thus hoping to secure his Persian flank. For one of his younger daughters, however, he had a revolutionary brainstorm. He decided to look west, across the Aegean, and use his younger daughter to forge an alliance with the rising power in the Greek world, Philippos of Macedonia. Because Pixodaros was a realist, because he knew that he was a minor dynast in an obscure little kingdom in Persian-dominated Anatolia, and because his younger daughter was no beauty, he offered her as a bride to Philippos's half-wit son Arrhidaios. Everybody knew that Arrhidaios would never amount to anything, in light of his mental limitations, but a marriage alliance was a marriage alliance and Pixodaros figured a half-wit was the best he could snag under the circumstances. Philippos accepted the proposal and the nuptial arrangements were set in motion.

This is where Alexandros's previous history with Karia came into play. Philippos had a second son, by another wife, who was nineteen at the time. This son, probably egged on by his mother, was in the midst of a fight with his father. When this second son found out about the proposed marriage of Arrhidaios to Pixodaros's younger daughter, he immediately (and irrationally) smelled a conspiracy by his father to deny him the throne of Macedonia and swung into action. He dispatched his own emissary to Pixodaros to offer himself as his daughter's husband. Pixodaros was naturally more than pleased to exchange a full-wit for a half-wit and promptly agreed to the upgrade. When Philippos found out, however, he confronted the second son, yelling at him, among other, less flattering observations: "Do you think that the daughter of a mere Karian, who's nothing more than a vassal of the barbarian king, is suitable marriage material for the future king of Macedonia?" (The half-wit Arrhidaios was not expected to become king of Macedonia, even though he was Philippos's eldest son.) In the end, neither son married Pixodaros's younger daughter. Philippos's second son, who came within a whisker of becoming the future pretender to the throne of Karia, was Alexandros.

Now, three short years later, Alexandros was once again entertaining hopes of becoming the ruler of Karia but there were at least three obstacles in his way. First, Memnon was at that very moment organizing the formidable defenses of Halikarnassos. Second, Orontobates, who had succeeded to the Karian throne upon the death of his father-in-law, could bring his own, substantial resources to bear in defense of his kingdom. Third, Alexandros's pose as the great liberator, coming at the head of a pan-Hellenic army to free the Greek cities of Ionia, would lose some of its force when used to justify an attack on the capital of the nominally independent, non-Greek kingdom of Karia. Hence, the detour on our way to Halikarnassos.

****

We hiked uphill for days (actually two days) before reaching the mountain fastness of Alinda, home of Ada, the legitimate queen of Karia (at least as far as Ada was concerned). Upon my first glimpse of the formidable walls of Ada's fortress, I had a moment of doubt as to the sanity of Alexandros's route but I needn't have worried. When we reached the last clearing before the walls, the gates flew open and a small, elegantly-attired delegation stepped out, to the sound of horns, flutes, and drums. In the midst of the group, eight bare-chested, middle-aged men carried an extravagant litter on their shoulders. Upon reaching the head of our column, the litter bearers lowered their burden and a lithe, alluring woman sprang out, located Alexandros, and prostrated herself in front of Boukephalas's hooves.

Alexandros appeared pleased. "Rise, young lady, and identify yourself."

"Your exalted highness. I'm Ada, queen of the Karians. We were anticipating your arrival as our nephew-in-law only a few short years ago but now we welcome you not only as our nephew but also as our conqueror."

Alexandros smiled and alighted from his horse, motioning to the rest of us to do the same. Ada stepped forward and embraced him, leaving a smudge on his cheek. "We've been looking forward to your arrival, your highness," she said. "May I present the members of the royal court?"

She was small but generously endowed, heavily made up, and wearing a fancy, glittering robe, which displayed her attributes and her many jewels in a flattering light. Resisting the ubiquitous misogyny of that era, I chose to direct my attention to her face. Having done so, I realized she might've had many desirable assets but youth was not among them. The cosmetologist who had painted her face was indeed an artist but he wasn't a magician. Under the layers of paint, I could discern the trembling of slightly sagging jowls, the crosshatching of imperceptible but unmistakable furrows of time, and the intimations of gathering folds of future chins. Letting my gaze drop below her neck, I realized it was only a marvel of sartorial engineering that kept her magnificent, jiggling bosom aloft and any supernumerary flesh safely sequestered. Fortunately for her, I doubted that either Alexandros or the other members of his bodyguard managed to see below her surface allure.

Ada introduced some of the people in her entourage, all of whom were male, middle-aged or older, and rather shabbily dressed. Alexandros listened amiably, nodding and smiling. Then she beckoned her servants to step forward with a long train of gifts, which appeared to be numerous and chintzy. Alexandros accepted them graciously. Finally, she invited Alexandros, along with his officers, into her fortress for a celebratory feast.

Alexandros laughed. "Every soldier in my army is an officer, my dear lady, so I hope you have a large banqueting hall."

Even under her layers of paint, the Queen of Karia visibly blanched. "I'm afraid, irresistible sire, that our accommodations may be too modest ..."

"Invincible," Hephaistion interrupted her. "We call him invincible, madam – Alexandros Aniketos."

Ada regained her color and then some. "I'm so, so, sorry," she stammered. "Your invincible highness, I'm afraid we don't have enough room to accommodate all your soldiers."

"An outdoor feast, then," Alexandros suggested jovially, "on the parade grounds of your fortress, perhaps."

"I suppose that might be possible," Ada agreed reluctantly. Then, trying to regain her footing, she grabbed Alexandros by the elbow and they proceeded to walk, arm in arm, into the fortified village, trailed by the rest of us.

The village was hardly large enough to accommodate an entire army. In the end, after Alexandros assured himself that there were no hidden assailants lurking within the fortress walls, he ordered the men to set up camp outside the walls and promised that the feast would be delivered to them. He then entered, with his usual crew of aides, into the large, stone house that functioned as Ada's castle.

We were ushered into a large dining room, furnished with comfortable, well-worn carpets and pillows, and told to make ourselves at home. Ada fluttered all around us, alternately issuing orders to her servants and fawning over Alexandros. Wine was brought in. After the usual prayers and libations, we were each handed a gold cup, filled to the rim. It turned out to be a remarkably rich, smooth, bright, and sweet vintage. "It's ambrosia," Alexandros crooned approvingly.

The servants brought in little tables for each of us, followed by platter after platter of food. We started out with flatbreads, served with olive oil and exotic fruits, such as oranges, pomegranates, and various berries. Then came the meat dishes. Some of them were recognizable, mostly mutton and poultry, but the rest were stews and kebabs whose ingredients I couldn't make out, although they seemed to consist mostly of vegetables such as eggplants, cucumbers, onions, olives, some kind of squash. All were uniformly delicious, some sweet and sour, some spicy, with a hint of saffron, cumin, coriander, and mint. Then came sweet pastries, nuts, dates, and figs. And throughout it all, the sweet wine kept flowing.

Alexandros, reclining between Hephaistion and Ada, was enjoying himself hugely. He drank beyond moderation, as usual, but didn't forget about his soldiers. "Go check on the men," he whispered to Seleukos. "Make sure they're equally well cared for."

Seleukos returned in a little while and whispered something in Alexandros's ear. Alexandros got up and was joined by Hephaistion. Soon, the rest of us were clustered around him.

"The men are getting fed," Seleukos was saying. "It's nothing fancy but it's wholesome and palatable. But there's no food left in the village. The locals didn't eat tonight and, by the looks of it, they won't have anything to eat tomorrow either."

"What do you mean?" Alexandros asked.

"I mean they're serving us the last of their food. These people have nothing."

I wondered at Alexandros's reaction to this intelligence. He turned to Ada and asked her to rise. "Come for a walk with me," he said.

We strolled through her "castle." It was immaculately clean, comfortably furnished, and elaborately decorated but all the rugs, chairs, tables, and chests were old, worn, and creaky. The paintings on the walls were cracked and fading. Many of the smaller rooms seemed abandoned and dilapidated. All the serving gold and silver had apparently been mobilized for our use in the dining room. There may have been dignity but there was no wealth in this household.

Ada seemed on the verge of tears but she kept her back straight and a smile on her face. "We have what we need. I'm a simple person, although I am also the queen of Karia."

Alexandros's voice was gentle. "I know, mother, I know." He took her in his arms. "I'll get you your kingdom back," he whispered, as she cried on his shoulder.

We stayed only long enough for our foraging parties to go out and replenish the food stocks of the villagers. Then Ada threw another banquet, during which she officially adopted Alexandros as her son and heir, and we were off to Halikarnassos to liberate the Karians from the clutches of their Persian oppressors and to restore Ada as their legitimate queen.

****

The harem was in an uproar. Two short days after finally arriving at their temporary home in Damaskos, and while still in the midst of unpacking their clothes, jewelry, and cosmetics, the women were told that Dareios himself was planning to inspect the harem that evening. This was akin to an announcement that Zeus was planning to descend from Mount Olympos for a little family visit, perhaps disguised as a swan. If anything, Dareios's arrival was viewed with more trepidation because, in addition to holding the power of life and death over the inmates (in this respect they were no different from anybody else in the Persian Empire), he also determined the pecking order of the women in his harem.

Unlike their permanent establishments in Ekbatana, Susa, Persepolis, and Babylon, this temporary harem was housed mostly in tents, enclosed within the walls of an old fort on the outskirts of Damaskos. Of course, these were not ordinary tents. Laid out on the parade grounds in the middle of the fort was an entire complex of colorful, gaily-decorated tents, some large, some bigger than large, and some enormous, erected along grassy "streets" and "avenues," and arranged according to a strict hierarchy.

The tent of Dareios's mother, Sisygambis, situated at the very center of the tent city, comprised six rooms, separated by light, linen walls, including an oversized sitting room suitable for entertaining visitors, a generously proportioned sleeping chamber, a dressing room, a prayer chamber, a dining room (in case she decided to skip a meal in the communal dining hall), and a small servants' room in which her night crew slept, ever vigilant for those urgent middle-of-the-night demands. All the walls had flaps, to keep the air fresh; the floors were covered in canvas, with lots of rugs, furs, comforters, and pillows strewn about; and the roof, with flaps of its own, was painted a robin's egg blue and kept high aloft by slender, decorated poles.

The tent of Dareios's number one wife, Stateira, was right across the "street" from her mother-in-law's tent and dwarfed it in size. Really, it was a whole complex of tents, housing not only the despot herself but also her two spoiled daughters, Little Stateira and Drypetis, her fractious young son, Ochos, and some of their many, many servants and slaves.

Barsine, her three girls and infant son, and their two serving girls lived in a large, one-room tent at the edge of the tent city. It was adequate for their needs.

The communal dining hall was a huge, military-style tent with row upon row of tables and benches, erected at one side of the tent city, next to the various food preparation areas. It was quite a comedown for the leading ladies of the harem because there was no throne, no dais, no indicia of superior rank. In fact, there was hardly enough room for the lower ranking women even to properly prostrate themselves when the leading ladies walked in. As a result, the leading ladies mostly ate in their own tents.

Flood Tide

The latrine was a labyrinth of enclosed cubicles and hallways, strategically placed above an open sewer. The ditch was supposed to be emptied each night by slaves but it stank to high heaven nevertheless. (It didn't help that the latrine, although it had canvas walls, had no roof, permitting the stench to permeate the entire camp.)

The eunuchs and most of the slaves were housed in the soldiers' quarters of the abandoned fort. These were bare, filthy, vermin-infested, fetid, and overcrowded rooms but they did have real walls and the remnants of a roof, which made them in some ways superior to the tents, at least during inclement weather.

News of the emperor's anticipated visit arrived shortly after the midday meal. Stateira suffered an immediate bout of intestinal incontinence, resulting in an endless relay of chamber pot runners, while two other teams of servants attended to both sets of her cheeks, trying hard not to mix up the unguents being applied to her nether regions with the creams getting rubbed on her face. Her eldest daughter, Little Stateira, who was twelve, did her best to emulate her mother. Although in robustly good health, she took to her bed and spent the afternoon imagining one malady after another, each one miraculously disappearing as soon as her attending nursemaids managed to round up the appropriate potions, ointments, tonics, and sweets. Her younger sister, ten-year-old Drypetis, didn't waste any time on hypochondria, proceeding directly to hysteria. She laughed uncontrollably one second and then burst into tears the next. Her attending nursemaids simply borrowed the potions, ointments, tonics, and sweets no longer needed by Little Stateira, which seemed to do the trick, at least until the next outburst. Ochos, the youngest of the three at eight years of age, contented himself by running around his mother's tent complex with his little sword, attacking the servants, trying to cut off their hair, slash their clothes, and gouge out their eyes. When one of the eunuchs took umbrage at the young prince's attempted assault and confiscated his sword, Ochos sprinted to his mother's room, demanding that the offender be executed forthwith. He might have gotten his wish, too, but fortunately for the eunuch, Ochos's mother was lying flat on her stomach at that moment, getting her rear end massaged, and didn't wish to be disturbed by her unmanageable son.

And all that activity was taking place in just one tent, albeit a large one. Across the "street," the children's grandmother, Sisygambis, was desperately trying to shed twenty or thirty years, checking her visage in a polished brass mirror every few minutes. Despite the feverish ministrations of her ablest makeup artists, the years proved remarkably recalcitrant, reducing the old lady to ferocious and profane screaming, which could be heard throughout the tent city. But no one paid any attention. They were all busy running hither and yon, trying to capture the magic that would enable them to entice the attentions of the emperor, if only for a night. Heck, if only for a blink of an eye, most would have been thrilled.

Barsine was not caught up in the excitement of the moment. She didn't consider herself part of the competition and didn't expect to receive any particular notice from the emperor. Ever since they had returned to the caravan, she had done her best to blend in and, with Kobad's assistance, she had escaped any punishment. In fact, everybody in the harem acted as if nothing had changed, and really, nothing had, except perhaps for the semiweekly nocturnal visits by Kobad the Eunuch.

Dareios arrived after they had finished their communal evening meal, after the royal ladies had primped some more, and after they had given up hope of seeing him that day. For some reason, he came into the fort wearing full armor. Perhaps he was afraid for his life, having to leave his usual bodyguard outside the walls. And who could blame him. As soon as the women heard he had arrived, they all dashed out of their tents, screaming for attention. The young eunuchs who were escorting Dareios toward Sisygambis's tent could barely restrain them.

Dareios smiled good-naturedly, pleased at the adulation. However, that didn't stop him from yelling at the women sternly. "Get back to your tents right now! I'll come and visit as many of you as I can but we can't have this kind of chaos." And when some of the women didn't comply with sufficient alacrity, he ordered the eunuchs to beat them. Most of the eunuchs were happy to oblige. "Careful, there!" Dareios yelled at a particularly enthusiastic eunuch. "We can't let these women get out of hand but we don't want to leave a mark on them either, you twerp."

Dareios was, by nature and experience, a cautious man. He had come to power only two years earlier, relatively late in life. And he was certainly not born to power. He had been a 38-year-old career soldier when he happened to catch the eye of his emperor, Artaxerxes Tritos Ochos, who appointed him captain of the imperial bodyguard. Ochos was a barbarous, brutal, bloodthirsty, but effective emperor, who managed to occupy the Persian throne for twenty-one years, during the last four of which it had been Dareios's responsibility to keep him alive. Despite his best efforts, Dareios had ultimately failed.

After twenty-one years in power, Ochos was poisoned by his own physician, who was supplied with the necessary poisons, incentives, and directions by Ochos's grand vizier Bagoas. Having arranged the murder of Ochos, Bagoas also made sure that, in the usual Persian fashion, all of Ochos's sons, nephews, and cousins were murdered as well. The only male royal survivor was Ochos's youngest son, Arses, whom Bagoas had kept alive to serve as the puppet emperor.

Flood Tide

Arses lasted two years. At that point, he made the fatal mistake of confusing his nominal title with actual power. Bagoas promptly poisoned him, too. Unfortunately, having killed Arses, Bagoas found himself fresh out of royal relatives. As a result, he was forced to look outside the family for the next successor to the throne. He hit upon an unassuming, reliable, 44-year-old career soldier named Kodomannos, who had been heard to say, when sufficiently inebriated, that his grandfather had been a brother of the father of the previously poisoned Artaxerxes Ochos. In fact, it was highly unlikely that Kodomannos was a distant offshoot of a junior branch of the royal family. The only thing certain was that his mother had been a royal chambermaid. He didn't strike Bagoas as someone who would assert too much independence.

After being anointed emperor, Kodomannos took on the name of Dareios Tritos, in keeping with his pretensions to having some connection to the prior ruling family. Once in power, much to everyone's surprise, Dareios turned out to be an accomplished survivor. His first act as emperor was to murder Bagoas, using the venomous vizier's own inexhaustible stock of fatal potions. Next, he secured his control of the empire in the customary way – by killing every potential rival. Two years later, he was forced to deal with the nuisance of some upstart Greeks trying to foment rebellion in the western satrapies of Anatolia. But first, he had to address the much more difficult problem of getting women living in a temporary harem to simmer down.

True to his word, Dareios peeked into the tents of most of his wives and concubines, exchanging a few words with each, but his first visit was with his mother. The dowager chambermaid, despite being treated daily as an (aged) goddess descended to Earth, continued to suffer from understandable insecurities, related to her humble origins, her lack of royal training, the evident vicissitudes of life, and the inexorable ravages of time. But she loved her son and Dareios reciprocated the affection. He spent his few minutes in Sisygambis's tent marveling at how enchanting, voluptuous, and young she looked. She was positively glowing by the time he left for the bigger tent across the "street."

Stateira had recovered from her ailments in time for her husband's arrival. Before she could launch herself at him, however, he told her he would see her in his bedchamber later that evening and she floated out of the tent in order to make the necessary preparations. With his wife safely out of the way, Dareios got down to the real purpose of his visit, which was to spend some time with his children, whom he hadn't seen for several months.

It took less than two hours for Dareios to complete his inspection of the harem. He had managed, during that short time, to speak to most of the wives and concubines, leaving each one more determined than ever to fight her way to the top of his totem pole. Naturally, he didn't speak to any of the servants or slaves whom he encountered along the way, all of whom were obliged to lie face down in the dirt as he passed, making conversation difficult.

Nor did Dareios get a chance to poke his head into Barsine's tent. Soon after he was gone, and while Barsine was still putting the girls to bed, Kobad pushed aside the entry flap. "Look, uncle Kobad has come for another visit," the oldest girl said brightly. "Go to sleep now," Barsine said, without turning around. "I'll be back soon."

****

We approached Halikarnassos from the northeast, making camp about a mile from the Mylasa Gate. Even before we had settled in, Alexandros dispatched a scouting party, led by Perdikkas, "to take the temperature of the defenders." They were back within an hour, nursing bruised bodies, dented armor, and wounded pride. "I think they're ready for us," Perdikkas reported.

Alexandros shrugged. "Get a good night's sleep, lads. We'll show them who's in charge tomorrow."

Memnon beat us to the punch. While we slept, he led a sortie of Greek mercenaries out of the Mylasa Gate and into our camp. By the time the alarm sounded, his men were back inside the walls of Halikarnassos, leaving behind four dead Macedonian sentries, a dozen seriously injured soldiers, a score of dead animals, many burning supply wagons and storage tents, and one furious Macedonian commander-in-chief.

"What in Haides happened?" Alexandros demanded to know. "Nobody, you understand, NOBODY, steals a march on me!" His voice was beginning to rise. "Least of all that son of a whore Memnon. All you guys were just lying there, making love to Morpheus, while this pervert hermaphrodite screwed us up the ass. I'd be better off surrounded by a bunch of lame dancing girls than you worthless wusses. Get out of my sight; it brings tears to my eyes to have to look at such a limp-dicked collection of flatulent fucks."

He was starting to splutter. The rest of us remained motionless, silent, afraid to breathe. "This will not stand," Alexandros continued, forcing his voice back to a lower register. "We are Macedonians, for Zeus's sake. We've got to conquer this shithole and kill those bastards, every last one of them."

Parmenion, who was after all the senior man in the tent, finally took a breath. "Yes, sire. We'll kill every last one of them." Then he paused, awaiting the next outburst. Alexandros said nothing.

"But it won't be easy," Parmenion resumed, somewhat tentatively. "This is a well-fortified, heavily-defended city." Still no response from Alexandros.

"Our siege equipment hasn't arrived yet," Parmenion added after a moment. "We have to get organized."

"On, shut up, you old fart," Alexandros finally exploded.

Kleitos, of all people, rose to Parmenion's rescue. "We'll get 'em, sire," he said bravely. "Don'tcha worry none. We'll cut off their dicks before they can pull 'em out of our asses."

Alexandros took a long, probing look at Kleitos ... and burst out laughing. "I don't even want to picture that. Now, let's get to work."

All of us, Alexandros most of all, knew that Halikarnassos would be a tough nut to crack. In order to defeat Orontobates's garrison, stiffened by Memnon's mercenaries, we would have to make our way across rickety, narrow, portable bridges, spanning a deep, wide moat. Assuming we succeeded in that task, we would be confronted by the towering walls of Halikarnassos, which were even taller, thicker, and more solidly built than the walls of Miletos. Beyond that, only three gates led through those walls – the Mylasa Gate in the east, the Tripylon Gate in the north, and the Myndos Gate in the west. Each gate was a massive, fortified structure, topped by catwalks and flanked by guard towers. If we somehow managed to breach the city walls, we could expect savage house-to-house, hand-to-hand combat, as we fought our way uphill toward the akropolis. And even if we succeeded in routing the defenders, they always had the option of withdrawing to the akropolis, a fortified city-within-the-city, with its own set of huge, crenellated walls and formidable watchtowers. In addition, the defenders could also withdraw to the fortress of Salmakis, on a spit of land projecting into the harbor, or to the King's Castle, splendidly protected on its own island across the harbor from Salmakis.

It didn't help matters that Halikarnassos's harbor was occupied by the Persian navy, with the bulk of our navy on its way back to the Greek mainland. Not only was there no possibility of a waterborne assault by our mariners through the city port, there was not even any likelihood of a successful siege, because the inhabitants and defenders of Halikarnassos could be resupplied indefinitely by ship.

"There are no easy options," Alexandros acknowledged, as if reading our thoughts, "which is what makes it fun. Instead of looking for the easy way out, we'll take the glorious road in – straight over the city walls." This time, no one was brave enough to raise an objection. "As soon as the siege equipment gets here," he added, in tacit acknowledgement of Parmenion's point. However, he certainly didn't apologize to the old commander for his earlier outburst. All of us would've been disappointed if he had.

Flood Tide

Landing siege equipment anywhere near Halikarnassos proved to be a tricky business, since the Persian navy not only occupied the harbor but also mounted regular patrols up and down the coast. Nikanoros, whose much diminished fleet could move no faster than the ponderous barges carrying the siege equipment, was taking his sweet time making the short voyage from Miletos to Halikarnassos. His ships, skulking like thieves in the night, from hidden inlet to serpentine estuary, were careful to stay out of sight during daylight hours. Alexandros didn't enjoy the wait. He alternated between chewing his nails, chewing our ears off, and chewing us all out. When he could stand it no longer, he dispatched companies of heavy infantry in futile sorties against the city walls, only to see them return bruised, bewildered, and demoralized.

Finally, five nights after we had made camp (and five nights after Memnon's lightning midnight raid caught us napping in that camp) the barges arrived – in the middle of the night – landing in a rocky, deserted cove, a good two miles from our camp. Every available man was dispatched to unload the ladders, shield walls, siege towers, catapults, battering rams, and raw lumber supplies before the barges were discovered by a Persian patrol boat. Once the materials were safely on dry land, we spent the rest of the night trudging back and forth, like a giant army of ants, hauling the disassembled pieces of equipment aboard horse-drawn wagons, dragged along the ground by oxen, or simply carried on soldiers' shoulders.

****

The next morning, I was sitting astride Pandaros, observing an anthill of activity. *What's with all the ant metaphors*, I thought. (When trying to breach the walls of a fortified city, a cavalry officer is about as useful to the siege as an erection is to a hermit, so I had plenty of time for contemplation.) In front of me, our trusty, light-armed, semi-barbarian Agrianians were busy running toward the moat, carrying baskets full of soil and rocks on their shoulders, dodging incoming missiles as they went. Our archers and other light infantrymen tried to protect them with a covering barrage of arrows and bolts, most of which fell harmlessly to the ground, well short of the defenders high up on their wall, neatly illustrating one of the benefits of holding the high ground.

After dumping their loads into the moat, the Agrianians ran back to pick up another load and test their luck once again. After a while, an enterprising group of foot soldiers harnessed teams of oxen to wagons and, sheltering beneath their shields, started ferrying loads of fill toward the moat. We lost some oxen in the process but after a few hours little mounds of soil began poking through the surface of the water in the moat.

I wondered how our effort to take Halikarnassos would turn out. Ever since the Battle of Granikos, I had been struggling to overcome my time sickness, that dizzying sense of uncertainty brought on by the loss of my ability to know what the future held in store, even in broad and hazy outline. I had known all along, of course, that unexpected accidents could happen, that time travelers were occasionally injured or even killed during their sojourns into the past, but the past itself was not supposed to change. When the pan-Hellenic invading army was not defeated at the Battle of Granikos and its leader, Alexandros, was not killed, the course of history had changed. Given the inertial tendency of the space-time continuum, however, it was only a matter of time before the torrent of history resumed its prior course. At least that was the theory drummed into our heads at the Academy. But how long it would take for temporal inertia to reassert itself was impossible to predict; it depended on the precise nature and severity of the violation and the consequent distortion. *When is the correction coming*, I wondered. *Will Alexandros's run in defiance of history end right here, under the walls of Halikarnassos, or will it end at the next battle after that?* I simply didn't know. And my previous knowledge of history was no help.

Questions about my own personal fate crossed my mind as well. *Will I live long enough to see the correction take effect?* The appearance of a slimy and wily antagonist, determined to bring about my death, diminished the prospects of my long-term survival. The solution sprang unbidden into my mind: *I simply have to kill Aristandros before he can kill me.* Unfortunately, this was more easily thought than done. Among other things, I was not a murderer. And, as always, there was the Prime Directive to consider.

On the other hand, surely both morality and the Prime Directive allowed for the possibility of self-defense. These excursions into the past were not supposed to be suicide missions, even when something went wrong. Besides, hadn't I already altered the flow of history by saving Kleitos's life? Perhaps killing Aristandros would simply help to redress the disruption.

Before I had a chance to consider means and methods, however, Seleukos rode up to join me in gazing uselessly at the efforts of our foot soldiers, putting a temporary stop to my ruminations.

****

While we sat there, contemplating onanistic hermits and other weighty subjects, our engineers were busy erecting colossal siege towers, mounting battering rams beneath tripod supports, building portable shield walls, and assembling complex catapults, which sprouted like an ungainly race of giants from the fields of Halikarnassos. By nightfall, two stretches of the moat were completely filled in and our troops started to roll the siege towers across the earthen dams. At the same time, a phalanx of heavy infantry, sheltering beneath shield walls, positioned one of the battering rams against Mylasa Gate and started to swing the massive, iron-tipped pole back and forth, producing a tremendous racket. No damage to the oaken panels was evident but the noise and ceaseless activity served as a useful diversion. In the sector between the siege towers and the battering ram, surreptitious sappers started digging mines under the wall, hoping to bring about its collapse. All through the night, the batterers kept up their clangor, the towermen stockpiled ammunition, and the sappers, under cover of commotion, shield walls, and darkness, continued their subterranean burrowing.

With the arrival of the first pinkish-gray streamers of dawn, our offensive resumed in earnest. Men clambered up to the top two levels of the siege towers, which placed them above, and only yards away from, the top of the wall, and started shooting arrows and throwing javelins, rocks, and flaming darts down at the defenders, who were running, evading, and ducking behind the crenellated parapet at the top of their wall. At the same time, the defenders did their best to dislodge our men on the towers. Periodic screams, followed by dull thuds, marked successful hits, although it was not always clear which side had scored. The battering rams provided a steady, satisfying, albeit ineffectual base beat to the staccato shrieks of wounded and dying men. The catapults roared periodically to life, sending huge boulders, burning barrels, and diseased carcasses arching over the wall. Beneath the cacophony of noise, the sappers continued their quiet, subversive work.

At midday, a portion of the wall, undermined by the sappers, finally gave way. Perdikkas and his hoplites were ready. With the noise of the collapse still ringing in their ears and a dust cloud still hanging in the air, they clambered over the pile of boulders and debris that had constituted the wall and poured into the city. They were met by a determined, organized phalanx of Memnon's mercenaries on the other side. A vicious, deadly contest ensued. It turned out that not only did Memnon have his troops lying in wait, he had also stationed archers and small catapults atop the houses nearest to the wall, which were pouring projectiles into Perdikkas's men who already had their hands full trying to fend off the skilled warriors confronting them on the ground.

After losing a dozen good men, Perdikkas ordered a retreat. Back on our side of the wall, he held a brief war council with Alexandros, Parmenion, and several other commanders. Aristandros was consulted; he requested time and sacrificial victims before rendering an opinion. While everyone else was dithering, Perdikkas added additional infantrymen to his troop and tried again. Soon enough, they were all back, carrying more dead and wounded soldiers. The skirmishes continued until nightfall but the only tangible result was a hospital tent filled with dead and dying Macedonian soldiers.

That night, while we slept, Memnon's mercenaries once again poured out through the Mylasa Gate and attacked our camp. This time our sentries gave timely alarm and we were not caught by surprise. The seven somatophylakes, including me, had slept in Alexandros's tent and the rest of the commanders were not far away. All of us had slept wearing our armor, with our swords close at hand. At the sound of the alarm, I attempted to rush out of the tent but was foiled by the presence of another bodyguard with the same objective in mind. Neither one of us noticed the other in the total darkness of the tent. We both went sprawling through the entrance flap and into the night. It was a minor miracle we'd managed to refrain from stabbing each other during our pratfall.

Visibility was marginally better outside the tent, with a modicum of illumination provided by the gibbous moon peeking through a gauzy cloud cover and by a supply wagon that had been set ablaze at one end of the camp. There was much more noise than light, however. Men were running around in total disorder, shouting orders, warnings, prayers, and imprecations. Their yelling was done predominantly in an assortment of Greek dialects because the men attacking the camp were mostly Memnon's Greek mercenaries and the men defending the camp were mostly Alexandros's Macedonian patriots. (The mercenaries and the patriots were both being paid at the going rate of one drachma per day but the patriots were fighting for the cause of pan-Hellenic liberation, not Persian hegemony.) In addition, metal clanged against metal, animals howled and brayed, and the surf beat against the nearby rocky shore, contributing a calming, reassuring roar. Pandemonium reigned.

It was impossible to tell friend from foe. The armor and equipment of Memnon's mercenaries was very similar to our own. It turns out that all fighting men look pretty much the same in the dark. Someone wearing a dull, dented helmet came roaring at me, his sword raised above his head. I shouted in turn and prepared to run him through with my javelin. He succeeded in parrying my thrust with his sword but our momentum caused us to bang into each other, chest to chest. "Is that you, Metoikos?" the other fellow asked. "Melas, you moron!" I yelled with relief, recognizing Kleitos's voice. We embraced.

I leaned close to Kleitos's ear, trying to be heard above the noise. "This is insane, brother."

He grinned in response. "Yeah, that's what makes it so much fun."

We stood side by side, peering into the chaos swirling around us.

"Where is Aniketos?" Kleitos yelled. "We've got to protect him."

"Just look for where the fighting is hottest."

Flood Tide

We advanced, shoulder to shoulder, toward the loudest noise. Other men recognized us and joined our group. We picked up speed, accreting comrades faster than a snowball rolling down a steep hill of freshly-fallen powder. We were at least a dozen strong by the time we encountered the enemy. At least I think they were the enemy. The other men with me slaughtered them before they had a chance to say much.

A pause in the action ensued. I scanned the darkness, trying to detect the motion of barely discernible shadows; I strained to filter out of the sounds of an imminent charge from the general tumult of a camp under assault; I tried to smell the odor of would-be attackers. It was an odd mental state, with my senses heightened to the point of retarding the tide of time itself. The silhouette of a large, heavily-armed man floated into view. He was shouting. I could hear the sound but the words didn't register. Ever so slowly, he jabbed his spear toward me. I easily sidestepped his thrust. Someone sliced off his arm at the elbow. A tight parabola of beautiful black fluid, with blood-red highlights, sprouted from the place where his joint used to be. I could have sworn the liquid hung motionless in the air. Then, in a blink of an eye, the spurting blood, the ragged stump, the man himself, all plunged to the ground and there was stillness amid the chaos once again.

What the hell am I doing here? I asked myself during the leisurely interval between one assault and the next.

Intellectually, I knew these attacks were coming thick and heavy but subjectively I had plenty of time for philosophical rumination between bouts of action. *Stay alive; comply with the Prime Directive; get back home.*

After a while, no further attacks came. Visibility in our camp improved greatly, the noise subsided to a conversational roar, the adrenaline level in my bloodstream normalized, and people started to move at regular speed once again, which at that moment happened to be the speed of a flock of chickens running around with their heads cut off.

It had been a small attack which, in hindsight, we beat back easily. Unfortunately, while we were busy fighting off the attackers, the night sky lit up with an ominous orange glow. Our siege towers, battering rams, and catapults were all aflame, accounting for the improved illumination. During our minor, groping skirmish, Memnon's incendiaries had been methodically destroying our siege equipment. Even more demoralizing was the sight, revealed by the brilliant glow of the surging flames, of the portion of the wall previously collapsed by our sappers: It had been completely rebuilt by the inhabitants of Halikarnassos during the night.

Alexandros accepted the loss of our equipment with equanimity, even a grudging admiration for our adversary. "It's only stuff," he said. "We can replace it." Projecting confidence and determination, he ordered the engineers to repair our siege engines as best they could, telling them, somewhat disingenuously, that there was plenty of wood in the surrounding forests. He ordered Philotas to take several squadrons of cavalry and bring back additional provisions (no easy task, because the harvest season had ended and we were mostly surrounded by inhospitable mountains, not the fertile fields of Ionia). He ordered the remaining cavalry commanders (including Seleukos, Kleitos, and me) to tether our horses and prepare our squadrons for fighting on foot, so that we could be more useful during our next attempt to breach the enemy's fortifications. And he ordered the sappers to get busy undermining two watchtowers on the northern side of the city wall, not far from the Tripylon Gate.

In due course, the two watchtowers toppled and the section of the wall between them collapsed. This time we didn't scramble over the rubble immediately. Instead, we massed our troops (including dismounted cavalry) and proceeded in a broad, orderly, deliberate, irresistible wave that washed across the tumbled remnants of the fortification.

To our surprise, no troops awaited on the far side. Instead, we were confronted by a brand new, massive inner wall, connected seamlessly to the still-standing portions of the outer wall. Apparently, the efforts of our sappers hadn't gone completely undetected. While they were hard at work digging, the Halikarnians were busy building the next wall. And Memnon's men were atop that new wall, waiting for our orderly, organized wave of soldiers to fill his pit of perdition between the rubble of the old wall and the implacable imperviousness of the new. Our tide of cheering attackers quickly turned into a seething, foaming, screaming, blood-soaked maelstrom of disorder, desperation, and death.

We lost close to a hundred men in the debris-filled fatal field before the rest of us managed to extricate ourselves from Memnon's trap. To add loss of honor to our loss of life, we were also forced to leave most of our dead behind as we struggled to make our way back across the jagged ruins of the old, collapsed wall beneath a lethal shower of enemy missiles from atop the insolent new one.

Alexandros, who had been in the midst of the killing zone with the rest of us, emerged unscathed but also uncharacteristically subdued. He retired to his tent, prohibiting anyone else, even Hephaistion, from joining him. When he emerged two hours later – ashen-faced and red-eyed – he ordered Seleukos to enter Halikarnassos, alone and unarmed, protected only by the kerykeion of an ambassador, and ask Memnon for a truce, in order to permit us to retrieve our dead. Memnon granted Alexandros's request. We spent the next day fasting, praying, and burning the bodies of our fallen comrades.

******

Flood Tide

Alexandros recovered his verve quickly. The morning after our day of mourning, he staged an elaborate sacrifice, with several different animals slaughtered, with much good meat burned on the altar, accompanied by paeans, dirges, and long, tedious entreaties addressed to all the relevant deities – Macedonian, Greek, Ionian, and Karian. Aristandros, also regaining his form, supervised the butchery and then spent a good amount of time peering into the resulting gore. When he rose to his feet, his white robe covered in blood, he was all smiles.

He addressed Alexandros but spoke loudly enough for all of us to hear. "Sire, you'll be in the Mausoleion before the full moon begins to wane."

"Does he mean alive or dead?" Kleitos whispered into my ear.

Alexandros noticed him leaning toward me. "Did you have something to add, Melas?"

"No, sire. I just wanted to ask Aristandros whether he saw you walking, riding, or getting carried into the Mausoleion."

Alexandros smiled. "That's a good question, Melas." Turning toward his soothsayer, he repeated my friend's question.

"You'll be strolling, sire ... with your friends by your side," Aristandros said confidently. Alexandros beamed and the crowd erupted in cheers. But Aristandros was not quite done. "However, I'm afraid that those two," he pointed to Kleitos and me, "may not be there with you." Nobody heard him, amidst the continuing ovation, with the exception of Kleitos and me.

Alexandros was elated. "Let's have something to eat," he yelled to his boisterous troops, "and then back to work. The full moon will be here in three days, so we have little time to waste."

****

The next two days were little different from the preceding few. Engineers worked to repair our equipment, sappers dug to undermine the enemy's fortifications, infantrymen banged their battering rams ineffectually against the city gates, and men on both sides died at a steady rate from disease, accidents, and the intentional infliction of bodily harm.

After two days, Memnon decided to end the stalemate one way or another. Shortly after midnight, while most of us slept, he launched another nighttime raid. Except this time, he attacked in force. At least a thousand of his best men poured out of Mylasa Gate and headed south, along the city wall, straight for our siege equipment. Our men, more prepared for the attack than the last time, rushed to engage the enemy and save our gear. Alas, Memnon's men managed to reach our armaments first.

It was a clear night, illuminated by a full moon and the glow of a dozen burning siege towers. Perhaps we were getting used to these nocturnal engagements but in no time we were drawn up in an orderly phalanx formation, ready to attack. Our cavalry squadrons, having forsaken their horses for the duration of the siege, were deployed at either end of the line. By chance, Kleitos and I, with our combined squadrons, found ourselves anchoring the terminus closest to the bay.

We enjoyed great numerical superiority over Memnon's mercenaries and were sure of a quick victory. On Alexandros's signal, we all rushed forward, singing and yelling as we ran, and tried to engage the enemy. However, Memnon's troops withdrew to the other side of the moat, across the earthen dams we'd built, making it difficult for us to take advantage of our numbers and impossible for us to outflank them. Savage fighting ensued between similarly armed, similarly trained, and similarly determined soldiers. We were still sure, however, that sooner or later we'd wipe these traitors out.

While we were all occupied trying to destroy the mercenaries in front of us, Orontobates led out the remaining Greek mercenaries and all of his own Persian troops through the Mylasa Gate. Before we knew what was happening, this force, which was almost equal in numbers to our own, hit us from the rear. Suddenly, we were surrounded on all sides. It proved impossible for us to maintain cohesion against the weight of heavy infantry coming at us from every direction. Our line disintegrated into small eddies of men fighting desperately while being gradually swamped and swallowed by the tide of opposing combatants.

Perhaps our men still outnumbered the enemy but any numerical superiority was nullified by the crush of soldiers from all sides. Not only were our men unable to maintain orderly lines with overlapping shields, they had a difficult time even deploying their weapons. They were squeezed together so tightly that, every time they tried to slash with their swords or thrust with their pikes, they were as likely to injure one of their comrades as a foe.

Our small group of erstwhile horsemen, holding the southern end of the line, was even less equipped to fight this kind of engagement than our infantry brethren in the center. We were used to the speed, maneuverability, and elevation afforded by our mounts. Surrounded and rooted to the ground, we were half way to defeat before we started to fight. We retreated, as best we could, along the city wall toward the coast. By the time we reached the rock-strewn beach, the leading edge of the rising sun conjured a shimmering path of golden shards across the choppy waters of the harbor. Unfortunately, it was not a path we could take. There were nine men left in our group, being pursued by perhaps thirty or forty heavily-armed Persians. I spotted an abandoned hunting hut on a nearby hill and told the remaining men to make a run for it. Only Kleitos and I managed to get to the hut alive, with the pursuing Persians hot on our heels.

Fortunately, the hut was solidly built and had only one door. When the first of the pursuing Persians stuck his head in, I stabbed him under his shield, my sword entering at the groin and travelling upward. At the same time, Kleitos stabbed him with a dagger in his left eye. The man collapsed in our doorway and didn't move. We managed to inflict two simultaneous and fatal wounds on the next man who contributed his corpse to the growing barricade forming at the entrance to the hut. *So much for never having killed a man with my own hands,* I thought as I searched in vain for some sign of regret in my conscience.

There was a short pause, while the Persians reconsidered their strategy. "No need for both of us to stand here," Kleitos observed with a laugh. "I'll take care of the next three and you can do the three after that. In the meantime, why don't you take a rest.'

"Maybe I'll take a nap," I replied, trying to match Kleitos's insouciance.

"That's fine. I'll wake you if I need ...." He was unable to finish the thought because two more enemy soldiers appeared, having sprung from either side of the door, and leapt onto the bodies blocking their way. Even though they had dispensed with their shields, the opening was still not wide enough for both of them and they became momentarily wedged between the doorposts. Kleitos ran them through, one after the other, before they could disentangle themselves.

"Decent speed," I said, "but you should've kept them from toppling back out. They would've made a fine door."

"Go have your nap, before I stuff you in the door."

I didn't actually take a nap. While Kleitos stood guard at the door, I enlarged an existing gap between two logs with my dagger to get a better idea of the disposition and activities of the men outside. I was surprised to see that they were mostly sitting down, resting. I couldn't see their commander, so I decided to create a crack on the other side of the hut. It turned out there was nobody on that side at all. *They must be congregating in the front, next to the door.*

I was about to make some witty observation to Kleitos when some movement far below the hill caught my eye. As luck would have it, I had the perfect vantage point to observe the progress of the battle under the city wall. What I expected to see was a massacre of our troops. In fact, the first thought that flashed in my mind was the realization that this was the destruction of the pan-Hellenic invasion force which was supposed to have taken place at Granikos. *I guess the instructors at the Academy were right after all. The flow of history is inevitable, even if it gets momentarily sidetracked from time to time.*

Even though this new turn of events meant the disturbance caused by my inadvertent violation of the Prime Directive would soon be rectified, I didn't derive any relief or satisfaction from that prospect. *These guys were my friends and comrades, after all. Too bad neither they nor I realized it until it was too late.*

As I stared at the melee far below me, I noticed a new element enter the fray. A cohesive, well-organized phalanx of hoplites advanced on the double from the direction of our camp. *Who are these guys?* I wondered. They were clearly Macedonian infantry but I had thought all of our men had rushed to protect our siege equipment and to attack Memnon's sortie during the initial engagement and had then become trapped when Orontobates brought out the second, larger force that hit us from the rear. Now, this new Macedonian phalanx was, in turn, charging into the soft posterior of Orontobates's combined Greek and Persian troops.

"Is that Parmenion leading them?" I wondered.

"What are you talking about?" Kleitos asked.

I hadn't realized I'd given voice to my thoughts. "Go over there and take a look," I said, taking over Kleitos's post by the door and pointing toward the chink I'd made. "See what you think."

Kleitos peered for a moment and then let out a joyous whoop.

"Keep it down! We're surrounded by forty blood-thirsty Persians who are discussing how to kill us right now."

"Who cares? Our guys are in the process of killing all the rest of them."

"Here, let me take another look." We switched positions once again. The fight had been joined in earnest. It was now Orontobates's force that was trapped and getting hit from both sides.

"I know who it is," Kleitos called from behind my back. "Take that, you son of a whore."

I turned around in time to see another dead Persian added to our collection. Kleitos, putting his foot on the man's chest, pulled out his sword and was cleaning it on the dead man's tunic. "These guys are not very smart, are they?"

"What do you mean, you know who it is?"

"Our guys, the ones who stormed Orontobates from the rear. I know who they are."

"Who are they?"

"They're the old veterans and the injured guys left behind to guard our baggage train. Parmenion must have gotten them organized when he saw what was going on."

"Well, they're winning the battle now. They're cutting Orontobates's guys to pieces. And now, I think Memnon's troops are also beginning to withdraw back toward the gate."

"Alexandros will be furious," Kleitos said.

"What do you mean? He'll be thrilled."

"What, at having his ass saved by Parmenion and a bunch of creaky old veterans? I don't think so."

As I watched, the retreat of Memnon's and Orontobates's troops turned into a disorderly rout. They were throwing away their shields and swords, running as fast as they could toward Mylasa Gate. Some of them stumbled and fell, only to be trampled by their fellow soldiers, desperate to reach safety. The narrow, rickety bridge across the moat collapsed under the weight of the panicked horde. The moat filled up with bodies, with more victims being pushed into the murky mire by the weight of the crowd behind them. Soon, men were able to cross the moat by skipping from body to body, although some of the stepping stones were still astir.

The gate was too narrow to accommodate the tremendous deluge of fleeing soldiers. I could see men getting crushed to death and falling into the roadway, only to have others climb over them. A small group of Persian officers tried to impose some semblance of order. With swords drawn, they formed a cordon outside the gate and tried to stem the flood of soldiers. They were quickly overrun and stomped to death. However, during the brief pause, the soldiers who had made it inside the wall slammed the gate shut. The new arrivals had no place to go, with additional waves of desperate soldiers crushing them against the unyielding walls and the now closed and barred gate.

In the meantime, our soldiers were pressing their pursuit of the fugitives. None of Memnon's and Orontobates's troops who had been left outside the gate survived. They were either trampled to death by their own comrades or killed by our men.

They were all dead, that is, except a small group of perhaps two hundred men, who decided to save their lives by running toward the hill which already held thirty or forty of their comrades and the two of us. One of the newly arriving men carried a flaming torch.

"Oh-oh," I said. "We may have a problem."

"What is it?"

"There are a couple of hundred Persians outside and one of them is getting ready to set our hut on fire."

Flood Tide

Uncharacteristically, Kleitos was silent. "Well, at least we won the battle," he finally observed.

I could see the flaming torch leave the Persian soldier's hand and arc, ever so slowly, toward our hut. Soon, there was smoke seeping in through the thatched roof, followed by a crackling noise, and then small tongues of flame started licking the rafters supporting the thatch. The smoke in the hut was getting thicker and the temperature hotter.

"We have to get out there and fight them in the open," I said.

"Unless we want to burn to death in here," Kleitos agreed.

"Even if we get outside, the odds might be against us."

"It's not a problem." Kleitos laughed. "All we have to do is take care of a hundred guys apiece." His laughter was overtaken by a coughing spell.

"Let's jump out together," I yelled through the smoke. It was getting very hard to breathe. "Once out the door, you go to the left and I'll go to the right. Let's try to ..." My words were cut short by the loud report of a rafter crashing to the ground in flames.

We rushed to the door, armed with a sword in one hand and a dagger in the other, ready to jump over the pile of bodies blocking our way, when we noticed the semicircle of men drawn up on the other side, waiting to catch us on the points of their swords, if and when we started the downward trajectory of our leaps. For a moment, we stood still, trying to suck some clean air into our lungs and clear our minds.

We both knew we would be dead within a moment or two. *I guess it's just the inertia of time, cleaning up some loose ends,* I thought ruefully. Surprisingly, I didn't experience fear or anger, only disappointment. *I wish I could've found out how it all turns out.*

I was brought back to the present by the heat at my back and the sound of Kleitos's voice. "I never really thanked you for saving my life," I heard him saying, in a remarkably calm voice, "all those many years ago, at the Dionysos ceremony."

"Best decision I ever made, my friend."

"It's been an honor serving with you, sire."

"I'm not a sire," I started to say but Kleitos interrupted me. "On the count of three," he said. "One, two, three."

We clambered out and, using the dead bodies as a springboard, launched ourselves into the seductive embrace of certain death. The altitude of our vaults might have surprised the men awaiting our landing. I, for one, came down on the head and shoulder of the man in front of me, instead of his sword, knocking him backward and clearing a small space into which I crumpled, as yet uninjured. I was back on my feet, ready to engage, by the time the men around me recovered from their surprise. Because of the corpse barricade behind us, and thanks to Kleitos's position to my left, only two or three men could attack me at the same time. I parried their jabs and blows, using my sword and my dagger. Gradually, and without conscious thought, I discerned a pattern in their attacks. I was no longer engaged in a sword fight but, rather, in an intricately choreographed dance. I knew, long before it happened, what their next stroke would be and my arms would move instinctively to thwart their thrusts before they even launched them. Although my sword and dagger flashed through the air too fast to see, melding into a bright blur of indistinguishable blocks, cuts, jabs, and slashes, time seemed to slow to a crawl. I had ample leisure, as I held off the men attacking me, to look over their heads and take in the entire hillside leading up to our hut.

A clamor at the bottom of the hill caught my eye. The commotion started to roll up toward us in defiance of the laws of physics. I lost sight of it for a moment, as I looked back at the swords trying to poke holes into me. The next time I saw the scrum of screaming soldiers, it had rolled half way up the hill. With a blink of my eye, the mélange of men and mayhem resolved itself into a single armored warrior, atop a very large black steed, slicing through a howling pack of frenzied Persians. The horse was instantly recognizable, by its size and by the white blaze on its forehead and face. The rider, covered in mud and gore, his white plume knocked askew, was equally unmistakable. *What's he doing here?*

Alexandros's unexpected appearance disrupted the autonomous rhythm of my sparring. A sharp, burning pain across my left triceps reminded me to pay attention to the task at hand. However, the rising uproar behind the men trying to kill Kleitos and me started to sap the momentum of their attack. As each man in turn snuck a peek over his shoulder and recognized the man in the middle of the melee, he stopped his assault, turned, and ran to join his mates in their cordial, communal, concerted effort to kill the Macedonian king.

Surrounded by two hundred baying enemy soldiers, cut off from the support of his bodyguard, Alexandros seemed not the least bit discomfited. He twirled the sword playfully in his right hand, then swooped and whirled, leaving a detached head suspended momentarily in midair. His movements were fluid, swift, and economical. Every time the surrounding mob attempted to surge in, Boukephalas and Alexandros, moving as a single fighting unit, cleared an oasis of dead and dying Persians.

Flood Tide

Far down at the bottom of the hill, a score of cavalrymen appeared. I recognized Perdikkas, Philotas, and Seleukos among them. They were resolutely slashing their way up to their king but Alexandros, disdaining their assistance, continued his rapid progress toward us. The gap between them remained stubbornly large. *I know how they feel*, I thought, having tried to keep up with Alexandros's reckless charges into the thickest fights once or twice myself.

The few enemy soldiers still possessing the power of locomotion melted away. Alexandros reached Kleitos and me before the rest of his men caught up to him.

"Nice fighting, sire," Kleitos said, by way of a greeting. "Thank you for saving us."

Alexandros laughed. "We never leave one of ours behind, Melas. You know that. Besides, I owed you one ... from Granikos. Now we're even."

"Yes, sire. Although you never owed me anything. I was simply doing my duty and, if I was able to help you in the process, that made it a special privilege."

Alexandros smiled and turned toward me, mischief tugging at the corners of his eyes. "But I'll be damned if I know why I saved you."

"It wasn't my time to die, sire." I laughed. "And you were the instrument of my destiny."

"Careful now, Metoikos. It's not too late for me to become the instrument of your destruction."

"Aye, aye, sire. I'm well aware of that."

"Aware of what?" Perdikkas asked, his group having finally caught up to Alexandros.

"Aware that you're painfully slow on that nag of yours."

Everybody roared, at Perdikkas's expense. He seemed a little dubious at first but finally joined in the laughter. The Macedonian army had somehow snatched victory from certain defeat and we all knew it. And I laughed the loudest of all. *I'm still alive,* I thought in wonder.

Chapter 10 – Mopping Up

It had been a close call. But for the timely intervention of Parmenion and the veterans, Alexandros's expedition might well have ended under the wall of Halikarnassos and Alexandros was a good enough soldier to know it. We withdrew back into camp and spent the rest of the day licking our wounds. There was no singing, no celebrations, no banquets, only the painful work of gathering the dead and wounded, getting the former ready for cremation and tending to the latter.

When night fell, most of us sat or lay in front of the tents, looking at the stars and marveling at our survival. It was a cold, breezy, cloudless night, silvered by the luminance of a full moon. And then, as the great sidereal disk wheeled inexorably toward midnight, the cool ambiance of the night gradually picked up a warmer, orangey undertone when fires began to blaze up in the city. As we watched, bonfire after bonfire sprang to life in the open squares and marketplaces of Halikarnassos, the flames licking the sky. *Must be some kind of celebration*, I thought but then the first of the houses joined the cavalcade of conflagrations.

"What are they doing?" Kleitos asked. We all had the same question and none of us had a good answer. Then we saw the ships. Taking advantage of the outgoing tide and the bright moonlight, ship after heavily laden ship left the harbor.

"They're evacuating the city," Seleukos said quietly, "and destroying anything useful that they can't take with them."

Kleitos started jumping up and down. "Hey, everybody! We've won! They're running away." His cries were picked up by the men around us and gradually rippled out through the camp. Soon enough, there was rejoicing everywhere.

We were summoned for a meeting in the king's tent. Once assembled, we found a glum Alexandros sitting quietly on his stool. "The bastard is getting away once again," he said in lieu of an opening statement. "I guess we could've used a navy just now."

Hephaistion hastened to reassure him. "They can flee to the ends of the Earth, Aniketos, but they can't escape your wrath."

"Well, they're doing a pretty good job of escaping just now," was Alexandros's dry response. "And I imagine Memnon is among them."

Hephaistion persisted. "You'll get him, Aniketos, that's for sure."

Aristandros joined in. "You'll be strolling into the Mausoleion tomorrow, sire, before the full moon begins to wane."

"Assuming the ashes cool down enough to walk on." I wasn't speaking to any one in particular but I kept my hand on my sword, just in case Aristandros proved incapable of taking a joke.

"The Mausoleion isn't burning," Seleukos observed. "They're not trying to burn down the city; only the supplies that might be useful to us."

Alexandros interrupted our by-play. "Get everybody ready. I want us through the gates at first light. Perdikkas will be in charge of breaking down the Myndos Gate, Parmenion will get through the Tripylon, and I'll take the Mylasa Gate.

"Ptolemaios, you and Kleitos will stay behind and secure the camp," he added flatly, almost as an afterthought. But his understated manner couldn't mask his evident irritation. "And organize some details to police the battlefield. I want all the loot collected, the enemy corpses stripped and burned, and our own fallen ready for the funeral rites by the time we get back. And make sure all the wounded are well cared for."

"Yes, sire," I said briskly, before Kleitos could protest, giving his tunic a little tug as I spoke, to make sure he got the message. This might have been a punitive assignment but we deserved it for getting into a pickle requiring Alexandros's deliverance, if nothing else. My wise-ass comment to Aristandros probably hadn't helped.

"And somebody go alert Queen Ada. I want her to enter the city with me." Alexandros was quiet for a moment. "And one more thing. Let's be careful tomorrow! You never know who might be lurking behind every corner and inside every house. All right, no time to waste." And with that, we were dismissed.

The anticipated door-to-door combat never materialized. When our troops arrived, garlanded with the first streamers of dawn, they found the gates unguarded and unbarred, ready to swing open at the slightest push. Once inside the walls, they entered a deserted and largely destroyed city. Perhaps the defenders intended only to burn militarily useful materiel but, with the aid of the stiff breeze, they managed to burn down almost every dwelling in the city. Only some of the larger, marble-clad public buildings survived. And the Mausoleion still towered over the smoldering ruins in all its gleaming magnificence.

Unlike the city itself, however, the three fortresses were far from empty. It turned out that, while the civilians might have been evacuated, the troops simply withdrew to the akropolis, the Salmakis Fortress, and the King's Castle and settled in for a long siege.

Alexandros's plans for restoring Queen Ada to her throne had to be scaled back for now. Instead of a grand banquet at the royal palace, which was inaccessible for the moment because of its vicinity to Salmakis, he organized a modest, open-air feast in the scorched agora, attended by Ada, her retinue, and a few of Alexandros's officers.

"She should feel right at home," Perdikkas was overheard whispering. "This is even more chintzy than the party she threw for us at Alinda." Fortunately for Perdikkas, Alexandros was too engrossed in his conversation with the queen to overhear his comment.

After all the wine had been consumed (there was hardly enough to get anyone drunk), Alexandros called for his scribe. "Kallisthenes, take down this official proclamation."

There was a brief delay, while Kallisthenes desperately searched for his lump of ink, which had somehow disappeared from its pouch. "There is plenty of soot around, Kallisthenes," Hephaistion suggested helpfully. "Just scoop up a handful."

Kallisthenes eventually found his block of dried, vegetable-gum-infused carbon black, broke off a small piece, dissolved it in water, sharpened his reed pen, unrolled a fresh sheet of papyrus, and looked up expectantly at his boss. Of course, Alexandros had long since lost patience and was strolling with Queen Ada toward her new official residence, trailed by his usual phalanx of aides, sycophants, and hangers-on.

"I'm ready, sire," Kallisthenes yapped, trying to catch up to the group.

In due course, the proclamation was reduced to writing. In it, Alexandros, in his capacity as liberator of Karia, restored Queen Ada to her throne and ordained the installation of popularly elected local leaders in all the towns and villages of her kingdom, provided the candidates were approved in advance by the queen and, tacitly, by Alexandros. "Have sufficient copies made, Kallisthenes, so we can dispatch messengers to read it in every agora in Karia." There was no pressing need to address the governance of Halikarnassos itself, given the current lack of available inhabitants subject to administration.

When the group arrived at Queen Ada's official new residence, which was one of the few dwellings in the city to escape the previous night's inferno, it proved to be a rather modest affair, hardly big enough to house the queen and her immediate retinue. "Don't worry, mother,"

Alexandros reassured her, "we'll soon have you in the palace."

None of the Macedonians ventured inside. Alexandros left behind a perfunctory guard of a dozen soldiers, mounted Boukephalas, and slowly made his way back to camp. He was chilled to the bone, tired, and uncharacteristically subdued when we saw him back at his tent.

****

Winter was fast approaching and, with it, the end of the fighting season. Alexandros had had his fill of Halikarnassos. His soldiers, who'd been marching and fighting steadily since the spring, needed a break. He needed a break. On the one hand, his army had successfully liberated Lydia, Ionia, and Karia. On the other hand, Memnon was still out there somewhere, organizing Persian forces not only to reverse Alexandros's successes in Anatolia but also to carry the war to the other side of the Aegean. This was likely to be a long struggle.

After mulling over his options, Alexandros called a general assembly of all troops under the walls of Halikarnassos and announced his dispositions for the winter. He had decided to send all his newlywed Macedonian soldiers home for a short furlough. "I want you to make some future warriors for me," he told them. His announcement was greeted with wild jubilation. "But

I need you back by spring." The acclamation continued unabated, perhaps even increased somewhat in volume. *I guess you can only make warriors so long, before you're ready to start making war again.* In the end, about a third of the troops decided they were newlyweds.

Alexandros put two brothers, Koinos and Kleandros, in charge of the soldiers returning home. "We'll rendezvous in Gordion. Be there by the spring equinox, at the latest. And bring back at least twice the number you're taking with you. Unlike the ordinary soldiers, you two are not going home to make babies, no matter what Parmenion may have to say about it.[15] Your job is to recruit – in Macedonia, Thessaly, the Peloponnese, and wherever else you can find able-bodied, patriotic Greeks who want to join our cause."

He split the remaining troops in half, telling Parmenion to take all the allied infantry and cavalry, plus most of the Macedonian Silver Shields, back through Ionia, Lydia, and Hellespontine Phrygia, to clean up any remaining pockets of resistance and meet us at Gordion.

Alexandros himself intended to take a more direct route toward Gordion, over the mountains, and await the

---

[15] Koinos was Parmenion's son-in-law. At times it seemed as if most of our commanders were related to the old man.

arrival of the rest of his army.[16] And he had one more command assignment. "Ptolemaios, you'll stay here in Halikarnassos, with your squadron. We'll bring your strength back up to two hundred horsemen, to make up for any casualties you may have suffered up to this point. Plus, I'm leaving you all of Memnon's mercenaries who have defected to our side. There are about three thousand of them. Your job is to provide security for Queen Ada."

"Yes, sire."

"And one more thing."

"Yes?"

"You will invest and reduce the three fortresses where Memnon and Orontobates and the rest of those bastards are hiding out. I don't want a single man to escape alive."

I was too staggered to respond. *It could take years to conquer those forts, even if we could besiege them effectively. Their fortifications were unassailable and two of the three could be easily resupplied by water. And he's giving me three thousand troops with suspect loyalties to do the job.*

"Meet us in Gordion but don't bother coming unless you're bringing Memnon's head with you."

---

[16] For maps of locations mentioned in this book, visit AlexanderGeiger.com.

I said nothing.

He smiled. "Don't look so glum, Metoikos. I'm leaving you all our siege equipment."

"Aye, aye, sire."

"Make sure you get the bastard this time. I'm counting on you." And with that, he clapped me on the back and left me in the shit.

****

I'm free. The thought flashed, unbidden and almost unperceived, as I watched Alexandros's army depart. *I have my own army now; I can do as I please.*

In truth, two hundred horse and three thousand infantry is not an army. It's not even a division. It's more like an armed band. And the armed band didn't belong to me; it belonged to Alexandros. Nevertheless, it was a heady thought. I was pretty sure my own squadron would follow me across the River Styx if I asked them. And the three thousand mercenaries could probably be persuaded to book passage on Charon's raft as well, if promised a sufficiently large bonus on the other bank. They had, after all, already demonstrated a flexible understanding of loyalty. Thus, it seemed reasonable to assume that, if I gave the order, they would march with me down to Egypt, where I could then await the arrival of the escape hatch while guarded by my own private band of desperadoes.

Of course, unlike the mercenaries, I had no intention of betraying Alexandros's faith in me. Even if I had been tempted, which I was not, it was impractical for me to try to fight my way through a thousand miles of Persian territory and then, once I arrived at my destination, to try to hold out for years against determined assaults by enemies near and far, while I awaited the appearance of the portal. Not even Xenophon's Ten Thousand would have been foolish enough to attempt such a feat.

No, on further reflection, it was not the temptation to go to Egypt that had sparked the stray, unwelcome thought; rather, that uncharacteristic, recreant flash was an underhanded attempt by my mind to keep me from focusing on the herculean task that awaited me right there in Halikarnassos. Cleaning the Augean stables was nothing compared to sacking three fortified, strongly defended positions, one of which occupied a commanding height above the city, the second of which we could not besiege effectively because it had unfettered access to the harbor, and the third of which we could not even get to, because it was on an island and we had no boats. Admittedly, Herakles had only one day to complete his task, while Alexandros had generously given me four months, but Herakles was a legendary hero and the son of Zeus, while I was a traveler stranded out of time, with only my squadron and three thousand untrustworthy mercenaries to assist me. On balance, I decided that we were both in equally deep dung.

I started out by finding comfortable quarters for all my troops in those public buildings in Halikarnassos that had managed to escape the flames. Next, I sent out my horsemen to fan out across the countryside and over the mountains and bring back all the provisions they could find within half a day's ride. When they returned, I organized a splendid banquet, attended by all my troops, as well as the queen and her entourage. The following morning, I ordered them to ride out a little farther and bring back more food. "You'll need to keep us provisioned for four months," I told them. Considering that winter was approaching and the countryside had been stripped already, theirs might have been the toughest assignment.

Finally, I addressed my mercenaries, who were presumably well-fed and rested by now. I told them to take off their armor, lay down their swords, and find some picks and shovels. "We're going to take those forts using your masonry skills."

It took my men less than a week to circumvallate the akropolis. After that, I left behind a skeleton crew to make sure no one got in or came out. "If you see a pigeon flying over there, I want you to shoot it out of the sky. If you see a rat scrambling up the wall, I want it dead before it gets to the top. Nothing comes in or goes out, got it?"

We changed the crew every eight hours and, as far as I could tell, they carried out my orders. When the defenders surrendered, two months later, of the original complement of three hundred soldiers, sixty were dead. The rest only looked that way. Contrary to Alexandros's instructions, we didn't put the survivors to the sword. I sent them, under guard, over the mountains, to Alexandros. I didn't inquire how many of them survived the journey. Worst of all, we didn't find either Memnon or Orontobates among the dead or the survivors.

While the defenders on the akropolis were starving to death, I turned my attention to Salmakis. We assembled and emplaced the siege engines left behind by Alexandros under the walls on the landward side of the fortress and engaged in desultory attempts to get under, over, or through the walls. After two weeks of no progress whatsoever, I bribed a local fisherman to take a half dozen of my most trusted men into the fortress from the seaward side, under cover of darkness. They opened a hidden gate in the wall and my mercenaries were only too happy to pour in and slaughter the defenders to the last man. We counted and burned 540 corpses. We didn't find the mortal remains of Memnon or Orontobates.

The King's Castle held out the longest. It took my mercenary masons more than three months to build a causeway from the nearest wharf to the island. First, I had the men scavenge throughout the ruins of Halikarnassos for large building blocks, which we dragged, ferried by raft, and dumped into the water. Once the larger stones started to poke above the surface, we carried smaller rocks and bricks to fill in the gaps. Finally, we used gravel, sand, and soil to create a smooth, wide roadway. Our construction held up against the waves long enough to enable us to get all our siege equipment across to the island.

The defenders, who could have left at any time, stood instead on the walls, hurling insults and shooting the occasional arrow. Finally, when all our men and equipment were in place, we launched a conventional siege, with sappers mining, rammers battering, catapulters barraging, and towermen assaulting. We outnumbered the defenders ten to one. Once our siege started in earnest, it took only two days for my men to take King's Castle. We didn't find either Orontobates or Memnon among the dead. How they had managed to persuade their men, after abandoning them in the lurch, to stay behind and sustain their doomed defense of the three fortresses, I'll never know.

The fragrance of the coming spring was already in the air by the time we finished our clean-up operations and settled Queen Ada in her palace. We set out – my squadron and my three thousand victorious mercenaries – on the road to Gordion. As I rode along, I experienced a new, different sensation. I'd managed to rid myself of my persistent case of chronotosis. I was still discombobulated and still had no idea what the future held in store for me but somehow I'd learned to live with it. Perhaps it was the exhilaration I'd felt upon escaping imminent death at the hunting hut or the satisfaction I'd savored upon completing my assignment at Halikarnassos or the experience I'd gained in the course of our entire campaign since Granikos but, at some point, I'd gotten over my sense of temporal dislocation. I realized my fellow soldiers had no idea what the future held in store for them either and they simply got on with it. I inhaled the clean, cool, verdant air. *If they can do it, so can I.*

****

When Dareios walked into her tent, Barsine was too stunned to prostrate herself. Her first thought was that her husband must have achieved a signal victory to warrant a personal visit by the emperor and she tried to find confirmation in his face. His stern visage reminded her instantly of her grievous breach of protocol. She threw herself to the dirt floor, fighting to still the pounding of her heart. Perhaps her long captivity was coming to an end.

"You may rise," Dareios said, not unkindly. Barsine was puzzled by his tone. Somehow, she had expected him to sound more enthusiastic. "Maybe you want to take a seat," he suggested. She shook her head, urging him with her eyes to get on with it. "I'm afraid we have received some bad news," he said.

"What?" she blurted out.

"Your husband is dead," he informed her, without further preamble. "I'm sorry," he added and it was possible he even meant it.

The tent started to spin. She decided to sit down after all. Dareios simply stood there, waiting for a response. Finally, she found her voice again. "What happened?"

Dareios shrugged. "He got sick and died." Seeing no visible reaction, he continued after a moment. "I sent my personal physician but there was nothing he could do."

The silence dragged on.

"What will happen to my children and me?"

Dareios smiled. His expression reminded her of a freshly fed feline. "You're the most beautiful woman in my harem." His tone was matter-of-fact but still not unkind. "I'm sure we'll find a place for you."

And with that, he turned on his heels and left the tent. Barsine sat quietly, alone, unable to cry.

Chapter 11 – Cutting the Cord

It took almost a month for the "newlyweds" led by Koinos and Kleandros to make it back to Macedonia. However, the closer they came to home, the more urgent their pace became. Finally, after crossing the Axios River, there was no restraining them.

The following morning, after striking camp, Koinos addressed the troops. "Alright men, listen up! I can tell by the tents at the front of your tunics that you're real anxious to get back to your wives." His comment was met by much laughter and cheering, the soldiers eagerly anticipating his next command. "You're free to go. Make your way home as best you can." More loud approbation. "We'll reassemble at this exact spot two months from today."

The men didn't need to be told twice. They turned and ran before Koinos could finish speaking. "Bring along your brothers and neighbors when you

271

come back," he yelled after them. "You bet," someone answered, and they were gone.

Koinos and Kleandros, accompanied only by their personal bodyguard, made it to the palace in Pella shortly after noon the following day. They were immediately ushered into the armory and met by Antipatros and Kassandros.

"Let's have your report," Antipatros ordered, without asking them to sit, "before Olympias finds out that you're here."

Koinos cleared his throat. "Sire, King Alexandros sends his greetings. There is much ..." He was interrupted by a loud commotion outside the door. "Get out of my way!" a woman screamed.

"I guess she found out," Antipatros said wearily. "Might as well let her in," he called out to the guards at the door.

Olympias burst in. "What's going on?"

"These men were about to tell us."

"Well, what're we waiting for?"

"Let's give them something to eat and a place to sit first."

Some food, wine, and chairs arrived, along with several high-ranking officers. Koinos and Kleandros spent the rest of the afternoon giving their audience a detailed report on the achievements of the pan-Hellenic army from the crossing of the Hellespont to the fighting at Halikarnassos. "And King Alexandros specifically wanted us to impress upon you his urgent need for at least ten thousand additional foot and twelve hundred additional cavalry, when we return with the furloughed veterans in the spring," they concluded.

Antipatros shook his head. "Well, that's not going to happen."

"But ...," Olympias started to object.

"Now, go wash up and get some rest," Antipatros added quickly, cutting short any further discussion. "We'll have a banquet tonight."

******

Sitting on his throne, Dareios towered over the assembled commanders, advisors, courtiers, bodyguards, and assorted hangers-on. He was a big man, taller than most of his contemporaries, and solidly built. He sat on a large, elaborately carved throne, which might have made a lesser man resemble a child in a highchair, but Dareios's broad shoulders filled the entire width of the seat while a small stool provided for his feet kept them from swinging freely in the air. The throne itself was placed on an elevated platform, with four steps leading up to it. The net result was to put Dareios's head almost ten feet above ground level. Anyone wishing to look at him was forced to crane his neck, even if allowed to stand, rather than kneel, while addressing the sovereign.

Although this was a temporary audience hall in dusty little Damaskos, built in less than a week, using stones salvaged from the tumble-down remains of an ancient temple that had once stood atop a nearby ziggurat, with a floor of packed dirt and a roof of thatch, the presence of the emperor imparted an aura of authority to the proceedings.

Dareios worked hard to maintain the trappings of power. He patiently bore the tall, gaudy, gold-bedecked hat that weighed more than his helmet and afforded a lot less protection. In his left hand he clutched an ornate, useless staff. His robe shimmered with gold and precious stones and was incredibly uncomfortable in the overheated chamber. His unruly beard had been carefully combed and set with an aromatic mixture of bear fat, beeswax, and oil. There was a trace of kohl around his eyes, which failed to conceal the heavy bags underneath or the deep crevices at the corners. Despite the best efforts of his cosmetologists, he still conveyed the impression of an impatient, powerful, uncouth warrior, perhaps not entirely by accident. Because of his life experiences, Dareios firmly believed that in Persia, power was the only reliable guaranty of survival.

He had convened this meeting to assess the current state of the war effort and to determine a way forward. Among the advisers present were his second-in-command, Mazaios, who held, among other posts, the satrapies of Babylonia and Mesopotamia; Orontobates, the former king of Karia; Arsamenes, the satrap of Kilikia; and Barzaentes, the satrap of Arachosia. Also present were a number of military commanders, including Nabarzanes, who had been given command of Dareios's cavalry; Pharnabazos, whom Dareios had appointed to take over the Persian navy following Memnon's death; and Autophradates, who had taken over Memnon's land forces. Finally, there was the Greek mercenary commander Charidemos who, in his own mind, was the obvious successor to Memnon.

Pharnabazos's assignment was to continue the island-by-island occupation of the Aegean envisioned by Memnon, in preparation for the Persian invasion of the Greek mainland. By the time Pharnabazos completed his report, it was clear to Dareios that Pharnabazos was no Memnon. The report of Autophradates, who had been tasked with the responsibility of containing Alexandros's forces along the seacoast, was equally dispiriting.

The next commander to step forward, Arsamenes, had been one of three satraps who had met with Memnon, a little less than a year earlier, at a small town called Zeleia, just east of the Granikos River, to plan the Persian resistance to Alexandros's pan-Hellenic invasion. He was also the only one of the four principals at the Zeleia conference who was still alive. (Of the other three participants at that fateful meeting, Spithridates, satrap of Ionia and Lydia, had almost succeeded in killing Alexandros during the ensuing Battle of Granikos, only to die as a result of the timely intervention of Kleitos Melas; Arsites, satrap of Hellespontine Phrygia, had fled from the battle, only to commit suicide in shame two days later; and Memnon, who had disappeared from the field at Granikos before Parmenion's phalangists could kill or capture him, went on to become Dareios's supreme military commander in the fight against Alexandros's pan-Hellenic army, only to be felled by a tiny, invisible salmonella enterica bacterium.)

At the Zeleia conference, Memnon had advocated a scorched earth strategy. He had been overruled by the three satraps, with disastrous results. In the wake of the defeat at Granikos, Arsamenes had learned his lesson all too well. After the fall of Halikarnassos, when Alexandros set out, with a fraction of his army, for Gordion, located on the central Anatolian Plateau, the route he chose took him through Kilikia, including the formidable Tauros Mountains pass known as the Kilikian Gates. As Xenophon had observed in his Anabasis, the Kilikian Gates could not be traversed if occupied even by a small defensive force. Arsamenes, in defense of his satrapy, stationed a more-than-adequate force in the pass, with instructions to hold it at all costs. With the remainder of his forces, he decided to implement Memnon's scorched earth policy with a vengeance. Instead of trusting in the ability of his troops to defend the Kilikian Gates, he proceeded to ravage the Kilikian countryside behind them, in order to deprive Alexandros of necessary supplies and spoils, in the event he somehow managed to get through the Gates. Arsamenes did such a thorough job that reports began to reach the defenders stationed in the Gates that there was nothing left for them to defend, because their homeland had already been despoiled by their own satrap. They melted away in the night, rushing back to aid their families and to salvage what they could of their possessions. Alexandros marched through the Gates unopposed.

Arsamenes, continuing to pillage his own people, retreated to his capital of Tarsos, intent on evacuating its inhabitants, removing all the treasure it contained, and then putting the city to the torch, before it could be occupied by Alexandros's forces. Alexandros, moving with his usual lightning speed, reached the city walls before Arsamenes had a chance to implement his plans. The satrap barely had enough time to run away and save his own skin. Alexandros entered the intact city, much to the relief of its citizens. Arsamenes ran all the way to Damaskos, where he was now recounting his military accomplishments to Dareios. Needless to say, Dareios was less than dazzled by his satrap's martial prowess.

Charidemos, who had not been blessed with a surfeit of tact, could not help but laugh at Arsamenes's report. "Your celestial eminence," he finally managed to spit out after catching his breath, "you must have competent commanders if you are to defeat this worm from the hinterlands of Macedonia. Give me an army and I will do the job. And forget this nonsense about invading Greece."

"What do you mean, nonsense?" Dareios interrupted. "That was Memnon's whole strategy."

"Well, Memnon is dead." Charidemos shrugged. "And besides, unless he could've somehow split himself in two, his strategy was never going to work anyway." Charidemos didn't need to spell out why he thought it necessary for Memnon to split himself in two. He was probably going to do it anyway but was stopped by the murderous look on Dareios's face. He quickly retreated. "I'm just saying, we should concentrate on defeating Alexandros right here and now. He is far from home, his communication lines are long and vulnerable, his army relatively small, and his supplies rapidly dwindling. If we hit him with a sufficiently large force, there's no way for him to survive. We'll wipe him out to the last man. It doesn't make sense to split our forces in two. After we wipe him out, there'll be plenty of time to turn our attention to Greece."

It didn't matter that Charidemos's advice was sound. Because it came from an obnoxious Greek mercenary, delivered in broken Persian, the satraps in attendance immediately fell into a competition to see who could disagree with him more vehemently. And because they were all shouting over one another simultaneously, it was impossible to tell what exactly they were proposing as an alternative but the negative tenor of their comments was fairly obvious nonetheless.

Finally, Dareios raised his hand to silence them. "I think he's right." His voice was quiet, once the hubbub had subsided. "How many troops do you think we'd need to be sure of victory?"

"A hundred thousand should do it, your incandescent brightness." Charidemos paused. "Provided at least a third of them are Greek mercenaries."

"I'm sick and tired of hearing about Greek mercenaries," Arsamenes yelled. "I didn't see them perform particularly well during the Battle at Granikos."

"That's because you ran away before the battle was joined," Charidemos sneered.

Had their weapons not been confiscated prior to their admittance into the audience hall, the argument could have easily escalated to bloodshed. As it was, Dareios merely nodded his head and the two men were forcibly separated by his guards.

"Field an army of a hundred thousand men shouldn't be a problem," Dareios said. "And I have the right commander in mind to lead them."

"Who?" several voices cried out.

The emperor peered intently at the commanders arrayed below him. "I am personally going to lead my army into battle." This time, there was stunned silence. "You forget I was a soldier once, before becoming the king of kings."

"You were the greatest commander Persia has seen since the death of the great King Kyros," Orontobates hurriedly interjected.

"Still am, son. I'm still alive, you know."

"You were, still are, and always will be the greatest ever, your highness," Nabarzanes put in.

Mazaios, relying on his seniority and standing with the emperor, finally brought a touch of pragmatism to the discussion. "We are all in agreement, sire, that you were and continue to be a great military leader. But that's just the point, sire. You are indispensable to this great empire. Why should you risk your life trying to swat down this little mosquito? We in this room are more than capable of getting the job done, while you continue to supervise the war effort, and the rest of the empire, from your throne right here in Damaskos, or Babylon, or

Persepolis, or Susa, or wherever your court may happen to be."

Charidemos couldn't hide his smile.

Pharnabazos noticed. "What are you laughing at, you foreign son of a whore?"

"I'm not laughing," Charidemos said. "I'm just envisioning our great victory." And then, remembering that Pharnabazos's mother was from Rhodos, he added in Greek, "You're half-Greek yourself, so you should know better. And the only son of a whore in this room is the guy sitting on the throne. If he's in command, we're all doomed." Charidemos was evidently unaware that the Persian emperor spoke fluent Greek.

Dareios rose from the throne, walked down the four steps to Charidemos, and physically lifted him off the ground by his girdle. "Kill him," he said calmly as he handed the hapless old soldier to his guards.

The guards dragged Charidemos out of the audience hall and, just beyond the front door, they ran him through, leaving him to bleed out into the dust. "If you lead this army against Alexandros, both you and your empire will die," Charidemos yelled on his way out.

****

Alexandros's growing fame as a military leader was exceeded only by his reputation for insatiable curiosity. Whenever he entered a new city or town, whether by accident, invitation, or conquest, he was met by hordes of touts, tour guides, and purveyors of ancient relics, natural wonders, and old wives' tales. There was no ostensibly historical site he would fail to tour, freak of fauna or flora he would not collect and ship back to Aristoteles, religious ceremony he would not grace with his presence and largess, bogus souvenir he would not buy, or hoary local shaman he would not hear out.

His arrival in Gordion was met by jubilation, due in equal parts to the joy of the Phrygians at the overthrow of their hated Persian overlords and their anticipation of the profits to be made from the influx of well-heeled, gullible visitors. Phrygians were an ancient Indo-European people, whose arrival in Anatolia (allegedly from Macedonia) has been lost in the mists of time. At one time, the Phrygians controlled almost half of Anatolia, from the Propontis (the small inland sea that connects the Aegean to the Black Sea) all the way to the southeastern edge of the central Anatolian Plateau. Then they made the mistake of allying themselves with the Trojans during the war against the Mycenaeans. After that came repeated assaults by Assyrians, Kimmerians, Amazons, Lydians, and finally Persians. The territory of the Phrygians shrank; a portion of Phrygia along the Propontis was split off and became known as Hellespontine Phrygia, with its capital at Daskyleion; and

Flood Tide

Phrygia proper, with its capital at Gordion, became a landlocked Persian satrapy in the middle of the Anatolian Plateau.

There was an interesting story told in Alexandros's time about the founding of Phrygia's capital, Gordion. According to legend, a long, long time ago, centuries before the Trojan War, a poor peasant named Gordias was minding his own business, driving his oxcart to market, when he happened to come across a convocation held in the precinct of a nearby temple in order to choose, with the aid of the gods, a successor to the recently deceased Phrygian king. After much debate, many sacrifices, several unsuccessful ballots, and near anarchy among the voters, none of the candidates was able to garner the mandate of the people. In desperation, the gods were consulted once again, and they advised the assembled Phrygians to elect as king the first man to ride up to the temple. That man happened to be Gordias.

Gordias turned out to be an able ruler. He founded Gordion as the new capital of Phrygia, married a minor Phrygian goddess named Kybele, and had a son named Midas, who expressed an ill-considered wish to have everything he touched turn to gold. But Midas's legendary, avaricious miscalculation occurred after his father was dead. Gordias, the humble peasant who became king, never forgot the source of his fortune and made arrangements to have the oxcart that had borne him to his kingship preserved for posterity. Needless to say,

Alexandros was told the story shortly after his arrival in Gordion and expressed an understandable desire to see the ancient conveyance for himself.

Before Alexandros could climb up to the Gordion akropolis, where the storied cart was housed, however, he had to deal with a number of administrative matters, among which was the arrival in Gordion of my cavalry squadron and mercenary contingent, after our successful mop-up operations at Halikarnassos.

"So where is the head?" Alexandros asked in lieu of a greeting when I showed up, empty-handed, at his headquarters in Gordion. We both knew whose head he was referring to.

"We didn't find Memnon's body, sire." I resisted the temptation to shrug, keeping both my shoulders and my voice level. "We did manage, however, to take the Halikarnassos Akropolis, the Salmakis Fortress, and the King's Castle in a few short months and with a minimum of casualties. But Memnon apparently got away once again."

Alexandros glared. "The man must be a ghost." He seemed genuinely angry.

"I'm sorry, sire. We'll get him next time."

"Oh no, you won't." Alexandros paused for dramatic effect. "Luckily for you, Metoikos, remorseless

Thanatos is a far more persistent hunter than you are. He always gets his man, sooner or later."

I had no idea what he was talking about and my blank look gave me away.

Alexandros was clearly enjoying my confusion. "And in this case, my friend, Thanatos finally caught up to Memnon."

"You mean, he's dead?" I asked uncertainly.

"That's exactly what I mean." He burst out laughing. "You did well, Ptolemaios." He clapped me on the shoulder. "And we don't need to worry about that bastard any more. I hear some kind of plague killed him."

Alexandros wanted to hear every detail of our operations at Halikarnassos and of our trip to Gordion. We were still engrossed in our discussion when a messenger walked in with a dispatch from Parmenion. Alexandros read it twice and shook his head. "That's the second similar message from Parmenion in two weeks." He handed the scroll to me.

I read the note. "What was the first one?"

Alexandros smiled. "That's a long story. Let's have something to eat and I'll give you all the details."

It was a small dinner party. Most of the command staff were still in the field, either with Parmenion's force or with various other detachments, but Hephaistion joined us, as did Kallisthenes, presumably to record any deathless declarations that might be delivered during our usual descent into drunkenness.

"So, that note from Parmenion I was talking about," Alexandros resumed after we had finished eating. "We had just entered Tarsos, on the heels of Arsamenes's precipitous withdrawal."

"The populace was overjoyed," Hephaistion chimed in.

"Well, that's subject to debate. Those guys on the riverbank may have been feigning their joy."

"What Aniketos is referring to," Hephaistion explained for my benefit, "is a welcoming committee of local dignitaries, who met us on the banks of the Kydnos, which flows through Tarsos. After the usual courtesies and thanksgiving ceremonies, one of the locals mentioned it was lucky we had arrived before the retreating Persians had had a chance to destroy the bridge because no one could have crossed the raging river, swollen by the springtime snowmelt in the surrounding Tauros Mountains."

"One thing led to another," Alexandros picked up the story, "and before I knew it, I'd made a wager with the locals that I could swim across the river."

"Even though he was exhausted and already had a cold," Hephaistion interjected. "It didn't go well."

"No, it didn't. Man, when they said it was ice cold, they weren't kidding. As soon as I hit the water, my whole body cramped up. I tell you, there wasn't a muscle I could move."

"He would've drowned for sure," Hephaistion agreed, "if one of the locals hadn't pulled a rope from somewhere and fished him out."

"It wasn't fun, I'll grant you that."

"By the time we had him on the shore, he was barely breathing, shivering uncontrollably, and white as Poseidon's hair. When we finally managed to rub a little life back into him and get him dressed again, he started to cough. We got him to a house, put him in bed, and covered him in animal pelts but he kept shivering uncontrollably. His skin became hot to the touch. We tried to feed him; he couldn't keep anything down. He was sweating profusely, gasping for breath, babbling nonsense."

Hephaistion shook his head, still unnerved by the recollection. "This kept up for two weeks; can you imagine that? The local doctors refused to treat him, afraid he was going to die, in which case we would've killed them for sure."

"You wouldn't have done that, would you?" Alexandros teased.

"Sure would've," Hephaistion affirmed mirthlessly. "The trouble was that Philippos of Akarnania was with Parmenion at this point and it took us two weeks to get him back. By the time he arrived, we were beginning to lose hope."

"Actually, I think I was getting better by then."

"Easy for you to say now. It didn't look that way at the time. Anyway, Philippos the Physician arrived, accompanied by a small cavalry troop. He took one look and started to mix some sort of purge. While he was busy doing that, one of the troopers handed a message from Parmenion to Aniketos."

"See, I was well enough to read it."

"Yes, you read it but said nothing. Instead, when Philippos handed his potion to you, you handed Parmenion's note to him."

Alexandros smiled at the memory.

"You were draining the cup while Philippos was reading the note. I'll never forget the looks on your faces."

"What did the note say?" I interrupted.

"In the note," Alexandros explained, "Parmenion told me that Philippos had been bribed by Dareios to poison me."

Hephaistion picked up the story. "As Philippos read the note, all color drained from his face. As Aniketos drank the purge, his face turned greenish white."

"It was the foulest concoction I'd ever tasted."

"When Philippos looked up from the note and saw the king drinking the potion, his look of consternation gradually melted into relief and then a tight smile, accompanied by a small nod. When Aniketos finished drinking, he looked up, a disgusted grimace contorting his face."

"Hey, give me a break. I was doing my best not to throw up."

"Anyway, I grabbed the note and read it. By the time I looked back, Aniketos was violently ill, retching and moaning and basically unconscious. I was sure the good doctor had killed our king."

"Fortunately, the purge worked, and I was much better by the next day, thus saving Philippos's life," Alexandros finished cheerfully. "That was Parmenion's first note."

"What do you mean 'first note'?" Hephaistion asked. "Has there been a second one?"

Alexandros handed him the scroll that had arrived while I was in the middle of my debriefing. It described in detail a conspiracy between Emperor Dareios and Alexandros of Lynkestis. Lynkestis, who was the last remaining member of that canton's royal house, was perhaps ten years older than Alexandros Aniketos. The two Alexandroi had had a complicated history. The future King Alexandros first met Alexandros of Lynkestis when they were both commanders in King Philippos's Companion Cavalry. After King Philippos's assassination, rumors surfaced that the House of Lynkestis had been involved in the assassination and was plotting to put a rival pretender on the Macedonian throne. These rumors, which bordered on the fantastic, were undoubtedly false. There were also other rumors, according to which the assassination had been incited and condoned by Philippos's wife Olympias because of her jealousy of Philippos's new and much younger wife and because of her concern that the newly-born son of the happy, half-young couple might one day displace her own son Alexandros as the heir apparent. These latter rumors were plausible and most likely true. In fact, perspicacious observers of the royal scene believed the rumors about the House of Lynkestis were invented and spread by Olympias herself precisely in order to deflect suspicion about her own involvement in Philippos's assassination.

Flood Tide

In the immediate chaos following the assassination of Philippos, the twenty-year-old Alexandros, who was somewhat insecure in his position and easily influenced by his mother, took the rumors about the House of Lynkestis to heart. The head of the House of Lynkestis, a former general named Aeropos, had been banished by King Philippos and had died in exile. His three sons, however, including the youngest, Alexandros, were still in Macedonia and very much alive. The newly acclaimed King Alexandros had the two older brothers arrested and executed, based on false confessions extracted under torture. On the other hand, he retained the youngest brother, Alexandros, in his position as a commander in the Companion Cavalry and, after the Battle of Granikos, promoted him to commander of the entire allied cavalry. (Two possible explanations for this disparate treatment were advanced by informed court observers. One was the fact that, immediately after the assassination, Alexandros of Lynkestis was the first man to publicly hail Prince Alexandros as the new king. The other was the fact that Alexandros of Lynkestis was the son-in-law of Antipatros, the senior advisor of both Philippos and, subsequently, Alexandros. Of course, these two explanations were not mutually exclusive.)

After the sack of Halikarnassos, when Alexandros was making his dispositions for the winter, he ordered Parmenion to take the allied cavalry, under Lynkestis's command, along with the allied infantry and most of the

Macedonian Silver Shields, and conduct a campaign to consolidate the army's gains in Ionia, Lydia, Hellespontine Phrygia, and central Anatolia. Therefore, Lynkestis was technically serving under Parmenion, who was not overly fond of the arrangement. He preferred to place his own relatives and admirers in as many subordinate command positions as possible.

In his note, which Hephaistion also had to read twice, Parmenion spun quite a tale. One of his foraging parties, Parmenion wrote, had captured a Persian spy named Sisines. Upon interrogation, this spy confessed that he had been sent by Emperor Dareios with a message for Alexandros of Lynkestis. The message, which was not written down because of its sensitive nature, was allegedly Dareios's response to a prior offer by Lynkestis to assassinate King Alexandros in return for Dareios's support of Lynkestis as Alexandros's successor. According to Sisines, he had been instructed to tell Lynkestis that Dareios wholeheartedly supported Lynkestis's plan, that he would pay Lynkestis a thousand talents of gold upon the successful execution of the assassination attempt, and that the Persian Empire would do everything in its power to support Lynkestis's claim to the Macedonian throne, provided Lynkestis agreed to remove the pan-Hellenic army from Persian soil immediately after the assassination. Fortunately, Parmenion added, Sisines was never able to deliver the message to Lynkestis. Unfortunately, Sisines also succumbed, shortly after making his confession, to injuries sustained during his capture and was therefore no longer available to corroborate Parmenion's note.

"What do you think?" Alexandros asked Hephaistion when he had finished reading.

"I think you should dispatch a squadron immediately to find Lynkestis and kill the bastard on sight. Metoikos here can be in command."

Alexandros leaned his head to the side and shot Hephaistion a skeptical look. "But Parmenion was wrong about Philippos the Physician, wasn't he? Maybe he's wrong about Lynkestis."

"Doesn't matter." Hephaistion was firm and unflinching in his response. "You can't take a chance. If he is guilty, he has to be eliminated, swiftly and covertly. If he is innocent, we'll manage to conduct the war without him."

"I'm not a murderer," I said quietly. Both Alexandros and Hephaistion ignored me.

"I'm not going to kill somebody on the say-so of one man," Alexandros finally decided. "I'll send a note back to Parmenion to take Lynkestis into custody and to keep an eye on him. We'll then investigate and, if necessary, have a trial. But we're not killing anybody based on this note."

Hephaistion stood up, ready to walk out. "Don't bother putting anything about this in your history," he told Kallisthenes on his way out.

Alexandros countermanded him. "No, go ahead and write down everything you heard. Just don't bother showing it to anybody until we find out how it all turns out."

And with that the meal was over.

****

Olympias arrived early for the symposion, carrying a covered wicker basket. She was dressed in a bright red peplos and matching red sandals, her décolletage decorated with a large, live water snake draped around her neck. She had just turned forty-four. The serving women preparing the dining room for the evening festivities were used to her eccentric ways and took no notice of her.

The dining hall was a spacious, rectangular room, with one entryway and no windows, a slate floor, with a black and white geometric mosaic in the center, and whitewashed walls, spruced up by colorful, fairly primitive murals, featuring still lifes of comestibles. Aside from the natural light streaming in through the entryway, a modicum of light was provided by oil lamps placed on small shelves built into the corners. In the evening, additional lighting could be provided by torches placed into sconces on the walls. There were seven couches arranged in a U-shape around the sides of the room, with three couches against each side wall and one larger couch against the narrower wall opposite the entrance. An upright chair had been placed, specifically for Olympias's use, in the far left corner of the room. A number of small tables were scattered in the middle, as well as a large, empty krater for mixing wine.

Olympias placed the basket underneath the larger couch at the far end of the room. She then tied a string to the lid that covered the basket and secured the other end of the string under the cushion that had been placed on her chair. "Don't you dare touch that basket!" she yelled to the staff in the room and walked back out. Given Olympias's reputation at court, there was very little risk anyone would disobey her order.

Olympias was born a princess, the daughter of the king of Epiros. She enjoyed a pampered, sheltered childhood, raised by nannies who filled her head with tales of romance, mysticism, and royalty. When she was sixteen, and already arrestingly alluring, she convinced her father to let her travel to Samothrake, a small, ruggedly beautiful island off the coast of Thrake in the northern Aegean. The island was home to one of the oldest, most important religious sanctuaries in the entire Hellenic world, known as the Sanctuary of the Great Gods. Pilgrims from all strata of Greek society, from humble peasants to famous intellectuals to powerful rulers, made the long, perilous journey for the once-in-a-lifetime experience of attending the annual mid-summer festival, participating in various rituals and ceremonies, making offerings, and being initiated into the chthonian mysteries. While on the island, Olympias met a twenty-one-year-old Macedonian prince named Philippos. It was love at first sight. They spent their entire time together, visiting the sites, attending the plays, walking the trails, and undergoing the initiation rituals, which she took seriously and he did not. Philippos also initiated Olympias into the mysteries of carnal intimacy. Upon parting for their journeys back to their respective kingdoms, Olympias had little hope of ever seeing the bright, energetic, handsome young prince again.

Philippos unexpectedly became the ruler of Macedonia two years later. He had not forgotten Olympias but when it came to royal marriages, kings wed for reasons of military necessity or national advantage, not romantic attachment. As it happened, Philippos was a great believer in cementing diplomatic alliances by means of conjugal concords. Two years after becoming king, Philippos – having already contracted three other marriages – perceived an opening for securing the western border of Macedonia and cementing a useful military alliance by marrying the younger niece of the then king of Epiros. The woman in question happened to be Olympias. (Olympias's father had died in the meantime and his younger brother had become king.) They were married when Philippos was twenty-five and Olympias twenty. Their first child, Alexandros, was born a year later.

It may have been that their marriage was a love match but the romance didn't survive beyond the honeymoon. Instead, it evolved into a more complex relationship. They were both brilliant, strong-willed, driven, ambitious, and ruthless individuals. Philippos was more gregarious, direct, powerful, tactically astute, and strategically farsighted. Olympias was more devious, conniving, conspiratorial, and deadly. She was also genuinely superstitious and pious, while he simply used religion as another tool to achieve his goals. Philippos was libidinous and indiscriminate in the pursuit of his pleasures. Olympias was willing to overlook his roving eye, as long as his dalliances, liaisons, and even future marriages didn't affect her power and standing at the court and didn't threaten the position of her son as Philippos's presumptive heir. They argued, fought, made love, plotted, inspired, helped, and pushed each other. They made an incredibly effective team.

Philippos was forty-two when he committed his fatal blunder. After a fight with Olympias, he decided to take, as his seventh (and, as it would turn out, final) wife the seventeen-year-old daughter of one of the leading aristocrats at the Macedonian court. She a year younger than their son Alexandros and a year older than their daughter Kleopatra. She even shared the name of their daughter. (To distinguish the two girls, the daughter of Philippos and Olympias was called Little Kleopatra while Philippos's new bride was known as Luscious.)

Luscious Kleopatra delivered to Philippos a daughter and a son in quick succession. Olympias's concern at the prospect of the infant boy displacing her son as Philippos's successor, farfetched as such a concern might have been, unhinged the former queen. When the dust settled, Philippos, Luscious Kleopatra, and their two infant children were all dead; Olympias's son Alexandros was king; and Olympias was the queen mother.

Not long after Olympias walked out of the dining hall, having left her basket behind, other guests began arriving for the banquet, walking in by twos and threes. It was going to be a small gathering, limited to Antipatros's immediate military advisors, invited to hear the report of Koinos and Kleandros on the progress of the Anatolian expedition and to discuss a response to Alexandros's demand for reinforcements. Olympias was included because it was impossible to keep her out.

Antipatros arrived, engrossed in an animated discussion with two of his most promising young aides, Krateros and Lysimachos, and took his seat on the larger couch at the far end of the room. He had a welcoming jest or personal inquiry for all the attendees. Olympias was the penultimate guest to arrive. She was greeted with wary courtesy by the men in the room, except for Antipatros, who ignored her altogether, pretending to be engaged in a deep discussion with Koinos. She took her seat on the chair in the corner, making sure the string was still under the seat cushion. (Women generally didn't participate in banquets, except as servants or entertainers, and they certainly didn't recline on couches in the presence of men.)

Kassandros was late, as usual. The libation had been poured and the prayers completed by the time he deigned to make his entrance, carrying a small bundle in his hand. He took his seat on the larger couch, next to his father, smiling broadly, evidently pleased with the world. He also ignored the queen mother, seated on the chair to his right. He placed his small bundle on the couch behind his back.

Kassandros, at twenty-five, was the youngest man in the room. He was also the youngest of Antipatros's ten children – and the most spoiled one. By the time he was born, his father, who was forty at that point, had become one of the leading supporters of the newly-elevated King Philippos. He was often away from home on military or diplomatic missions for his king but each time he returned he brought back extraordinary, exotic gifts for his favorite little boy. During his absences, the little boy played with his expensive toys, abused the nannies charged with his upbringing, tortured and killed small animals, and ruled as an absolute despot in the household of his mother.

It was a great relief to all when the fifteen-year-old Kassandros was invited by King Philippos to join the coterie of young scions of Macedonian nobility who served as the fellow students, training partners, and playmates of a thirteen-year-old Alexandros at the royal finishing school established by Philippos for the benefit of his son at Mieza. By the time I arrived at the school, as exotic specimen and hand-to-hand combat instructor, Kassandros had already been given a nickname by his fellow students: He was known as the Frog Killer. The sobriquet managed to capture, with that remarkable insight, concision, and acerbity of which only children are capable, the two salient characteristics of young Kassandros: He liked to torment little animals and was deathly afraid of hunting the big ones. (He was thirty-five, and the murderer of several people, before he managed to bag his first boar in a hunt.)

When Alexandros departed for Asia, almost a year earlier, leaving Antipatros behind as regent, he expected the sly old general to rule Macedonia and to dominate the rest of Greece on his behalf. Unfortunately, in the haste of his departure, he neglected to make his dispositions clear to his mother. Or perhaps he had and Olympias was just constitutionally incapable of accepting his arrangements. Either way, she had spent the year interfering with Antipatros's efforts to govern Macedonia, undermining his authority at court, and fostering dissent among the people. In her free time, she sent countless missives to her son filled with strategic suggestions for the campaign in Anatolia, rumors of conspiracies against him among his commanders, and reports of treasonous malfeasance by Antipatros, his sons, and the other generals left behind in Pella. Antipatros bore her constant meddling with patience, if not good humor, reassured by his knowledge that the troops admired and respected him and despised her. He also realized that the one thing sure to set Alexandros off was any report that Olympias was not being treated with the respect due her by virtue of being his mother. Kassandros, on the other hand, lacked his father's tact, maturity, self-confidence, and acumen. A fierce struggle quickly developed between the son of the regent and the queen mother, which conflict they waged, face-to-face and through proxies, day after hate-filled day.

Once Kassandros had finally taken his seat, the banquet proceeded smoothly. The guests washed their hands. The serving girls brought in platter after platter of food and distributed it on the small tables placed in front of the couches, making sure everyone's wine cups were kept filled.

As Olympias picked at her food with her right hand, she surreptitiously fingered with her other hand the string running from beneath her chair cushion to the cover of the basket stationed under the sprawling figure of Kassandros. Her patience, never a strong suit, was being severely tested. She could hardly wait to release her venomous viper. She had been assured by her principal snake wrangler that a bite of this species brought on inexorable, albeit lingering and painful, death but she had to wait until Antipatros left the couch. It would have been unfortunate if the snake bit the regent, rather than his hateful son.

The serving girls cleared the plates, brought in more bread so guests could clean their fingers once again, placed sweet cakes and fruit on the tables, and topped off the wine cups. Koinos gave a detailed report on the status of the war in Anatolia, ending with Alexandros's request for more troops. Krateros reviewed the available manpower in Macedonia and the possibility of recruiting additional warriors from the adjoining kingdoms of Epiros and Thessaly, from the friendly barbarian tribes to the north and east, and most importantly from the allied cities of the Hellenic League. A lively debate ensued about the merits of each group of fighters.

When Antipatros finally joined the discussion, he was pragmatic and trenchant. "The so-called allies will soon be our enemies. The Persians are occupying island after island, hopscotching their way toward the Greek mainland. Our allies aren't oblivious to the developments in the Aegean and they're getting understandably nervous. At the same time, Dareios's agents are busy siphoning off their men of military age, promising them money and adventure as mercenaries, while other agents are bribing their leading politicians, fomenting rebellion. And then there is Sparta and its Peloponnesian allies. They've never become members of the Hellenic League and they're itching to take us on, while most of our troops are in Asia. And trust me, my friends, if our so-called allies in the Hellenic League ever get the idea we're beatable, they'll immediately switch sides to Sparta. I hate to tell you this but we're not universally beloved by our allies, who resent our preeminence in Greece. They've all forgotten what life was like when Sparta enjoyed a brief period of ascendancy. So, we have no troops to spare. And the sooner our king manages to wrap up his adventure on the other side of the Hellespont and bring our troops back home, the better off we will be. In the meantime, we need to cut off his lifeline of troops and materiel from here to there."

Kleandros tried to explain the benefits Macedonia would realize as a result of the liberation of the Greek cities of Ionia and as the result of being accepted as the leaders of the entire Greek world. "Just think about the profits Athens reaped from their Delian League during Perikles's time." Koinos mentioned the fact that King Alexandros had sent a direct, written order requesting more troops. The notion of Macedonian hegemony over the Greek world had some appeal to the commanders in the room but in the final analysis they were practical men and the regent's warnings about a coming rebellion against Macedonia carried a great deal of weight with them.

Olympias was uncharacteristically silent, wishing devoutly that Antipatros would get up and leave the room and therefore reluctant to say anything that might launch him into another oration. Kassandros, in the meantime, was also quiet, busy unwrapping the little bundle behind his back and palpating its contents. It was a mouth-watering mound of sweetmeats, just like the ones the serving girls were putting out on the tables, except that this one was infused with a deadly toxin, purchased at great expense from an itinerant Persian poisoner. He was waiting for Olympias to be distracted, perhaps by getting into a fight with his father, before pulling his special treat out from behind his back and slipping it onto the dessert plate in front of her.

The serving girls cleaned up some of the scraps from the floor and then withdrew, making room for the dancers with their tambourines, a flutist, and a lithe contortionist. All the performers were young women, wearing nothing more than sheer chitons and enticing smiles. While the dancers jiggled and sang and shook their little drums, the acrobat stood on her hands, causing her chiton to flutter down to her armpits, bent her back and legs until her toes were almost touching the floor behind her head, and then twirled on her hands, making sure that all the guests were afforded an ample view of her charms. The discussion faltered, as most of the men watched entranced, some forgetting to breathe, others beginning to pant.

Periodically, the performers would take a little break, while the serving girls would make sure no one was running short of wine. Small eddies of conversation sprang up once again on the couches, while the entertainment continued in the middle of the room. Every now and then, one of the girls would venture too close to a couch and then giggle at the grabbing and fondling that would inevitably follow. Men would get up and leave, some alone, some accompanied by one of the girls. Eventually, they would all come back and resume their former places.

Finally, Antipatros got up to answer the call of nature, to Olympias's evident relief. She had no way of knowing whether the call had been sounded by his bladder or by some other part of his anatomy but he had staggered out alone and therefore she had to assume it was the former, giving her only a short window to act. She pulled on the string to release the snake. She wanted to watch the snake slither up and bite Kassandros's buttocks but she couldn't because every time she glanced in his direction, she caught him looking intently at her. Finally, unable to stand the tension, she got up and left the room.

As soon as she was out of sight, Kassandros, seizing his chance, reached behind his back to retrieve her dessert. Instead of the sticky dough, however, his fingers felt something cold, hard, and scaly. Whirling around, he found his hand resting on the snout of a dead snake, with the telltale bulge of the deadly treat lodged only a few inches behind its head. An involuntary yelp escaped his throat as he jumped off the couch. Olympias, having heard the outcry, rushed back into the room. They faced each other across the dining hall, staring, a sudden understanding striking both of them simultaneously. And at that moment Kassandros's face broke into a lopsided, malevolent grin. He clenched his left eye in a wink, pregnant with the promise of mayhem. Olympias smiled back, a bright, cocky smile, but one that stopped well short of her eyes, which remained cold as ice.

****

I'm not a murderer. The sentence, which I had said out loud to Alexandros and Hephaistion during their discussion of Alexandros of Lynkestis and which they had both ignored, continued to echo in my mind. I might not be a murderer – yet – but the notion of killing Aristandros had been silently growing in my mind, like a malignant brain tumor, below the level of conscious thought at first, then as an occasional daydream, and finally as an ever-present obsession.

I was strolling through the narrow lanes leading to the Gordion palaistra, lost in thought. Although we were all encamped in our usual tents outside the city walls, most of the officers made a point of exercising at the palaistra every day, followed by a bath and a visit to one of the public houses located nearby. Since my arrival, I had wrestled and bathed daily as well but had yet to avail myself of the food, wine, and serving wenches on offer.

Flood Tide

Gordion was an ancient city, at least a thousand years old. Alas, its streets and alleyways gave no evidence of cleaning, much less reconstruction or repair, in all that time. Unless you were a native, getting from one corner to the next required constant vigilance, agile path selection, and exceptional balance and dexterity. To begin with, sewage flowed freely down the center of every street, with unexpected bends, loops, and windings to keep the traveler on his toes. As I leapt from one patch of terra firma to the next, I also had to avoid all the beasts of burden, carts, and pedestrians coming the other way; I had to be careful not to land in freshly deposited dung; I had to dodge drenching deluges of household offal being dispensed with careless abandon from above; and I had to devise a route that would eventually get me where I wanted to go. Trying to get to the palaistra whilst lost in thought was probably a mistake.

A pair of existential enigmas preoccupied my mind. On the one hand, I had to decide, once and for all, how best to defend against the threat posed by Aristandros. And, on the other hand, assuming elimination of the threat was the right response, I still had to figure out the most effective means of accomplishing that goal.

I was on the verge of resolving the first of those puzzles when a devious ditch snuck, unobserved and unexpected, under my foot. *Oh, crap!* was my first reaction as I extracted myself from the thick, smelly mélange. As usual, my first reaction was right on the nose. The rest of the way to the palaistra my thoughtful analysis was accompanied, with metronomic regularity, by the slushy sound of my soaked left sandal hitting packed dirt and by the pungent odor released with each energetic stride. To make matters worse, I was walking in circles.

There were no two ways about it – I had to kill Aristandros. He was clearly trying to kill me. Short of talking him out of his inexplicable enmity, which happy outcome didn't seem to be in the cards, my only choices were either to run away or make him disappear. Neither one of us was leaving voluntarily, that was for sure. One of us would have to be taken out.

I rehearsed my mantra: *Stay alive; comply with the Prime Directive; get back home.* How many times had I wrestled with this issue? And yet, it was somehow different this time. Finally, I was ready to do more than simply ruminate. The time had come for me to act.

I marched ahead more resolutely than ever, only to realize I was about to step into the exact same disgusting puddle that had claimed my left foot the last time around. The good news was that I had managed to stay my stride in the nick of time. The bad news was the irrefutable confirmation that I had lost my way.

Undaunted, I forged ahead. *How exactly am I going to kill him?* It had to be swift, clean, sure, and unattributable. (Interestingly, not once did I worry that the famous seer would somehow foresee what I was planning to do to him. Some things are just not worth considering.)

The obvious answer was to wait until our next battle, seek Aristandros out, and inflict a fatal, combat-related injury. After all, men died in battle all the time, sometimes even at the hands of their comrades. Mistakes happened, especially in the heat of struggle. The only problem with this approach was that I had never seen Aristandros anywhere near combat. Among the many uncanny attributes of his clairvoyance was an unerring ability to disappear from sight the moment there was the slightest hint of danger.

I tried out many lethal scenarios in my mind and rejected each one. My left shoe was almost dry, albeit still quite smelly, and I was pretty sure I had finally found my way to the palaistra, and still, no viable means of putting an end to the slimy soothsayer's viability came to me.

"You look a little peaked, my friend."

I looked up to see Kleitos's smiling face. "I'm having some trouble finding the palaistra today."

He clapped me on the back in his usual enthusiastic fashion, almost knocking me into the path of a heavily laden donkey. "Well, today is your lucky day, Ptolemaios. I'll take you. Fancy a little wrestling match when we get there?"

I laughed. "You've got no chance, Kleitos. How many times have I pinned you?"

"There's always a first time. And you don't seem yourself today. What's bothering you?"

"Nothing, really. Just lost in thought."

"Oh, c'mon. I know you better than that."

Eventually I confessed. "I've been thinking about Aristandros. He's been predicting mayhem and misfortune for both of us."

"Don't give it a second thought. He's full of shit."

I stopped dead in my tracks. "That's it!"

"What, what? What did I say?"

"Never mind, my friend. You've given me an idea." Suddenly, I was skipping over the puddles. "And, just to be clear, you've got no chance."

We wrestled, and bathed, and drank together. I let him win at drinking but neither of us was really keeping track.

****

Waiting for the insidious diviner to walk in was getting tedious. It would have been nice if I'd been able to predict the slimy soothsayer's arrival time but only he had that knack. So, patience became a necessary ingredient of my plan. A strong stomach proved to be a requirement as well.

The latrine at the palaistra, unlike the rudimentary affair at our camp, required a long walk through shadowy passageways, followed by dressing alcoves and enclosed individual stalls. It turned out that Aristandros had become a habitué of the palaistra during our stay in Gordion. *All I've got to do is surprise him the next time nature calls, cut his throat, and let him fall into the trench below with all the other waste.*

It was a perfect plan, at least in my own mind. The ancient walls of the latrine were rough, damp, and rancid but they were also sound-proof. Numerous dark corners provided convenient hiding places for a would-be assassin. Individual stalls afforded ample privacy for the terminal act itself. The overpowering stench would nicely mask the smell of a decomposing body. And finally, it was clear to me that no one had looked into the offensive trench deep beneath the sitting plank that ran the length of the stalls in ages, much less actually cleaned it. I would be safely ensconced in my own era long before anyone thought of flushing out the trench.

Someone entered the building. His footsteps were light and swift. *Doesn't sound like Aristandros, unless he's in a real hurry.* Instead of hiding, I decided to start walking out of the latrine, acting as if I'd just finished my business.

It turned out to be Philotas coming in. He gave me a curt nod and a curious grin. "Must've have been a tough turd."

I raised an eyebrow, taken aback. "What do you mean?"

He pointed to the dagger in my hand. "Had to cut it off, eh?" He sniggered.

Somehow, I'd forgotten the weapon clenched in my fist. I shrugged, felt my face turn red, and kept walking. Once outside the building, I hid the dagger beneath my tunic and turned toward the exercise arena, taking an intense interest in some wrestlers practicing their moves. I knew Aristandros was on the premises and I really didn't want him to see me.

After an interminable wait, Philotas finally came out. However, before I could go back in, a pair of men I didn't know decided to utilize the facilities. *This will not do. I can't be seen loitering outside the latrine all day long.* Once the coast was clear, I entered again, resolved to stay hidden inside the foul-smelling building for as long as it took.

At some point, I fell asleep, sitting in one of the alcoves. I was awakened by a familiar footfall. I recognized it instantly. *Aristandros!*

Flood Tide

I crept out of my hiding place, holding the dagger at the ready. The steps were getting fainter. *He's on his way out.* I ran after him. He reached the exit before I caught up. I stopped in the corridor, letting my daggered hand fall against my side and my chin sink against my chest.

Well, at least he never noticed that death was at hand while he shat. So much for his clairvoyance. Somehow, I didn't find much solace in the thought. I resolved to kill him next chance I got. But this time I would keep it clean and odor-free.

****

Koinos and Kleandros parted company as soon as the winter snows began to melt. Kleandros set off for the Peloponnese to continue recruiting, while his brother prepared for the return trip to Asia. Koinos and the "newlyweds" made it back to Gordion shortly after the vernal equinox. They brought reinforcements as well: Three thousand Macedonian infantrymen, including two battalions brought over by Krateros and Lysimachos, five hundred cavalry, and a few hundred recruits from the rest of Greece. Notwithstanding Antipatros's opposition, Alexandros's reputation for martial prowess and generous bonuses proved irresistible to many unemployed young men, especially Macedonians, who were anxious not to miss out on whatever looting opportunities might still remain. However, Koinos also brought to Alexandros a rather stark message from his regent back in the home country: Unless the expeditionary force returned to Macedonia before the fall, there would be a rebellion in Greece, led by Sparta, which the forces remaining under Antipatros's control might not be able to resist.

Alexandros summoned a meeting of the general staff and read Antipatros's message to us. "I guess that means we have six months left to consolidate our gains, secure the Greek cities of Ionia so they never revert to Persian rule again, and then make our way back home."

"We'll be vulnerable to the Persian navy during our crossing back," Parmenion observed, "now that we have no navy of our own. At least not one capable of opposing the Persian fleet."

Alexandros glared at him. "Well, they won't know we're crossing until we're on the other side, will they? Unless somebody here decides to tell them," he added ominously.

Parmenion ignored the king's last remark. "There is another issue, sire. The cities of Ionia will have a tough time defending themselves against maritime assaults if the Persians control the Aegean Sea."

"Don't worry about that, old man. We'll rebuild our navy over time, making sure it's more reliable than the last one. And until then, the Ionians will just have to fend for themselves. We'll leave a garrison in each city to help them out and maybe we'll put you in overall command of the maritime provinces once again."

"I am at your service, sire, as always."

Alexandros nodded. "There's just one more thing I'd like to accomplish before going back."

Hephaistion perked up, right on cue. "What's that, Aniketos?"

"I'd like to beat the Persian army one more time, so they'll think long and hard before venturing this way again."

"Dareios would be crazy to take us on in a set piece battle, when he can simply wait us out," Parmenion said. "Plus, he's doing a fine job hitting our vulnerable flank by shifting the war to the Greek mainland. Why would he risk a battle here?"

"Because he is a king!" Alexandros was astonished at his deputy's obtuseness. "He won't sit still while we ravage his provinces. And he may never get them back, even if we leave. Not just Ionia, but Phrygia, Karia, and all the rest. It's not like these people enjoyed being Persian vassals. Once they get a taste of freedom, they'll fight like sons of Ares to keep it."

Seleukos quietly joined the discussion. "I think he'll attack," he agreed. "His commanders, or his courtiers, will kill him if they detect any weakness. And letting us rampage inside his empire, even for a short time, would be perceived as a sign of weakness."

"Alright then, there you have it." Alexandros clapped Seleukos on the back. "Let's get ready for a fight. We'll meet again tonight to make some specific plans. In the meantime, I have something else to attend to."

One more local attraction remained that Alexandros absolutely had to visit before leaving town. For some reason he chose me to keep him company. We climbed up, along with a couple of bodyguards and half a dozen tour guides, to the Gordion akropolis to take a look at the fabled founder's oxcart. If the accounts of the guides were accurate, this relic was close to a thousand years old. But what was truly remarkable was the large knot of cornel-bark strips that fastened the yoke to the pole of the cart. Although the bark had lost its elasticity over the years, I still found it difficult to believe it could have survived at all for a millennium.

There was a legend associated with this knot, the guards told us. Evidently old Gordias wanted to make sure no one unhitched his oxen while he was not looking, so he was careful to tuck in the ends of all the ribbons making up the complex knot, leaving no tips exposed. He did such a good job that no one was able to untie the knot afterward. The passage of time, which turned the bark rock hard, eventually made the task impossible.

Once that happened, some enterprising and imaginative local promoter invented the story that whoever managed to loosen the knot would become lord of Asia.[17] Many tourists came to try their luck and none succeeded.

Needless to say, Alexandros, when he heard the old legend, was intrigued. "This is even better than one of Aristandros's predictions," he told me. He then spent a good hour tugging and pulling at the petrified bark, making no progress whatsoever. Finally, in frustration, he whipped out his sword and, before the astonished guides could intervene, he sliced right through the knot. At first, there was a flabbergasted silence but then our bodyguards started to whoop and holler. "He did it! He did it!" they yelled.

Alexandros was delighted. "I'm going to be the lord of Asia," he told everyone present. The tour guides congratulated him absent-mindedly, busy composing in their minds the next legend they could tell future visitors about the time a Macedonian king came to their obscure

---

[17] The geographic term "Asia" had a somewhat variable meaning back then. To the Greeks, whose knowledge of Asia came principally from Herodotos, it covered a hazy expanse of land stretching eastward from the Aegean Sea but how far it extended, nobody knew. When Alexandros first crossed the Hellespont "to conquer Asia," what he really meant was conquering the maritime provinces of Anatolia and, in his heart of hearts, he would have been pleased simply to gain control of the Troad and Ionia.

little provincial capital and sliced right through a thousand-year-old cornel-bark knot.

"I'm going to be the lord of Asia," Alexandros repeated to me as we made our way back down the hill.

In response, I did my best impersonation of Hephaistion. "You already are, sire. You just have to consolidate your hold on this land before returning to Macedonia."

Alexandros shook his head. "I can't get it done in six months. We'll be lucky if I can get Dareios to attack us before the fall and even if he does, and we beat him, it will still take years before we can get firm control of these provinces. The truth is, most of them don't want to be part of the Hellenic League any more than they wanted to be part of the Persian Empire."

Since I happened to agree with the king's sentiments, I maintained a discreet silence. I was surprised, however, at the bluntness of his assessment.

Alexandros, as if reading my thoughts, resumed. "You're different from my other commanders, Metoikos. I can be more direct with you."

"Thank you, sire."

He laughed. "It's not a compliment. Sometimes I think you're too independent in your thinking. But I know you won't run off blabbing to the others, because you're an outsider to all of them."

I drew back, feigning offense. "I've been here almost ten years, sire."

"I'm not sure ten generations would be enough. But don't worry about it. Let me ask you instead: What do you think I should do? It sounds like Antipatros is in trouble. My first responsibility is to Macedon. But if I leave, we'll quickly lose everything we've achieved here."

"True," I agreed.

"And now I've been told I'll be lord of Asia. I can't be lord of Asia if I'm sitting in Pella."

I nodded. "It would be somewhat harder."

"And another thing's been bothering me, although I'd never admit it to the other men. I don't see how we can ever hold any part of Asia as long as the Persian navy controls the seas. It's like holding a castle while the enemy roams the surrounding countryside. And I don't think we'll ever beat them on water. We Macedonians aren't made to be sailors. The Athenians are sailors and they did beat them at Salaminos but I can't trust the Athenians. Deep down, they look down on us as outside interlopers. Every time they've had a chance, they've allied themselves with our adversaries. If Antipatros's reports are to be trusted, they're in the pay of the Persians right now and plotting with Dareios and with Sparta to attack us."

"I think I may have a solution for dealing with the Persian navy, sire."

That stopped him in his tracks. "You do? Let's hear it."

"It's simple to describe but hard to execute. It came to me while we were standing atop Mount Grion, watching our navy race against theirs to see which one reached Miletos harbor first."

"It's funny you say that. I reached the opposite conclusion watching that race. It's true that Nikanoros got our men into the harbor first but looking at the number of warships they had and looking at the fact we were counting on unreliable allies to fill out our meager numbers, I decided right then and there that our navy couldn't stand up to theirs in the long run."

"I know, sire. That wasn't my idea. What I learned at Miletos was that we completely neutralized the superiority of their navy by denying them access to land anywhere near the city. They couldn't get provisions, couldn't get fresh water, couldn't get respite from the pounding of the sea. Eventually they had no choice but to sail away, leaving Miletos at our mercy."

"I remember."

"Well, what would happen if we occupied every port from the Hellespont down to Egypt? Eventually, they would have to go away, no matter how many ships they had and no matter how few we had."

He gave me a long, searching look. "I knew you were an independent thinker," he finally said. And then he just stood there, silently, for a long time.

I wonder whether I made that suggestion to make my trek to Egypt easier, I asked myself, *or because it was strategically sound?*

"It would mean cutting Antipatros loose and leaving him to his own devices." He shrugged. "Let's go back to the tent and discuss it with the boys."

We started to walk again. "I mean, discuss our plan to occupy every port. Not the part about cutting Antipatros loose. That's only between you and me."

"I understand, sire."

We practically sprinted the rest of the way, exchanging nary a word.

Chapter 12 – Issos

By the end of spring 253 Z.E., Alexandros was ready to implement his new strategy of depriving the Persian navy of its bases of operations in the eastern Mediterranean. Before leaving Gordion, he appointed Antigonos Monophthalmos, one of his father's old generals, satrap of Phrygia. This was a vital post because Alexandros's lines of communications (and potential escape routes) to the Hellespont all led through Phrygia and the adjoining Hellespontine Phrygia. Unfortunately, Alexandros could only spare one infantry battalion for Antigonos's use, which was hardly sufficient in the event the locals decided to rebel or Dareios decided to dispatch a detachment to attack. But Alexandros was not overly concerned about lines of communications back to Macedonia and he was certainly not thinking about potential escape routes. And besides, he needed all the troops he could muster for the forthcoming drive down the coast toward Egypt.

Flood Tide

The army that marched out of Gordion was smaller than the combined forces that Alexandros had had at his disposal when he crossed the Hellespont a year earlier. He brought with him some 37,000 men who then joined up with Parmenion's expeditionary corps of 10,000 warriors already present on the Asian side of the Hellespont, making for a combined force of around 47,000 men. During the previous year's fighting, we had lost fewer than a thousand men to death, illness, or disabling injury but several thousand more had to be left behind on garrison duty in various cities we had liberated in the course of our campaigning. Notwithstanding the reinforcements brought over by Koinos, Krateros, and Lysimachos, we marched out of Gordion with fewer than 41,000 men, consisting of slightly less than 6,000 cavalry, 22,000 heavy infantry, and about 13,000 light infantry and auxiliaries.

Dareios, in the meantime, was busy in Babylon assembling a huge army, determined to obliterate this cheeky little intruder from Macedonia once and for all. Theoretically, his empire could have furnished him with a million soldiers or more but there were practical constraints on the size of the army that massed, maneuvered, and eventually marched from the banks of the Euphrates: The countryside could only feed so many hungry troops and horses; Dareios's patience had its limits and some of the local levies were taking an incredibly long time to make their way to the heart of Mesopotamia; and, most importantly, Dareios realized that, when it came to the lethality of an army, quality was more important than quantity. He wanted an army of trained professionals, rather than reluctant conscripts. He ended up with some of each. His army comprised 11,000 heavy Persian cavalry, 10,000 Persian Immortals,[18] 12,000 Greek mercenaries, and some 70,000 infantry conscripts. In other words, although his army numbered more than 100,000 soldiers, only 33,000 of them were truly elite fighters. The rest were Persian Pussies.[19]

For their own reasons, both Dareios and Alexandros were anxious to confront each other in a pitched battle. For Dareios, it was almost a matter of self-preservation. The continued presence of a foreign invader within the ambit of the Persian Empire for more than a year was anathema, not only to Dareios but also to Persian nobility, to Dareios's bodyguards, and to rank and file Persian soldiers alike. Unless Dareios managed to deal with the pest from across the Aegean, his hold on power

---

[18] The Persian Immortals were very good, highly trained, dedicated infantry soldiers. However, they were as mortal as the rest of us. They acquired their appellation as a result of the practice instituted by an early emperor of keeping additional unit members in reserve, which made it possible to replace any fallen soldiers immediately, in the midst of battle, thus maintaining the unit's strength at 10,000 fighters, regardless of the extent of their casualties. By Dareios's day, there was no reserve, just the 10,000 Immortals. Their numbers were likely to diminish in the course of battle.

[19] That was not their official name.

would become rather tenuous. And of course, in Persia, there was only one tried-and-true mechanism for replacing the buttocks pressing down on the hard, wooden seat of the large imperial throne.

Alexandros, on the other hand, had to prove that his victory at Granikos had not been a fluke, that he really was destiny's darling. Unless he could defeat Dareios in the field, and do so relatively soon, the entire Macedonian enterprise on the Asian side of the Hellespont was doomed to inevitable collapse. And the failure of the pan-Hellenic expeditionary adventure in Anatolia would likely lead to the end of Macedonian hegemony on the Greek mainland as well. In addition, on a more mundane level, Alexandros was once again short of money. Finally, on a more transcendental plane, he liked the idea of a battle, which he was sure he would win.

Dareios and Alexandros spent the summer of 253 Z.E. chasing each other, hoping to precipitate a set piece contest on a field of their choosing. Dareios meandered northwest, across the fertile plains of Mesopotamia, making his way slowly toward Anatolia. In addition to his 100,000-man army, he was dragging along a huge baggage train, including his courtiers and his harem. Nobody wanted to miss the spectacle of the Persian army wiping out the Greek invaders and Dareios, confident of victory, wanted as many witnesses to his triumph as possible.

The summer was long gone by the time the entire horde crossed the Euphrates, near the Town of Thapsakos, and headed west, toward the Amanos Mountain Range, which runs parallel to the Gulf of Issos. At this point, Dareios finally decided that his army needed more speed and mobility and sent the bulk of the baggage train, along with most of the harem, back to their temporary quarters in Damaskos. However, he kept his family, along with a few of his favorite ladies and their accouterments, with the army. There was a limit to the sacrifices an emperor should be asked to make simply to win a battle.

Alexandros made his way across Kilikia, through the Kilikian Gates, back to the coast, and then south along the Gulf of Issos. He was assuming that Dareios would bring his army to the Mediterranean coast somewhere to the west of Damaskos and then travel north, along the coast, because, by sticking close to the sea, he could keep his army supplied and supported by his navy. Dareios, however, had chosen a different route, believing that a battle on the open plains on the eastern side of the Amanos Mountains would enable him to take advantage of the numerical superiority of his forces, particularly the two-to-one advantage of the Persian cavalry over their Greek counterparts. He was also sure that Alexandros would stay away from the narrow strip of land between the sea and the western foothills of the mountains, precisely because he would not wish to be exposed to possible raids by the Persian navy.

Alexandros, by contrast, liked the idea of fighting on a narrow field of battle, which would neutralize Dareios's numerical superiority, make it much more difficult for the Persians to outflank the Greeks, and reduce the scope for initiative by the Persian cavalry, which was the Persians' most formidable arm.[20]

****

The night we reached the small fishing village of Issos at the apex of its eponymous gulf, Alexandros convened the usual command meeting in his tent. Parmenion, who had been put in charge of the advance scouting units, rushed in breathlessly, anxious to share all the good news his scouts had collected.

"This is the perfect location," he told us. "Issos sits in a bowl, surrounded by mountains on three sides, with the bay on the fourth. There are only three passes through these mountains. My men have occupied all three of them. If Dareios tries to cross through any one of them, we'll know immediately and we can rush up reinforcements. The Persian army will never get across."

"I thought they were marching up the coast," Alexandros interrupted.

"No, sire. My scouts tell me they're on the far side of the mountains. I believe we should simply hunker

---

[20] See Map 7 at AlexanderGeiger.com.

down right here and wait for them. This is the perfect defensive spot."

"I think you're wrong, Parmenion. Those troops your scouts saw are merely a detachment of Persians, sent here by Dareios to keep us bottled up. His main force is coming up north, along the coast, to wipe us out. And besides, we don't hunker. We're going to march south and meet them head-on."

"We can't stay here," Hephaistion chimed in. "The harvest was brought in a long time ago. Winter's coming. We'll eat these folks out of house and home in short order and then what?"

Philotas cleared his throat. "Then we'll forage along the coast and bring back more food."

Perdikkas literally shouldered Philotas aside. "Unless you get ambushed by the Persians along the way."

"We don't hunker," Alexandros repeated. "And that's final."

We marched out the next morning, leaving only our baggage train and our sick and wounded behind, guarded by a handful of old veterans who, Alexandros worried, might slow us down. His plan was to march south as rapidly as we could and surprise Dareios's main force before they were ready to face us. Dareios, in the meantime, was marching north, on the other side of the mountains. The two armies passed, like ships in the night, oblivious to each other's movements.

******

Dareios was the first to realize that the two armies had missed each other. He circled behind Alexandros's back and made his way to the Gulf of Issos through the Amanic Gates, which had been left unoccupied when Alexandros's army set off on its march south, along the coast, the previous day. Alexandros, unaware of the Persian movements, guided his own troops through a narrow pass at the southern end of the Amanos Mountains, known as the Assyrian Gates, and then force-marched them another thirty-five miles in a single day, to a Phoenician seaport called Myriandros, where he waited for Dareios's army to come marching up the coast from the south. He waited in vain.

Dareios, in the meantime, fell upon the fishing village of Issos from the north and captured our baggage train, along with the sick and wounded soldiers we had left behind. Dareios's troops slaughtered every person left in our camp, sparing only a half dozen of the veteran guards, and pillaged our baggage train, which must have been a disappointment. There was no treasury, because Alexandros had almost no money left by this point, and there were few luxurious possessions, because most of the spoils we had captured in the course of our campaigning during the previous year had been spent on assuaging the men's hankering for female company and on other frivolous pursuits.

Dareios had his army march to a small river just below Issos, called Pinaros, where he established the Persian defensive line. His soldiers set to work erecting a palisade along the northern bank of the river and then, just to make it even more difficult for any attackers to get across, they drove stakes into the side of the riverbank, with sharpened points aimed up and out. After all the defensive preparations were completed, Dareios's army set up camp, stretching northward, beyond the village of Issos, around the bend of the gulf, as far as the eye could see. Fenced off toward the back of the camp was the imperial precinct, housing Dareios's own command tent, the tents of the royal family and the emperor's favorite ladies of the harem, his traveling treasury, and the various opulent accouterments the army had dragged across the plains of Mesopotamia, the Euphrates River, and the Amanos Mountains.

When all the preparations were completed, Dareios met with his commanders in the reception room of his tent complex. He listened to a number of reports about the disposition of troops, the state of defensive fortifications, and incoming intelligence from returning scouts. After the reports were finished, Nabarzanes had a question: "How do we know Alexandros will turn around and attack our fortified position, instead of simply continuing on his current course south, ravaging Lowland Assyria and Phoenicia in the process?"

"He'll turn around." A confident, cocky smile spread across Dareios's face. "He's got no other way to get back home. Plus, he's a hothead who wants to have a fight. And just to be sure, I've made arrangements to send him an invitation to battle that he won't be able to resist."

This last statement raised an instant clamor in the tent, everyone asking at once what the emperor had in mind.

Dareios beamed. "Just step outside and take a look."

When the commanders exited the tent, they were treated to the sight of six bedraggled, chained, nearly nude old soldiers lined up next to a roughly hewn stone block, surrounded by Persian soldiers. One after the other, the Macedonian veterans were forced to place their right arms on the rock, only to have their hands chopped off at the wrist. Then, with geysers of blood spurting from their stumps, their arms were plunged into a cauldron of boiling pitch, cauterizing their wounds.

"Send them back to Alexandros," Dareios ordered when the gruesome butchery was completed. "Tell your leader the king of kings sends his greetings," he added, in Greek, as the men staggered away.

******

Alexandros learned of the arrival of the Persian army at Issos and the slaughter of our sick and wounded comrades long before he laid eyes on the six maimed veterans. He immediately turned us around and marched us back to the Assyrian Gates. We completed the seventy mile round trip in two days, getting across the pass just before nightfall. The days were growing short. As we made camp in the foothills of the Amanos Mountains, we could see the campfires of the enemy winking into life in the valley in front of us. There were many more flickering fires in the distance below us than there were stars overhead but we were too tired to absorb either the beauty or the menace of the scene. We simply wanted to get some sleep.

Alexandros spent the cold, clear night reconnoitering the enemy. He walked, alone, the nine miles from the pass to the Pinaros River, then climbed to the top of the mountain ridge and circled all the way behind the enemy camp. He roused us at dawn for a meeting of the general staff.

He was bouncing cheerfully on the balls of his feet, bursting with energy. "We have them exactly where we want them." He was actually rubbing his hands. "The valley opens up very gradually, which will limit the scope of their cavalry play. By the time you get to the river, the valley is still only about three miles wide, so we'll be able to throw a dense infantry line all the way across, from the seashore to the foothills. Besides, it looks to me like they're planning to play defense along most of the width of the valley. You should see the defensive fortifications they've built for themselves on the northern bank of the river.

"I think they'll hit us on our right side, the side closest to the mountains, first. There is a lot of activity in the foothills. So, I think they'll send some commandos through the trees on the mountainside with the idea of getting beyond our line and then descending from the trees in a surprise attack from behind. And then, once they've got the right end of our line in disarray, they'll send the opposing, left end of their line across the river, hitting our right end with everything they've got."

"It isn't going to be much of a surprise if you're telling us about it now," Perdikkas observed.

Alexandros shook his head. "Nah, the surprise will be on them. We'll actually extend our line, so it'll be more than three miles long. We'll add an extra leg beyond our right end, angled back, so it'll be ready to catch anything that comes down from the hills. Plus, we'll put our best men on the right side."

"How many troops do they have?" Parmenion asked.

"Well, that doesn't really matter, does it? It's how you use 'em that counts. But to answer your question, they've got their Immortals, so that's a myriad. And then, they've got more than ten thousand in the damned mercenary corps."

"More than ten thousand mercenaries?"

Alexandros nodded. "Yes, that's what I counted. And I think they'll put them all on their left side, as the shock troops that will hit our right."

"So, between the Immortals and the Greek mercenaries, they've got as many heavy infantry as we have," Parmenion observed. "And I imagine they've got some other troops as well."

Alexandros laughed. "Of course, they've got myriads and myriads of Persian Pussies but their job will be to get in the way of their own army and then to lead the flight from the field, once we hit them."

"What about cavalry?" Parmenion asked.

Alexandros grew serious for a moment. "They got twice as much cavalry as we do but, as I said, the terrain will limit their utility. Unless they can break through our infantry line, they'll be pretty useless."

"Nobody breaks through our infantry line," Hephaistion called out. The men who would actually command the infantry line kept their silence.

"Alright, here's the plan. We march out in a column and then, as the valley opens up, we spread out into a line. Parmenion, you'll be in overall command of the left side. I'll give you half the hoplites but they'll be mostly allied troops. Perdikkas will be in overall command of the right side; he'll get the Silver Shields. I'll be in charge of the cavalry, with Philotas reporting to me and the rest of the cavalry commanders reporting to him. Parmenion, you'll also get all the new recruits on your side, so Krateros, Lysimachos, and Koinos will all be serving under you, but I suggest you hold their units in reserve until we see how the situation develops.

"Ptolemaios, you'll be an infantry commander for the day. You'll be under Perdikkas but I have a special assignment for you. You'll be in charge of the units forming the dogleg on the right. It'll be your job to catch anything coming down from the hills."

I snapped to attention. "Yes, sire!"

"The Agrianians and other light infantry will operate under their own commanders. We'll see as the battle develops how best to use them. Speaking of which, everything I just said is tentative. Be ready for new orders once we see how they're actually deployed.

"And now, let's observe the solemnities."

****

Our entire army assembled at the mouth of the pass. Aristandros, resplendent in his white robe, appeared as usual to do his shtick. Animals were slaughtered and their viscera inspected. Aristandros announced that all the signs were propitious. "You will win the battle today, led by the decisive stroke of your great leader, Alexandros Aniketos," he called out to the troops. Choice cuts of meat were burned on the altar and appropriate offerings made to all local deities, as well as any gods who might have had regional jurisdiction. In a special and somewhat unusual touch, a spectacular chariot, which we had captured at Halikarnassos, drawn by four matched horses, was driven into the bay and the unfortunate animals drowned, in order to appease Poseidon and also, presumably, forestall any untimely intervention during the battle by the Persian navy.

With the religious rites out of the way, and with the Persian army massing in orderly ranks on the far side of the Pinaros River, Alexandros invited the troops to a sumptuous meal, complete with hot vegetable dishes, cooked meat, plenty of bread and olive oil, and accompanied by fine, albeit strongly diluted, wine. As we were finishing our repast, Alexandros mounted a wagon and addressed the troops.

Flood Tide

"Look ahead, men, to that river in the distance. If you look really hard, you can see greatness there, awaiting us. By the time this day is done, we'll have once again wiped out the barbarian horde. All the auguries this morning were favorable but I didn't need any auguries to know that our arms are irresistible. The last time our brethren marched across this land, some seventy years ago, there were but ten thousand of them, yet the combined might of all the Persian Empire couldn't stop them. And there are a lot more of us today. We're hardened, battle-tested, undefeated, invincible!" The cheers built gradually after each adjective until the entire army was on its feet, roaring.

"And they, they're still the same cowardly, barbarian savages they have always been." At that point, Alexandros beckoned the six maimed veterans up to the wagon. It took a moment for the soldiers to figure out what they were looking at but when the realization finally sunk in, utter pandemonium broke out. The men snatched up their weapons and were ready to rush down on the enemy right then and there. With some difficulty, Alexandros finally managed to quiet them down.

"Let's maintain our discipline today," he yelled. "Listen to your commanders, follow your orders, protect the man next to you, and do what you do best. Now let's go kill the bastards. Fall in!"

Alexandros mounted his horse; the maimed veterans waved their blackened stumps; their comrades saluted them; and the pan-Hellenic army set off for its appointment with destiny.

By the time all our units were assembled in a long, orderly column, the sun was nearing its zenith. The Persian troops had been standing in their serried ranks for hours, while we feasted, mustered, and finally marched, at an easy pace, into the steadily widening valley. As the foothills receded, our column gradually transformed itself into an ever-widening line. It was a beautiful, sunny, peaceful, late autumn afternoon.

Even though I had been given command of an infantry battalion, I was on horseback, trotting alongside my troops on my trusty Pandaros, straining to see the entire battlefield. Alexandros, astride Boukephalas, surrounded by his royal cavalry squadron, was not too far behind us, unmistakable in his gleaming armor and large white plume. I was jealous to see Kleitos riding close by his side. We were all trying to discern whether the Persians had in fact deployed as Alexandros had predicted but it was hard to tell. Dareios sent a screen of cavalry and light infantry across the river and their movement obscured whatever dispositions the emperor had made behind his defensive palisade.

Their screen melted as we approached, their horsemen and light infantry scrambling back over the river to join their own units. Alexandros halted our advance, while still well out of archery range, and inspected our line, riding back and forth in front of us, making small adjustments with a nod of his head or the wave of an arm. At the same time, he was keeping an eye on the enemy. They were not lined up as he had expected. The placement of their units was beautiful, orthodox, symmetrical, perfect for a parade-ground review. How effective it would prove to be in a dynamic engagement remained to be seen.

The emperor's personal bodyguard, with their splendid armor and gold-butted spears, was stationed precisely at the center of the line, surrounded by the ten thousand Immortals. Behind them, Dareios himself was standing tall, atop his large, ornate, ceremonial chariot, partially shielded by his chariot driver on one side and his head steward, waving a large palm frond to keep him cool, on the other. Flanking the Immortals on either side were the Greek mercenaries, split into two equal, 6,000-men divisions. Completing the rest of the right side of their line, all the way to the shore, was the Persian heavy cavalry, both the men and the horses gleaming in their silver armor. The left side of their line (that is, the side of the line opposed to the units commanded by Perdikkas, including my battalion) was made up of Persian infantry and Persian light cavalry. The conscript infantry battalions were held back, behind the front line, for use as reserves, Dareios's opinion of their fighting abilities being evidently as low as our own. Archers were stationed immediately in front of their entire line and we could see some light infantry soldiers lurking in the woods above us.

Parmenion has his work cut out, I thought. It was clear to me that the heaviest Persian thrust would come on the seaward side of the front, not the mountainside, as Alexandros had anticipated. And the threat of troops descending on us from the woods behind our line seemed to have been exaggerated. Alexandros made some quick adjustments. He sent the entire Thessalian and allied Greek cavalry back to Parmenion to support the left end of our line, making sure their movement was concealed behind the infantry phalanxes making up Parmenion's end of the line. However, he kept the entire Companion Cavalry for himself, hidden and massed behind Perdikkas's end of the line. He reinforced the middle of our line, across from the Immortals, using all the available reserves, under Krateros's overall command. They would not have an easy time of it either. Finally, he dispatched two companies of Agrianians, along with some other light-armed troops to deal with the soldiers trying to get behind the right end of our line up in the woods.

With the adjustments carried out, we resumed our slow advance, singing loudly. Alexandros halted us once again, just outside archery range. We were now close enough to see the faces of the enemy and to scream insults at them. The Persians yelled back at us. Neither side understood the words of the other but the meaning was unmistakable. We waited, hoping they would abandon their strong defensive position and attack us. Dareios was too good a tactician to allow them to charge and they were disciplined enough to await his command. It was getting to be late in the afternoon and the two armies were still standing there, yelling at each other. *If we wait another hour or so, the sun will sink into the gulf on our left and we can all return to our respective camps.*

Finally, Alexandros nodded his head, the trumpets sounded, and Krateros's phalanxes in the middle charged.[21] The men started at a slow run and picked up speed as they reached the river. The sky above them darkened with incoming salvos of arrows, most of which they were able to catch on their shields. However, once in the swiftly moving current of the river, they found it impossible to maintain the precision of their ranks and they started to clamber, willy-nilly, up the opposite bank. It was difficult going. The bank was five or six feet tall, slippery, and topped by a palisade. Waiting behind the palisade were the Immortals and the Greek mercenaries. They were tough, experienced fighters. Neither the Persian Immortals nor the Greek mercenaries expected any quarter from Alexandros. They would either prevail or die on the battlefield. At the moment, however, most of the dying was being done by our infantrymen, fighting uphill, with poor footing, without the support of an

---

[21] For an animated depiction of the Battle of Issos, visit AlexanderGeiger.com

organized line, trying to kill, in hand-to-hand combat, hardened enemy soldiers protected by a wooden fence.

As soon as the middle of the line engaged, the Persian heavy cavalry poured across the river and fell upon Parmenion's end of the line, made up mostly of allied hoplites. Our Greek warriors maintained the cohesion of their ranks and resisted the heavily armored men and beasts but the weight of numbers began to tell. Small gaps developed here and there and became more and more difficult to plug. The Thessalian and allied horsemen tried to help where they could but were no match for the Persian cavalry.

At the same time, on our end of the front, at the foot of the mountains, we charged the Persian infantry opposed to us. However, as we ran, we opened a corridor between units wide enough for squadrons of Companion Cavalry to ride through. Before we even had a chance to engage the enemy, our cavalry, led by Alexandros, roared through, leaped over the palisade and scattered the Persian Pussies standing in their way. It was no contest. In minutes, the Persian infantry was fleeing the field. Alexandros didn't take the time to pursue them, veering instead to his left and riding straight for Dareios's chariot. The presence of thousands of Greek mercenaries, Immortals, and the emperor's personal bodyguard between the two kings didn't detain Alexandros. The Macedonian cavalry wedge, with Alexandros at its point, was irresistible. Dareios's defenders fought fiercely and well, dying where they stood, but dying nonetheless. They were getting slashed, pounded, and trampled under the hooves of the Companion Cavalry. Alexandros, ignoring a dagger wound in his thigh, came close enough to look into Dareios's eyes. Dareios, snatching a javelin from one of his bodyguards, hurled it at Alexandros and missed. The horses hitched to the chariot, unaccustomed to the violence of battle, spooked and reared. Dareios was in danger of being thrown to the ground. At the last moment, one of Dareios's bodyguards offered him his horse. Dareios vaulted onto the animal's back and sought refuge behind the lines. The Macedonian cavalry was continuing its slaughter, while our infantry units, at Perdikkas's end of the line, did their best to pursue the fleeing Persians.

Alexandros, seeing Dareios in flight, turned Boukephalas, in order to give chase. Before he could move, however, a messenger from Parmenion reached him and informed him that the middle of the line, under Krateros, had made no progress trying to cross the palisade and that the seaward end of the line, under Parmenion, was in desperate trouble, unable to fend off the Persian cavalry. Reluctantly, but without hesitation, Alexandros broke off his pursuit of Dareios. Instead, he led the Companion Cavalry across the battlefield and charged into the back of the Persian cavalry, who suddenly found themselves trapped between Parmenion in front of them, Alexandros behind them, and the Gulf of Issos to their side. At the same time, they learned their emperor had fled the battlefield. Caught in two minds, unsure whether to continue their charge or to follow their leader and flee, they did neither. In short order, they were slaughtered where they sat.

In the meantime, Perdikkas's phalanxes also circled behind the Greek mercenaries and the Immortals and attacked them from the rear. With the resistance at the riverbank easing, the middle of our line was finally able to gain the palisade and a generalized slaughter of the Greek mercenaries and Persian Immortals ensued. The conscript levies that Dareios had kept in reserve watched the developments with interest and ran for their lives long before anyone attacked them.

In a matter of minutes, a closely contested fight turned into a generalized rout. Alexandros, accompanied only by a small squadron of riders, resumed his pursuit of Dareios. I held back my battalion momentarily to make sure our Agrianians had dealt with any remaining Persian elements in the woods above us. It became quickly apparent that the few enemy troops in the woods before the battle had by now joined the wholesale flight of the Persian army. With that threat removed, we hurried to catch up to the rest of Perdikkas's line. Unfortunately, our progress was slowed by all the carnage under our feet. We reached a second river meandering across the plain, which had separated the battlefield from the Persian encampment area. The waterway, once a fairly deep and swiftly moving stream, was choked with dead bodies. My men were able to get across without getting their feet wet, skipping from corpse to corpse.

The rest of the hoplites under Perdikkas's command reached Dareios's camp before we arrived. Alexandros had left no orders concerning the treatment of any captives or the disposition of booty. The Macedonian infantrymen, remembering what Dareios had done to their comrades, took no prisoners. They looted the camp and killed any men they found. (Most of the men were actually eunuchs.) They raped the women, then killed some of them, while saving others for later use. Any children and domestic animals they tended to ignore, in pursuit of more valuable plunder. However, they refrained from invading the imperial precinct, scrupulously saving its contents as Alexandros's personal share of the spoils.

Alexandros continued his pursuit of Dareios until well past midnight, attempting to pick up the trail of the escaping monarch in near total darkness, oblivious to the risk of ambush he and his men were running. Finally, near collapse from total exhaustion, Alexandros broke off the search and turned back.

****

Where in Haides is he? I had checked in all the expected hiding places without success. Aristandros had vanished like a scorpion sensing an owl nearby. If his death was to appear as a casualty of the battle, I had no time to waste. And yet, here I was, riding aimlessly through what had been the Persian camp the night before.

The wreckage of the camp was brightly lit by countless fires, some set intentionally by our soldiers trying to keep warm and others caused accidentally by carelessly overturned lamps and braziers. The initial pandemonium had died down to a sustained uproar, punctuated by the occasional shriek or triumphant shout. Despite my ostensibly urgent errand, I was simply drifting, floating along on the softly narcotic afterglow of mortal combat. Amidst the fighting, I was not an outsider; I wasn't worried about the Prime Directive; I forgot about timesickness; I didn't wonder what the future held in store for me. I was simply trying to survive; trying not to make any mistakes that could cause the men in my charge to lose their lives; and, if I was honest about it, trying to make sure that our side won. I realized I wasn't supposed to be partisan but it was becoming increasingly clear to me that, somewhere along the line, I had taken a side. I hated to admit it but I had enjoyed that feeling of camaraderie, belonging, and certainty of mission that only fighting in a battle could bring. The last thing I wanted to think about was Aristandros.

My reverie was interrupted by the eruption of a distraught, screaming woman from a tent a few paces in front of me. Her chiton was torn, her hair disheveled, her face blood-streaked. Two young Macedonian soldiers, whom I recognized as members of the battalion I had commanded earlier that afternoon, wearing nothing but loincloths, emerged from the tent in hot pursuit. In her desperation, the woman threw herself in the dirt right in front of Pandaros's hooves. "Sire, please save us," she pleaded, in perfect Greek.

I alighted from my seat and picked her up. The two soldiers, who evidently recognized me as well, hesitated. I spun the woman toward me, taking a good look at her face. "I'll take this one."

The taller of the two tensed, ready to spring at me. He cocked his right fist. Then he thought better of it. "I guess that's fair." His voice lacked conviction or enthusiasm.

Still, I was a commander and armed to boot while he was wearing nothing but an undergarment. I wished I could remember their names; unfortunately, it wasn't my usual command and, unlike Alexandros, I didn't know the name of every Macedonian in the army. The soldier shrugged. "C'mon, Doberos, let's let the commander have her. Besides, there's two more in there anyway."

Doberos seemed dubious. "But they're not as pretty as this one."

The tall one laughed. "Since when did you start looking at their faces?"

"I appreciate it, fellas." I prepared to mount up again. The woman leaned in toward me. "My children are in there," she whispered. I looked at her again. Under the grime and blood and anguish I saw intelligence and determination. "I have four small children in there," she repeated. "Please don't let them die."

I recalled the last time I had decided to save a youngster, a lifetime ago. If I had managed to resist that impulsive act, I would have been back at the Academy at the end of my three-day excursion, none the worse for wear, instead of being stuck in this alien time and place. "I changed my mind, fellas." I pushed the woman away. "Do as you see fit."

She reared at me like a cobra. "You surprise me, sir. You looked like a decent man." And without a further word, she grabbed the dagger hanging at my belt and whirled against the two soldiers who were standing there, beginning to shiver. Given her speed and vehemence, she might well have killed one or both of them. They certainly seemed too startled to put up much of a fight.

I lunged after the woman, grabbing her by the arms and immobilizing her. Doberos, taking advantage of the opening, seized her wrist and forced her to drop the dagger. His compatriot, in the meantime, punched her in the face, knocking her to the ground.

"Alright, lads, that's enough. She's just a woman, you know."

"Yeah, she was gonna kill us, woman or not."

"I know, but still. Anyway, let her be. And besides, why are you two naked and unarmed? Get dressed, get your armor on, gather up whatever loot you have managed to collect, and move on."

They grumbled but proceeded into the tent to retrieve their gear. They seemed safe enough to me; their passions had apparently subsided during our extended interlude. The woman on the ground, however, clearly thought otherwise. She pulled herself to her feet and ran after them. Reluctantly, I followed as well, tying Pandaros up at the entrance.

The tent was dark and very warm. Upon ducking in through the flap, I almost tripped over the trussed-up body of the woman. The two soldiers were evidently not going to take any further chances with her. Dominating the middle of the tent was a huge bale of booty. I couldn't make out exactly what was in the jumbled pile but there was a lot of it. "You've been busy fellas, haven't you?" I laughed. "I'm amazed you found time for women."

Doberos's drew back his shoulders. "We always have time for the women, sir."

As my eyes adjusted to the gloom, I picked out two young girls behind the bundle of booty, huddled in the corners, shaking. And behind them, not uttering a peep, were four small children.

"Tell you what, lads. You'll need a horse to carry all that stuff back to our camp. You can use mine. I'll stay here, in the meantime, and look after these women."

The taller one smirked. "Who would've thought a milquetoast cavalry commander could be a three-wench guy? I guess the deepest rivers flow with least sound, as they say."

"Yeah," Doberos agreed, "and the guys with the shortest pricks are the horniest."

I smiled. "Now, now. Don't make me yank mine out. You might get hurt by the whiplash."

They seemed pretty well sated, libidinally and materially. With a modicum of discontent, displayed more for the sake of form than out of conviction, they dressed, loaded poor Pandaros down, and set out for our camp, leaving me in the dark, warm tent.

The woman on the floor rolled to her back. "Let's get it over with."

"I'm not going to rape you," I assured her, as I loosened her bindings. "It's not my custom to interfere in other people's affairs."

She sneered. "I guess you don't consider killing people interference."

"I try not to kill people," I told her quietly, "although it's sometimes unavoidable in my line of work. But in any event, I'm not going to rape you."

"What are you going to do with us?"

"That I haven't figured out yet." We sat quietly for a moment. "Bring your children closer, so I can have a look."

She nodded to the two frightened girls in the back and they brought the youngsters toward me. There were three girls and a boy. The oldest, a girl, couldn't have been much older than seven or eight. The youngest, the boy, was just learning to walk. All four seemed to be preternaturally self-possessed, not appearing nearly as frightened as the two girls, who, at sixteen or eighteen years of age, perhaps understood their peril more clearly.

I patted one of the little girls on the head. "They're brave little kids."

"They've seen a lot. You're less scary than some." She stood up and rubbed the welts on her arms. "Let me see whether I can find you some food. There might still be some hidden outside."

I rose to my feet and blocked her way. "We're fine as we are. I don't want you to go anywhere."

"You can come with me, if you'd like."

"We can send one of the girls," I finally said.

The girl returned with a pitcher of water and handed it to me. "This is all I could find."

I gave the pitcher to the woman. She poured some on her face and washed the blood off. Wherever her wound was, it had stopped bleeding. For the first time, I was struck by her beauty. "Your Greek is perfect," I said, "better than mine."

"It ought to be. I'm Greek, at least on my mother's side, and you're obviously not."

"So, what's a Greek woman doing in Dareios's camp?"

The woman shrugged. "We were kept as hostages."

"Does that mean you're somebody important?"

"Well, I used to be, ... when my husband was still alive."

"Who was your husband?"

"He was a mercenary commander in Dareios's army. Dareios kept us hostage to make sure my husband did his job."

"Did your husband have a name?"

"Yes. His name was Memnon of Rhodos. Perhaps you've heard of him."

I nodded, too stunned to speak. *No wonder people believe in gods.* After all the times her husband had slipped through my fingers, what were the odds his widow and children would land in my lap by random chance?

"What are you laughing at?" she asked, her suspicion tinged with hope.

"You don't want to know."

Perhaps I could keep her as my share of the booty. In all my travels, I'd never met anyone like her. I couldn't begin to imagine what she'd endured and yet, here she was, full of life, spunk, and courage. And she was beautiful, too, I had to admit.

It was an alluring prospect but then the Prime Directive reasserted its hold on my conscience. Despite my chafing under its yoke for the past ten years and despite my inadvertent violations, some minor but at least one resulting in a demonstrable deflection in the river of time, I was more determined than ever to adhere to its dictates. Perhaps it was precisely because of all the sacrifices I'd made and the heavy price I'd paid that adherence to the Prime Directive had become a deeply ingrained article of faith.

She and her family needed a guardian but it wouldn't be me. It couldn't be me. Acquiring an instant family and perhaps siring a few additional children into the bargain was one guaranteed way to alter the future. My objective was not to settle down in this world; it was to make my way back to my own. Even if I had to kill somebody to get there.

After a long moment of silence, I looked into her eyes. "Let me take you to the imperial precinct. It hasn't been looted. The soldiers are saving it for King Alexandros, as his personal booty. You and your children will be safer there."

Her face lit up in a wistful smile. "I used to play with Alexandros once upon a time." I must have looked surprised. "It was a long time ago, when we were both little children."

It was getting close to dawn by the time she finished recounting her entire story. "Don't tell anybody that those are Memnon's children," I advised her as I walked the entire group toward the imperial precinct. "Tell them they're your servant girls' kids. That way, they'll have a better chance of growing up. And, as long as you keep the same girls in your service, you'll get to see your children without jeopardizing their future." I realized my suggestion sounded fairly impractical. "Do you think you can convince your children not to betray your secret?"

"They're smart kids. And they'll forget I'm their mother soon enough."

Neither one of us believed that but we had reached the imperial precinct and there was nothing more to say. I turned the group over to the sentries guarding the precinct. "This lady and her attendants are part of the imperial harem," I told the guards. "They're reserved for King Alexandros. See to it that no harm comes to them." The guards nodded in acknowledgement and escorted the ragged little cluster of captives into one of Dareios's tents.

I started making my way back to our own camp. I walked fast, feeling strangely pleased with the world. I never did find Aristandros that night.

******

"So, this is what it's like to be a king." Alexandros was immersed up to his neck in steaming-hot water. Two eunuchs who had somehow managed to escape the massacre were washing his hair, massaging his shoulder muscles, adding aromatic oils to the water.

The bronze bathtub was stationed in the middle of a large tent dedicated solely to Dareios's cleaning and grooming needs. The floor was carpeted with rugs and furs. There were pillows strewn everywhere. Even the tent walls were hung with shimmering tapestries. Tables of inlaid wood held golden goblets and plates. Two braziers in the corners provided heat and some light. On one side of the tub, a small ebony table held the emperor's perfumes, unguents, and cosmetics. On the other side stood a matching ebony chair, containing a built-in chamber pot. The emperor's luxurious, purple "harem robe" was laid out across a couch.

"You know, if Leukonides[22] could see me now, taking a hot bath in Dareios's bathtub, he'd kill me for sure."

Hephaistion laughed. "It's your bathtub now, Aniketos. And if Leukonides could see you now, he'd congratulate you on that charge you led against Dareios."

"That really was something," Perdikkas agreed. "Turned the tide of battle."

Leonnatos, one of Alexandros's bodyguards and member in good standing of the Mieza clique, who had fought side-by-side with Alexandros during most of the cavalry charge against Dareios, walked into the tent at that moment. "What turned the tide of battle?"

---

[22] Leukonides was the drill sergeant charged with the responsibility of turning young Alexandros and his mates into soldiers during their years at the Mieza boarding school. He was notoriously intolerant of any indulgence in luxuries.

"We did!" Alexandros roared, rising from his bath. "Now get me some wine."

One of the eunuchs rushed to a side table to retrieve a golden goblet, while the other eunuch dried the king with a thick, fluffy towel. "Maybe I should put on Dareios's robe, what do you think?"

The king's aides, reclining on soft furs and pillows and sipping their own cups of wine, said nothing. Alexandros walked over to the couch and slipped into Dareios's robe. It was way too big for him. "How do I look?"

"You look ready to sample the wares in the women's tent next door," Hephaistion told him.

"Maybe you should put a little more kohl around your eyes first," Philotas quietly observed.

Alexandros ignored his comment but he did take the robe off and put on his own tunic.

Just then, some soldiers brought Dareios's abandoned chariot into the imperial precinct, intending to present it to Alexandros as another battle trophy. Although the king didn't see the fabled vehicle being dragged in, its arrival was noted by the emperor's family, cowering in a nearby tent. Inferring that the emperor must be dead, the ladies of the court, including the emperor's mother, wives, and daughters, launched into a loud chorus of lamentation and wailing.

"What's that ghastly racket?" Alexandros demand to know.

Mithrines, the Sardian traitor, spoke up. "It's the king's family, your majesty. They think the emperor's dead."

"Go out there and shut them up," Alexandros ordered.

Leonnatos, who was the only one in the tent still wearing his armor, walked out, called over a couple of the sentries, and marched into the imperial ladies' tent. The ladies, assuming the soldiers were there to do them harm, as would certainly have been the case had they been captured by a Persian potentate, increased the volume of their keening. Leonnatos, not understanding a word of what they were saying and unable to stand the noise, drew his sword and threatened the loudest lady, who happened to be Dareios's first wife Stateira. That only made things worse. Stateira, in her best histrionic form, collapsed to the floor and called upon the gods to save her, making sure her plea was loud enough to be heard by the gods all the way back in Babylon. Leonnatos, at his wits' end, spun on his heels and walked back out.

"They're very unhappy about something, sire," he reported to Alexandros, "But I can't understand them."

"Mithrines, go back with him and find out what's going on," Alexandros ordered.

Leonnatos and Mithrines were back in a moment, with the noise level unabated. "They think Dareios is dead and they're sure you're going to kill them, your majesty. They don't seem inclined to shut up. Perhaps killing them might be the best solution."

Alexandros laughed. "I think we can do better than that. Let's go pay the ladies a visit." And with that, the entire group, wearing only their tunics, made their way over to the imperial ladies' tent.

As soon as the men walked in, the ladies ceased their wailing. Stateira, quickly assessing the entire group, threw herself at Hephaistion's feet, assuming that the tallest and handsomest man present must be Alexandros, and started to beg and cry loudly. Mithrines, instantly apprehending her mistake, kicked her discretely in the ribs, while pointing with his finger toward Alexandros.

Stateira, without missing a beat, leapt from Hephaistion to Alexandros, displaying remarkable agility for a woman of her age and girth. She slithered forward and clasped Alexandros's knees to her bosom, importuning him, in Persian, all the while.

The king looked at her uncomprehendingly. "She thought Hephaistion was Alexandros, sire," Mithrines explained.

"Tell her we are all Alexandroi," the king said, as he struggled to extricate his legs from her clutches. As soon as he succeeded, he turned around and walked out of the tent. "Keep them safe and securely confined," he called over his shoulder. "They may yet make valuable hostages."

****

After a relatively short orgy of looting, pillage, rapine, and murder, Alexandros passed word through his commanders that order should be restored and it quickly was. He decided it would be futile to chase after Dareios just then. He let the soldiers keep whatever booty they had managed to seize, including the women.

It occurred to me that, for the first time since the invasion, our progress was going to be impeded by an extensive baggage train and a large contingent of camp followers, wherever Alexandros decided to go next. Would he decide to pursue Dareios, resume our long trek toward Egypt, or declare our mission accomplished and return to Macedonia? And what exactly would I do?

In the end, Alexandros kept none of the spoils the soldiers had reserved for him. He generously gave it all away to his friends, to various commanders, and to common soldiers who had distinguished themselves during the battle, keeping only one trophy for himself – a captured woman named Barsine.

Flood Tide

Author's Note

Ptolemaios, known to English-speaking historians as Ptolemy I, was born circa 364 B.C.E. (the date is disputed) and died circa 282 B.C.E. He accompanied Alexander III of Macedonia, also known as Alexander the Great, on his military campaigns, rising through the ranks to become one of Alexander's leading commanders. Book One of the Ptolemaios Saga covered the period 343 to 334 B.C.E. This volume carries the story forward to the end of 333 B.C.E. It is the author's hope to recount the history of Ptolemy to his death, and beyond, in subsequent volumes.

Ptolemy left behind a memoir describing his experiences during Alexander's campaigns. Unfortunately, Ptolemy's memoir is now lost. However, a distant echo of Ptolemy's history continues to reverberate in our collective memory because it was utilized as original source material by ancient historians writing during Roman imperial times, such as Lucius Flavius Arrianus (Arrian), Quintus Curtius Rufus (Curtius), and possibly Lucius Mestrius Plutarchus (Plutarch), whose works are still extant today. Modern histories of the period covered in this book are in turn based largely on these ancient Roman accounts.

The Ptolemaios Saga is an attempt to reconstruct Ptolemy's lost memoir. Of necessity, some of the narrative, much of the characterization, and almost all of the dialogue were invented by the author. However, all the principal characters mentioned in this book were actual historical figures; the major events really happened; and the minor characters and events interpolated by the author, it is hoped, do no violence to the historical record.

The spelling of the characters' names is an accurate transliteration of their names in Greek. The spelling of place names is inconsistent. Those places that have well-known English names have retained those names. Places less well known in the English-speaking world have been given their Greek names, transliterated into the English alphabet. The author regrets the inconsistency.

Finally, although this is a true story, albeit embellished by the author, there is no historical evidence to suggest that Ptolemy I was a time traveler.

April 15, 2019

Alexander Geiger

Flood Tide

Additional Materials

Additional materials, including sources, illustrations, maps, battle depictions, an author's blog, and descriptions of upcoming volumes, are available at AlexanderGeiger.com.

Acknowledgements

The author wishes to express his gratitude to the following individuals who kindly read (and, in some cases, re-read) the manuscript of this novel and offered numerous helpful suggestions and corrections, ranging from fixing typographical errors to pointing out infelicitous phrasing to urging a restructuring of plotlines: Helene Geiger, Kathy McGowan, Aviva Schwarz, David Schwarz, Alan Unsworth, Michelle Alterman, Larry Bruck, Susan Falk, Ken Krevitz, and George Rifkin. Special thanks to Scott Schmeer of Prometheus Training, LLC for the cover design.

Any remaining mistakes are attributable solely to the obduracy of the author.

Alexander Geiger

About the Author

The author is a history buff who has always wished he could travel back in time to visit some of his favorite historical figures, places, and events. The entire Ptolemaios Saga is an account of one such extended trip, intended to witness the dawn of the Hellenistic world. The men and women who lived, strived, fought, and loved during this seminal age didn't know their ideas, exploits, and accomplishments would reverberate all the way to the present day but, boy oh boy, did they leave a mark. Imagine being able to see, through the eyes of Ptolemaios Metoikos – who was actually there – all the adventures, sights, and colorful figures of that vibrant, memorable, and thrilling era. It's the author's hope that you will enjoy the ride.

In real life, the author is a graduate of Princeton University and Cornell Law School and a retired commercial litigator. He lives with his wife in in Bucks County, PA.

Please email all comments, questions, suggestions, or requests for author interviews and appearances to Alex@AlexanderGeiger.com.